Although Danielle Steel was born in New York, she spent her formative years living in Paris. She decided to make the journey back to New York after she had finished her education. One of her first jobs in the city was for the pioneering PR firm, Supergirls Ltd, where she was involved in creating PR campaigns and hosting parties for clients. During a spell working in advertising, Steel started publishing poems in women's magazines. Since then she has written at a furious pace and has enjoyed huge success, with 57 bestsellers, over 100 international bestselling novels in print, and more than 600 million copies sold.

You can discover more about the author at www.daniellesteel.com

Facebook
www.facebook.com/DanielleSteelOfficial

Twitter @daniellesteel

MAGIC

Once a year in the City of Light, a lavish dinner takes place outside a spectacular landmark. Selected by secret invitation, the guests arrive dressed in white; and when the night is over, hundreds of white paper lanterns bearing everyone's wishes are released into the sky. This year, a group of close friends stand at the cusp of change. Jean-Philippe and Valerie are high-flying, successful and devoted to their young family. But a once-in-a-lifetime opportunity in China may lead to separation — and temptation. Benedetta and Gregorio run an Italian clothing empire in Milan, but Gregorio has a weakness that will ignite a crisis in their company, and their marriage. And screenwriter Chantal and Indian tech entrepreneur Dharam arrive as friends, but their paths will be set on dramatically different courses before the night ends . . .

DANIELLE STEEL

◆

MAGIC

Complete and Unabridged

CHARNWOOD
Leicester

First published in Great Britain in 2016 by
Bantam Press
an imprint of Transworld Publishers
London

First Charnwood Edition
published 2018
by arrangement with
Transworld Publishers
Penguin Random House
London

A catalogue record for this book is available
from the British Library.

ISBN 978–1–4448–3648–6

To my beloved, wonderful children,

May there always be magic in your lives!
    Look for it!
    Believe in it!
    Cherish it!
You are the magic in my life!
I love you with all my heart and love,

                              Mommy/ds

1

The White Dinner is a love poem to friendship, joy, elegance, and the beautiful monuments of Paris. And each year it is an unforgettable night. Other cities have attempted to emulate it around the world, with little success. There is only one Paris, and the event is so revered and respected and perfectly executed that it is hard to imagine it in any other city.

It began some thirty years ago when a naval officer and his wife decided to celebrate their anniversary with their friends in a creative, unusual way, in front of one of their favorite monuments in Paris. They organized about twenty of their friends, everyone dressed in white. They arrived with folding tables and chairs, linens for the table, silver, crystal, china, maybe flowers, brought an elegant meal with them, set everything out, and shared a glorious celebration with their guests. The magic began on that night.

It was such a success that they did it again the following year, in a different but equally remarkable location. And each year ever since, the White Dinner has been a tradition, and more and more and more people attend, to celebrate the evening in the same way, entirely dressed in white, on a night in June.

The event remains by invitation only, which is respected by all, and over the years it has become one of the most cherished secret occasions held in Paris. The all-white dress code is still mandatory, including shoes, and everyone makes a real effort to dress elegantly and follow the established traditions. Each year the White Dinner is held in front of a different Parisian monument, and the possibilities are vast in Paris. In front of Notre Dame, the Arc de Triomphe, at the feet of the Eiffel Tower at the Trocadero, in the Place de la Concorde, between the pyramids in front of the Louvre, in the Place Vendôme. By now the White Dinner has been held in a myriad of locations, each one more beautiful than the last.

Over the years, the White Dinner has grown so large that it is held now in two locations, with the total number of invited guests approaching fifteen thousand. It's hard to imagine that many people behaving properly, arriving looking elegant, and following all the rules, but miraculously they do. 'White food' and meals are encouraged, but above all a proper meal must be served (no hot dogs, hamburgers, or sandwiches). A real dinner is meant to be brought along, set out on a table on a white linen tablecloth, eaten with silver utensils, with real crystal and china, just as in a restaurant, or a home where honored guests are being entertained. Everything one brings must fit in a rolling caddy, and at the end of the evening, every scrap of garbage or debris must be put in white garbage bags and removed, down to the last cigarette butt. No sign of the revelers must remain in the beautiful locations chosen that year for the White Dinner. People must appear and disappear as gracefully as they arrive.

The police turn a blind eye to it, although no permits are taken out for the event, despite the vast number of participants (taking out permits would spoil the surprise), and remarkably, there are no crashers. An invitation to the White Dinner is much coveted and celebrated when received, but those who are not on the guest list never show up and try to claim they are. There have been no bad incidents or hostilities at the event. It is an evening of pure joy, reinforced by respect for fellow guests and love for the city.

Half the fun is not knowing where it will take place that year. It is a formal secret kept religiously by the six organizers. And wherever it will happen, people are invited in couples, and each couple must bring their own folding table and two chairs, both of regulation size.

The six organizers inform 'subheads' of the evening of the first location where people are meant to gather. All invited guests are to show up with their caddies, tables, and chairs, at one of the initial sites at precisely eight-fifteen P.M. The two groups will dine in two different locations. The excitement begins to mount when the first locations are revealed, which revelers are informed of only the afternoon of the event. It gives one some rough idea of where the actual dinner might be held, but it's all guesswork, since usually there are several possible beautiful locations within easy walking distance of that first location. All day people try to guess where they will be having dinner. People arrive promptly at their first location, dressed all in white and equipped for the evening. Friends find each other in the crowd, call out to each other, and discover with delight who is there. Spirits are high for half an hour in the meeting place, and at eight-forty-five precisely the final destination is revealed, no more than a five-minute walk from where they are.

Once the location is announced, each couple is assigned a space the exact size of their table, and they must set up in that space, in long neat rows. People often come in groups of couples, friends who have attended the event for years, and dine side by side with their individual tables as part of the long rows.

By nine o'clock, seven thousand people have reached the spectacular monuments that are the lucky winners for the night. And once they have arrived and been given their table location assignment, measured by the inch or centimeter, tables are unfolded, chairs set down firmly, tablecloths spread out, candlesticks produced, tables set as for a wedding. Within fifteen minutes, the diners are seated, pouring wine, happy, and beaming in anticipation of a spectacular evening among old and new friends. The excitement and the finally revealed secret of the location make the participants feel like children attending a surprise birthday party. And by nine-thirty, the festivities are in full swing. Nothing could be better.

The dinner begins about an hour before sunset, and as the sun sets, candles are lit on the tables, and after nightfall the entire square or place where the event is held is candlelit, as seven thousand diners clad in white, toasting each other with shimmering crystal glasses, silver candelabra on the tables, are a feast for the eye. At eleven P.M., sparklers are handed out and lit, and a dance band plays halfway through the evening, adding further merriment. At Notre Dame the church bells toll, and the priest on duty offers a blessing from the balcony. And precisely half an hour after midnight, the entire crowd packs up and disappears, like mice scampering into the night, leaving no sign that they have been there, except the good time that will be remembered forever, the friendships that were formed, and the special time that was shared.

Another interesting aspect of the evening is that no money changes hands. No fee is charged to be invited, nothing has to be purchased or paid for. One brings one's own meal and cannot buy one's way into the White Dinner. The organizers invite whom they choose to, and the event remains pure. Other cities have tried to make a profit from doing similar dinners and immediately corrupt the event by including rowdy people who don't belong, pay any price to be there, and spoil the evening for everyone else. The White Dinner in Paris has stuck to the original model, with great results. Everyone looks forward to it, as the date draws near. And in thirty years, the secret of where the actual dinner will be has never leaked, which makes it even more fun.

People wait all year for the White Dinner and

are never disappointed by the event itself. And unfailingly, it is a night one could never forget, from the first moment to the last. The memories of it are long cherished by those who are lucky enough to be asked. And everyone agrees, magic happens there.

★ ★ ★

Jean-Philippe Dumas had been attending the White Dinner for ten years, since he was twenty-nine years old. And as a friend of one of the organizers, he was allowed to invite nine couples, to form a group of twenty seated together with their individual tables tightly placed side by side. He chose his guests carefully every year, and along with good friends he had invited before, he tried to include a few new friends who he thought would be respectful of the rules of the event, get along with his other guests, and have a good time. There was nothing haphazard or casual about his guest list. He took it very seriously, and if he included anyone who didn't appreciate the evening, or wasn't fun to be with, or tried to use it as a networking opportunity, which it emphatically wasn't, he replaced them the following year with other friends. But mostly he brought back regulars who begged to come every year.

After Jean-Philippe married seven years earlier, his American wife, Valerie, came to love the dinner as much as he did, and they carefully selected their guests together every year.

Jean-Philippe worked in international investments at a well-known firm. Valerie had met him two weeks after she moved to Paris. Now, at thirty-five, she was the assistant editor of French *Vogue*, and the leading candidate to become editor-in-chief in two years, when their current one was slated to retire. Eight years before, Jean-Philippe had fallen in love with her at first sight. She was tall, sleek, smart, with long, straight dark hair. She was chic without being tiresome about it, had a great sense of humor, and enjoyed his friends. She had been a wonderful addition to the group, she and Jean-Philippe got on famously, and after they married, they had had three children, two boys and a girl, in six years. They were the couple everyone wanted to spend time with. She had worked at American *Vogue* in New York straight out of college, before she moved. She took her work seriously, but still managed to be a good wife and mother and somehow juggled it all. She loved living in Paris and couldn't imagine living anywhere else. She had made a big effort to learn French for him, which served her well at work too. She could speak to photographers, stylists, and designers now. She had a heavy American accent he teased her about, but her French was fluent. They took their children to her family home in Maine every summer, so their children could get to know their American cousins, but for Valerie, France had become home. She no longer missed New York or working there. And she thought Paris the most beautiful city in the world.

They had a wide circle of friends and a good life. They lived in a wonderful apartment. They entertained often, and sometimes cooked for friends, or hired a cook for informal dinner parties. Their invitations were much coveted, especially to the White Dinner.

Valerie had met Benedetta and Gregorio Mariani at Fashion Week in Milan right after she had gone to work at Paris Vogue. They hit it off immediately, and Jean-Philippe loved them too. They had invited them to the White Dinner even before Jean-Philippe married Valerie, when they were still dating. The Marianis had been regulars ever since and flew in from Milan every year. This year Benedetta was in a white knit dress she had designed that showed off her excellent figure, and high heels, and Gregorio was wearing a white suit he'd had made in Rome, with a white silk tie, impeccable white shirt, and immaculate white suede shoes. Gregorio and Benedetta always looked as if they'd just stepped off the pages of a fashion magazine. Both their families had been involved in fashion for centuries, and they had managed to combine their talents to the benefit of both houses. Benedetta's family had been making knits and sportswear that were famous around the world, and they were doing even better now than previously with her talent for design. And Gregorio's family had been making the finest textiles in Italy for two hundred years. They had been married for twenty years, and Gregorio had been working with her ever since, while his brothers ran the family mills and supplied them most of their fabrics. They were slightly older than Jean-Philippe and Valerie, Benedetta was forty-two and Gregorio was forty-four and they were always fun to be with. They had no children, as they had discovered that Benedetta was unable to conceive, and had chosen not to adopt. Instead, she lavished all her love and time and energy on their business and worked side by side with Gregorio, with impressive results.

The one painful aspect of their marriage was Gregorio's weakness for pretty women, and occasionally scandalous dalliances that caught the attention of the press. Although she deplored his infidelities, it was something Benedetta had long since decided to overlook, since his indiscretions usually blew over quickly and were never serious attachments. He was never in love with the women he had affairs with, and he seemed no worse than the husbands of many of her Italian friends. She disliked it when Gregorio had an affair, and she complained about it, but he was always contrite, insisted he loved her passionately, and she always forgave him. And his rule on the subject was never to sleep with the wives of his friends or Benedetta's friends.

Gregorio was hopelessly attracted to models, particularly very young ones, and Benedetta tried not to have him at fittings for that reason. There was no point putting temptation in his path, as he had no trouble finding them for himself. He always seemed to have some young girl hanging on his every word, while his wife turned a blind eye. But there was never any sign of his infidelities when they were out together.

9

He was a devoted husband who adored his wife. He was strikingly handsome, they were a very attractive couple, and always fun to have around, and they both looked ecstatic as they stood around the Place Dauphine, with Jean-Philippe and their friends, waiting to hear where the dinner would be located that night. Everyone was guessing, and Jean-Philippe thought it would be Notre Dame.

As it turned out, he was right, and as the location was announced at exactly quarter to nine, a gasp of delight, cheers, and applause went up from the crowd. It was one of everyone's favorite locations. The rest of their friends had arrived by then, and they were ready to move on for dinner.

Chantal Giverny, another of Jean-Philippe's closest friends, was a regular every year. At fifty-five, she was slightly older than the other guests and had been a successful screenwriter for many years. She had won two Césars, had been nominated for an Oscar and a Golden Globe in the States, and was always creating something new. Her dramatic work was powerful, and she occasionally did documentaries on subjects that were meaningful, usually related to cruelty or injustices to women and children. She was writing a screenplay now but wouldn't have missed the White Dinner for the world. She was one of Jean-Philippe's favorite people, and his confidante. They had met one night at a dinner party and had become fast friends. They had lunch frequently, and he always asked for her advice. He trusted her judgment implicitly, and

10

their friendship and the time they spent together were gifts to both of them.

Chantal had been thrilled when he and Valerie got married and thought they were perfect for each other. She was the godmother of their first child, Jean-Louis, who was now five. She had three grown children of her own, none of whom lived in France. She had devoted herself entirely to them after she was widowed when they were young, and Jean-Philippe knew that it was hard for her to have them all living far away. She had brought them up to be independent and pursue their dreams fearlessly, which they had. And now Eric, her younger son, was an artist in Berlin; Paul, her older son, was an independent filmmaker in L.A.; and Charlotte, her daughter, went to the London School of Economics, got an MBA at Columbia, and was now a banker in Hong Kong. And none of them had any interest in moving back to France, so Chantal was alone. She had done her job too well. Her flock had flown.

She always said she was grateful that her work kept her busy, and she visited her children from time to time but didn't want to intrude on them. They had their own lives and expected her to have her own. Her only regret was that she had been so dedicated to them, and busy with them, that she had made no effort to get seriously involved with a man while they were young. And by now she hadn't met a man who interested her in years. So she worked harder than she might have if she'd had someone to share her life, or if her children lived near. But she was busy and happy and never complained about her solitude, although Jean-Philippe worried about her and wished she'd meet someone so she wouldn't be so alone. Once in a while, she admitted to him how lonely it was to have her children so far away, but most of the time she stayed busy with her friends, had a positive attitude about life, and she added fun and intellectual sophistication to every occasion.

The rest of their group that night had also been to the White Dinner before, as Jean-Philippe and Valerie's guests, with the exception of a lovely Indian man they had met in London the year before. Dharam Singh was from Delhi, one of the most successful men in India, and a technology genius. He was consulted by high-tech firms all over the world and was a charming, unassuming, very attractive man. He said he had business in Paris in June, so they had invited him to the dinner, especially for Chantal, since she didn't have a man to bring and needed someone at her table. Jean-Philippe was sure they'd get along, although Dharam's taste seemed to run to very beautiful, very young women. If nothing else, the Dumases were sure that Dharam and Chantal would be good dinner partners and find each other interesting.

Dharam was fifty-two and divorced, with two grown children in Delhi. His son was in the business with him, and his daughter was married to the richest man in India, had three children, and was a spectacularly beautiful woman. Dharam's white suit, made by his tailor in London, made him look very handsome and exotic, as he sat across from Chantal. She had brought the tablecloth and table settings, and the meal, and he had added caviar in a silver bowl, champagne, and excellent white wine.

Chantal looked lovely that night and as always younger than her years with a trim figure, still youthful face, and long blond hair. She and Dharam were already deep in conversation about filmmaking in India and enjoying each other's company as he opened their champagne, and he had brought a bottle for Valerie and Jean-Philippe too. Several of the tables shared their food, and there was a congenial, festive atmosphere throughout. It was amazing to think that seven thousand people were dining elegantly and having a good time. And by nine-thirty everyone was sitting and the party was under way, as wine was poured, hors d'oeuvres were passed around, old friends were rediscovered, and new ones were made.

There was a table of younger people just behind them, with some very pretty girls in their midst, whom Gregorio and Dharam had already spotted, and then pretended not to notice, focusing on the people at their table. Jean-Philippe and Valerie had put together an attractive, lively group who were clearly having a good time as everyone laughed and had fun, as the sun set slowly, and the last rays reflected off the glass of Notre Dame. It was an exquisite sight. The church bells had tolled almost as soon as they had arrived, greeting them. And the priest had come out on the balcony to wave at them and make them feel welcome.

Half an hour later the sun had set, and the entire square in front of Notre Dame was candlelit, with candles on every table. Jean-Philippe strolled around to make sure that all his guests were having a good time. He stopped to talk to Chantal, and for just a flash of an instant, she saw a serious expression in his eyes, which concerned her.

'Is everything all right?' she whispered to him when he bent to kiss her. She knew him well.

'I'll call you tomorrow,' he answered so no one else could hear. 'Let's have lunch if you can.' She nodded, always willing to be available to him if he needed her, or just for a friendly lunch to chat and laugh. He moved on to his other guests just as Gregorio's cellphone rang. He answered in Italian and switched immediately to English as Benedetta stared at him with a worried look. He got up hastily and walked away to continue the conversation, and Benedetta joined Dharam and Chantal's banter at the table next to theirs and tried to look unconcerned.

Chantal had seen the pain in her eyes. She suspected it was the latest of Gregorio's affairs. He was gone for a long time, and Dharam drew Benedetta into their conversation gracefully. He had been trying to convince Chantal to visit India and suggested locations she had to see, among them Udaipur, with its temples and palaces, which he said was the most romantic place in the world. She didn't say that she had no one to travel with, which would have seemed pathetic. And he was shocked to discover that Benedetta had never been to India either. He was still trying to entice both of them when Gregorio returned to the table half an hour later with a nervous glance at his wife, and said something cryptically to her in Italian.

Dharam had been liberally pouring the wine for all three of them in Gregorio's absence. Benedetta had looked more relaxed for a minute, until her husband returned to the table. She answered him rapidly in Italian. He had just told her he had to leave. He was speaking softly so the others wouldn't hear him, and Chantal and Dharam chatted so as not to appear to be listening.

'Now?' Benedetta asked him with a tone of severe irritation. 'Can't it wait?' She had been living with a difficult situation for the past six months and didn't like it intruding on the time they spent with friends, particularly tonight, although she knew that the cat had been out of the bag for some time and was all over the tabloids. But no one had been rude or unkind enough to bring it up to her.

'No, it can't wait,' Gregorio answered tersely. He had been having an affair with a twenty-three-year-old Russian supermodel for the last eight months, and the girl had been foolish enough to get pregnant six months before, with twins, and refused to have an abortion. Gregorio had had other affairs, many of them, but he had never fathered a child with any of them. And given Benedetta's inability to conceive, the fact of the girl's pregnancy was excruciatingly painful for her. It had been the worst year of Benedetta's life. He had promised her that it was an unfortunate mistake and he wasn't in love with Anya, and as soon as she had the babies, he would disengage from her. But Benedetta wasn't sure how willing the girl would be to let go of him. She had moved to Rome three months before to be closer to him, and he had been running back and forth between the two cities for those three months. It was driving Benedetta to distraction.

'She's in labor,' he added, anguished to have to discuss it with her here. And if that was true, she was three months early, Benedetta realized.

'Is she in Rome?' Benedetta asked in a pained voice.

'No. Here.' He continued in Italian. 'She had a job here this week. They just admitted her to the hospital an hour ago, in early labor. I hate to leave you, but I think I should go. She's all alone, and she's terrified.' He was mortified to be explaining it to his wife, the whole thing had been an agonizingly awkward situation for months, and the paparazzi had had a field day with it. Benedetta had been very elegant about it, and the Russian girl was less so. She called him constantly and wanted to be with him in situations that were absolutely impossible. He was a married man, and he intended to stay that way, and had told her so from the beginning. But she was on her own in a hospital in Paris, in labor three months prematurely, and he didn't feel he had a choice but to go to her at once. He was a decent human being after all, in a terrible situation for both him and his wife. And he knew that abandoning her at the White Dinner

16

wouldn't sit well with her.

'Can't you wait until this is over?' Anya had been sobbing hysterically on the phone, but he didn't want to explain that to Benedetta. She knew enough.

'I don't think I should. I'm really sorry. I'll just slip away quietly. You can say I saw friends at another table. No one will realize I'm gone.' Of course they would, but worst of all, she would know that he was gone, and where, who he was with, and why. The joy of the evening was over for her at that moment. She was still trying to absorb the fact that he was going to have two children with someone else, while they had none.

He stood up then, not wanting to argue with her but determined to go. However unfortunate their alliance and Anya's pregnancy, he didn't want to leave her in the hospital in labor, panicked and alone. Benedetta was sure it was just a ploy to get him there and it would turn out to be a false alarm.

'If she's all right, please come back,' she said, looking tense, and he nodded. It was embarrassing to have to cover for him, once they noticed that he was gone, which they were bound to do while she sat at their table without him, and left by herself when it was over.

'I'll try,' he said, still speaking to her in Italian. He gave her an uncomfortable look, and then without saying anything to their host or the other guests, he disappeared into the crowd, as people milled from table to table, visiting with friends between courses. He was gone in an instant, while Benedetta tried to appear as though

17

nothing had happened and she wasn't upset. Chantal and Dharam were still talking, and a little while later Chantal excused herself to say hello to someone she knew at another table. Benedetta was trying to calm her nerves from Gregorio's hasty departure, when Dharam turned to her with a gentle look.

'Did your husband leave?' he asked cautiously, not wanting to pry.

'Yes . . . he had an emergency . . . a friend had an accident, and he went to help him at the hospital,' she said, fighting back tears while trying to sound nonchalant. 'He didn't want to disrupt the party by saying goodbye.' Dharam had seen the tense looks exchanged between them and could tell that she was upset, and he did his best to cheer her now.

'How wonderful. It must be destiny,' he responded. 'I've been trying to get you to myself all night. Now I can woo you relentlessly without his interfering!' He smiled broadly, and she laughed. 'In a romantic setting like this, we should be madly in love by the time he gets back.'

'I don't think he is coming back,' she said sadly.

'Perfect. The gods are on my side tonight. Let's make a plan immediately. When will you come to India to see me?' He was teasing her to raise her spirits, but he was more taken with her than he would have dared to admit otherwise, and she chuckled at his performance, as he handed her a white rose from Chantal's vase on their table. She took the rose from him and smiled, just as the band started playing in front of the church. 'Would you like to dance?' he asked. She didn't really want to, knowing where Gregorio had gone and what was happening, but she didn't want to be rude to Dharam, while he was being so kind to her. She got up and followed him to the dance floor, as he held her hand in the crowd. He was a good dancer, and dancing with him took her mind off her troubles for a while. She was smiling when they came back to the table and found Chantal deep in conversation with Jean-Philippe, who looked up when he saw them.

'Where's Gregorio?' he asked Benedetta, and Dharam answered for her.

'I paid two men to remove him and tie him up, so I could seduce his wife. He was becoming quite a nuisance,' Dharam said as the others laughed, and even Benedetta was grinning. And Jean-Philippe got the instant feeling that he shouldn't inquire any further about his friend. The look in Benedetta's eyes said that something unpleasant had happened, and Dharam was trying to distract her. He wondered if the couple had had an argument and Gregorio had stormed off. If so, Jean-Philippe had missed it, but he had seen Gregorio create scenes before. And he knew from Valerie that all was not rosy between them at the moment.

The story about the pregnant supermodel was all over the fashion world, and she had told him about it months before. But Jean-Philippe would never have mentioned it to Gregorio or Benedetta. He just hoped that they'd survive it, as they had before when he got involved with young women. He'd been pleased that they had agreed to come to the dinner that night, but it was unfortunate, especially for Benedetta, that he hadn't stayed. Jean-Philippe was grateful to his Indian friend for helping Benedetta save face and salvage the evening. Dharam was talking animatedly to Benedetta and Chantal when Jean-Philippe walked away to check on his other guests. Everyone seemed to be having a wonderful time.

Dharam had been taking photographs all evening with his cellphone, to show his children how beautiful the evening was. He was so glad he had come. They all were. Even Benedetta, thanks to Dharam being so kind and humorous with her. And he had plied her with excellent champagne to raise her spirits. Both she and Chantal were having a good time with him and the others in their group. Some delicious desserts were passed around, and plenty of wine and champagne. Someone else had brought a huge box of fabulous chocolates they shared generously, and another table provided delicate white *macarons* from Pierre Hermé.

And at eleven o'clock Jean-Philippe handed out the regulation sparklers to his guests, and suddenly the entire square was ablaze with twinkling, sparkling lights being held aloft and waved as Dharam took photographs of that too. He had chronicled the entire evening with photos and videos. It touched Chantal when he said he was doing it to show his children. She couldn't imagine sending photographs of the evening to hers. They were very independent, and not interested in her activities, and would probably think her silly if she sent them photographs of the White Dinner and might wonder why she was there. Their vision of her was of someone who stayed home working and had no particular life apart from them. As a result, she told them very little about what she did, and most of the time they didn't ask. It never occurred to them. They were far more engaged in their own activities than hers, not out of any malice, they just never thought of her as a person who had a life that might be of interest to them. Meanwhile, Dharam was having them all pose for the photographs to send his son and daughter, convinced that they would want to know all about it. His whole face lit up when he talked about them.

The party was still lively as people visited from other tables and began to mill around a little more than they had earlier. And as Chantal turned to greet a cameraman she knew, who had worked on a documentary she did in Brazil, and another screenwriter, she noticed the good-looking younger people at the table behind them. They were handing out paper lanterns from a huge box. One of the men at the table was showing everyone how to set them up, and he handed several lanterns to Jean-Philippe's guests too. The lanterns were about three feet tall and had a small burner at the bottom that was lit with a match, and as the small fire burned, the paper lantern filled with warm air. Once it was fully inflated, he held it aloft, high over his head, and let it go. They watched the lantern sail up into the sky, as the fire within continued to burn. The others could see it sailing through the night sky, brightly lit like a shooting star, carried on the wind. It was an exquisite sight, and the guests around him were excited as they lit their own. The man giving them away told them to make a wish before they let them go, once they were lit by the flame at the base and full of warm air. They were gorgeous to watch. Chantal was mesmerized by the sheer beauty of it, as Dharam took a video and then helped Benedetta light hers. He reminded her to make a wish as they held on to hers and then released the delicate lantern into the night.

'Did you make a good wish?' Dharam asked her seriously after hers sailed into the sky, and she nodded, but didn't tell him for fear it wouldn't come true. She had wished for her marriage to return to what it was before Anya had come into their lives.

The others were busy lighting their lanterns too, as the man who had brought them continued to help everyone, and then he turned and saw Chantal. Their eyes met for a long moment. He was a handsome man in white jeans and a white sweater, with a thick mane of dark hair, and looked to be about Jean-Philippe's age, somewhere in his late thirties. The girls at his table were beautiful and considerably younger, in their twenties, like her daughter's age.

He spoke to her directly, never taking his eyes from hers. 'Did you do one yet?' She shook her head. She hadn't. She'd been too busy watching

Dharam and Benedetta do theirs, and Jean-Philippe's had been one of the first.

The young man walked over to Chantal then and held one out. He lit it for her, and they waited for it to fill with warm air as he told her it was the last one. It seemed to fill more quickly than the others, and she was surprised by the heat from the small flame. 'Hang on to it with me, and make a wish,' he instructed her quickly, holding it with her so they didn't let it go too soon. And just as it was ready, he turned to her with an intense look. 'Did you make a wish?' She nodded, and then he told her to let it go, and at the moment they released it, it sailed straight up into the sky, like a rocket, heading for the stars. She stood and stared at it like a child watching a balloon float away, with total fascination, as he stood beside her, keeping his eyes on the lantern with her. They could see the fire at its base burn brightly until they could barely see it anymore, and then he turned to smile at her.

'It must have been a good wish. That was a powerful one — it went straight up to heaven.'

'I hope so,' she said, and smiled back at him. It had been one of those perfect moments that you know you'll never forget. The whole evening had been that way. The White Dinner always was. 'Thank you. That was beautiful. Thank you for doing it with me, and giving me the last one.' He nodded and went back to his friends, and a little while later she saw him looking at her again, and they exchanged a smile. He was sitting with lovely young girls, and a pretty woman across from him.

The next hour passed too quickly for all of them, and at twelve-thirty Jean-Philippe reminded them all to wrap up. The witching hour had come. And like seven thousand Cinderellas, it was time to leave the ball. The white garbage bags came out, and what needed to be was thrown away. The rest they put back in their caddies, the silverware, the vases, the glasses, the remaining wine and food. Within minutes all the accessories had disappeared, the tablecloths, tables, and chairs were folded, the lines of elegant tables had vanished, and seven thousand people dressed in white quietly left the square in front of Notre Dame, with a last glance over their shoulders to where the magic had taken place. Chantal thought about the beautiful lanterns again, burning their way gently through the sky, and she saw that the table of people that had brought them had already left. The lanterns had vanished from the sky by then, carried by the wind to where others would see them and wonder from where they had come.

Jean-Philippe asked around to make sure everyone could get home. Chantal was planning to take a cab. Dharam had offered to take Benedetta back to the hotel since they were staying at the same one. And the others all had rides too. Jean-Philippe promised to call Chantal in the morning and arrange to meet for lunch, and she thanked him for another unforgettable evening. The White Dinner was her favorite day of the year, and everyone else's who was lucky enough to come. And with the beautiful paper lanterns soaring up into the sky, she thought this had been the most magical one of all.

'I had a wonderful time,' Chantal said to Jean-Philippe as she kissed him goodbye. He helped her into a cab with her caddy and table and chairs and asked the driver to assist her when she got home.

'So did I,' Jean-Philippe said, beaming at her, as Valerie waved while she loaded up their car. Dharam and Benedetta were just getting into a taxi to go back to the George V. And the others were heading for cabs and cars and the nearest Metro station. It was an orderly unraveling of what had been a perfectly orchestrated event. 'See you tomorrow,' he called after Chantal, as her taxi drove away and she waved from the window. And suddenly Chantal wondered if her wish would come true. She hoped it would, but even if it didn't, the evening had been flawless and unforgettable, and she smiled all the way home.

2

Dharam was a perfect gentleman when he escorted Benedetta to her room, carrying her folded table and chairs for her, while she rolled the grocery caddy behind her. She had brought their table decorations from Italy, and borrowed the plates and silverware from the hotel. He asked if she would like to have a drink downstairs at the bar, but she wanted to wait in her room to hear from Gregorio. It would be a conversation she didn't want to have in a public place. She told Dharam she was tired, and he understood. He said he had had a delightful evening thanks to her, and would send her the photographs and the video, and get her email address from Jean-Philippe. He didn't want to bother her for it then. He could see that she was worried again now that the party was over and there were no distractions. Clearly, something had happened for her husband to disappear the way he did. And just as clearly she was upset about it. She thanked him again for his help and kindness through the evening and said goodnight.

And as soon as she was alone, she lay down on the bed. She checked her cellphone, and there were no text messages or voicemails. She had checked it discreetly periodically through the evening and had heard nothing from him. And she didn't want to call him and catch him at an awkward moment when he couldn't talk to her. She lay there waiting to hear from him, and by three A.M. she had heard nothing and fell asleep.

★ ★ ★

Gregorio got to the hospital just before ten P.M. and Anya had already been admitted to a room in the maternity ward. She was being examined by two doctors when he walked into her room. She was lying on the bed sobbing and reached her arms out to him immediately. She was in mild labor, and she hadn't started dilating, but the contractions were consistent and strong, and the IV of magnesium they had started an hour before hadn't stopped them. Their concern was that the babies were still too small and too undeveloped to be born. Both doctors agreed that there was only a very small chance of saving them if she delivered them now, because of the stage of gestation and the fact that they were even smaller than usual because they were twins. And Anya was hysterical after what they said.

'Our babies are going to die!' she wailed as Gregorio held her in his arms. This was not the scenario he had wanted to be involved in. He had hoped everything would go smoothly at the appropriate time, and he could make a gracious exit from her life, with financial support for her and the twins. He had never wanted her to have them, or to get pregnant at all. Because of a casual, playful indiscretion, he had wound up in a situation he had never been in before and didn't want. And now it was even worse.

27

The obstetrician had been candid with them that the babies were likely to die or be damaged, and he would have to deal with a possible tragedy, not just an unwanted birth. And he was worried about his wife too. He couldn't leave Anya for long enough to call Benedetta and reassure her. He could just imagine the state she was in. She had been patient with his indiscretions before, but this time was infinitely more upsetting. He had never gotten anyone pregnant. And now there would be two children he didn't want, with a girl he barely knew, who had been asking him to leave his wife for her, which was out of the question. He had never misled any of the women he got involved with, and always told them he loved his wife. And no one had ever asked him to leave her. But as soon as Anya got pregnant, she had become totally dependent on him, like a child herself, and Gregorio was not equal to the pressure she put on him. It had been a nightmarish six months, and now the possibilities the doctors had outlined to them that night were horrifying. He felt sorry for Anya, as she sobbed in his arms, but he wasn't in love with her, not that that mattered now. They were in this together, and there was no way out. He had to see it through. There were two tiny lives at stake, and both could be seriously impaired if they survived, which was an awesome responsibility too. He couldn't imagine Anya handling that at twenty-three, and she had the maturity of a sixteen-year-old. She clung to him like a child that night, and he never left her side. It was a terrible situation.

Gregorio was shaken by it too.

The contractions slowed for a little while, then picked up at midnight and got stronger again, and then she started dilating. They had given her an IV of steroids to try and increase the babies' lung capacity if they were born, but it was too early, and at four o'clock in the morning, they told them it was unlikely that her labor could be stopped. A special neonatal team was brought in while she was closely monitored and labor began in earnest, but instead of the joy of anticipation normally associated with a birth, there was a sense of dread and resignation in the room. Whatever happened now, they all knew it wouldn't be good. The only questions were just how bad it would be and if the twins would survive.

Anya was terrified and screamed with every pain. They gave her no drugs to ease the contractions, so as not to risk the babies further, but eventually they gave her an epidural to lessen the pain, and to Gregorio it all looked fierce. She had tubes and monitors everywhere, and as the labor progressed, both babies began to show signs of distress with each contraction, but she was fully dilated so they told her she could push. Gregorio was horrified, watching what she was going through, but stayed staunchly at her side. He finally forgot about his wife entirely, all he could think about was this poor pathetic girl, clinging to him in terror and sobbing between contractions. She was almost unrecognizable in the condition she was in. This was not the racy, flamboyant girl he had met and slept with on a lark.

Their son was born first, at six A.M. He was blue when he emerged, a tiny infant who didn't look fully formed and had to fight for his first breath. He was whisked away the instant the cord was cut and rolled down the hall in an incubator to the neonatal ICU with two doctors and a nurse. With a respirator already in place, the infant was struggling for his life. His skin was so thin you could see his veins through it. His heart stopped an hour after he was born, but he was revived by the team attending to him, and they told Gregorio that his chances for survival were not good. As he listened to what they said, tears rolled down Gregorio's cheeks. He hadn't expected to be so moved by the sight of his first child being born, and in such dire distress. The baby looked like a creature from another world, with wide staring eyes that were begging them to help. Gregorio couldn't stop crying as he looked at him, and Anya was incoherent from the pain.

The little girl came twenty minutes later, slightly bigger than her brother, and with a stronger heart. Each weighed less than two pounds. But her lungs were as inadequate as his. They put her on a respirator, and a second team whisked her away. Anya began hemorrhaging after the second birth, which took them time to control and required two transfusions, and Gregorio saw that she looked gray. And then they mercifully gave her something to make her sleep, after the trauma she'd been through, and they warned both of them again that the babies might not survive. Both were in critical condition, and it would be a long time before they were safe, if they lived. The days ahead would be crucial. The doctors spoke to Gregorio again after Anya was sedated and unconscious. He went to see the babies in their incubators then and just stood there and cried, he was so moved by the tiny beings, his children. It had been a hard night for him too, and the worst lay ahead. He had no idea what he would say to Benedetta now. This was all so much more intense than anything he had imagined. He had believed it would all work out somehow, and now clearly it wouldn't, or not for a long time. There was no escaping reality and the consequences of his actions.

A nurse told him that Anya would sleep for a few hours from the shot she'd been given, and he realized that this was his chance to go back to the hotel. It was eight in the morning by then and he hadn't called Benedetta all night. There had been no chance to do so, and once Anya woke up, he might not be able to get away again. She had no family in western Europe, just a mother in Russia she hadn't seen in years, and no one else to help her. He was it. And there were the babies to think of now. He had felt instantly attached to them, which had come as a shock to him.

He took a cab back to the hotel and walked into the George V feeling as though he had returned from another planet. Here everything seemed normal and the way it had been the night before, when they left for the White Dinner. It seemed odd to see such ordinary life around him. People leaving for meetings, going to breakfast, walking through the lobby, checking in. He went up to his room and found Benedetta sitting at the desk with her head in her hands, staring at the phone. She was in despair and had been awake nearly all night, waiting to hear from him. He was still wearing his clothes from the night before, and noticed that there was blood on his white shoes, which made him feel sick when he remembered how it had gotten there. There had been blood everywhere when Anya gave birth. They had given her two transfusions. The delivery had been a terrible scene.

'I'm sorry I didn't call you last night,' he said in a dead voice as he walked in. She turned to him with anger mixed with fear, and saw tragedy in his eyes. 'I couldn't.'

'What happened?' She looked frantic.

'They were born two hours ago. They may not survive. It was the worst thing I've ever seen in my life. It may just be too early for them to be saved. They're doing all they can. They don't even look complete or ready to be born. And they both weigh under two pounds.' He acted as though he expected her to grieve with him, and Benedetta just stared at him in misery.

'What are you going to do now?' she asked him with a look of anguish. He had two children now, by someone else. And she could see that they were very real to him. She hadn't expected that.

'I have to go back. She has no one else. And I can't just walk out on them. They're fighting for their lives, and they could die at any time. I have to be there, for her and for them.' He sounded surprisingly noble, and Benedetta nodded, unable to speak. She felt shut out of what was happening to him. It was the hardest day of her life. 'I'll call you later and let you know what's happening.' He was pulling clothes out of the closet as he spoke to her, and changing as she watched. He didn't take the time to shower or eat — all he wanted was to get back.

'Should I wait here?' she asked in a flat voice.

'I don't know. I'll tell you later.' He realized that it might be all over by the time he got back to the hospital. He put his wallet in his pants and looked at Benedetta sadly. 'I'm sorry. I really am. We'll get through this somehow, I promise. I'll make it up to you.' Although he had no idea how, and she didn't see how he could. And if the twins survived, he had two children now. He walked over to kiss her, and she turned away from him. For the first time in their life together, she couldn't face him, and maybe not forgive him either. She didn't know yet. 'I'll call you,' he said gruffly, and then left the room in a hurry, and as soon as he did, she burst into tears. She went back to bed and cried until she fell asleep. And by then Gregorio was back at the hospital, sitting between the two incubators, watching his newborn babies fight for their lives, with an army of people tending to them, and tubes attached to every part of them.

He went back to Anya in her room an hour later, when they told him she was awake, and he spent the day consoling her, and whenever he

33

thought he could leave her for a few minutes, he went back to see the babies. It was nearly six o'clock when he remembered to call Benedetta, and neither her cellphone nor the hotel room answered.

She had gone out for a walk, and ran into Dharam as she left the hotel. Her hair was pulled back in a ponytail, she was wearing jeans and flat shoes, and she looked ravaged. He felt instantly sorry for her, and tried not to let it show. She made distracted small talk as they walked out of the hotel, and he turned to look at her. She was smaller than he remembered, and he realized she'd been wearing high heels the night before. She was a slight, delicate woman and seemed fragile to him now, with huge sad eyes that dwarfed her face.

'Are you all right?' he asked her gently. He didn't want to be intrusive, but he was worried about her. She appeared as though something terrible had happened. He wondered if it had to do with her husband leaving the night before. Unlike Jean-Philippe and Valerie, he knew nothing of the fashion world gossip and Gregorio's affair with the Russian model.

'I . . . yes . . . no.' She started to lie to him and then couldn't, as tears ran down her cheeks, and she just shook her head. 'I'm sorry . . . I was just going out to get some air.'

'Do you want company, or do you want to be alone?'

'I don't know . . . ' She was confused and he hated to let her leave the hotel by herself. She was so distracted she didn't seem safe alone. She

34

was in no condition to be on the streets on her own.

'May I come? We don't have to talk. I don't think you should go out alone.'

'Thank you.' She nodded and he followed her out of the hotel and fell into stride beside her. They walked for several blocks before she spoke. And then she glanced at him hopelessly, as though the world had come to an end, and for her, it had.

'My husband started having an affair with a model several months ago. He's done it before, which is embarrassing, but he always came to his senses and got out of it very quickly. This time the girl got pregnant, with twins. She gave birth to them three months early this morning. And now my husband is entangled in all the drama of two babies who may die, a young girl who needs him, and these are his first children. We have none. It's an incredible mess, and I have no idea how we'll survive it. And this could go on for months. I don't know what to do now. He's at the hospital with her.' The story tumbled out as tears ran down her cheeks, and Dharam remained calm, although he was stunned.

'Maybe you should go home,' he said quietly. 'That might be better than waiting for news in a hotel room, on your own. It might take a while for things to calm down. You can't sort it out right now.' Everything he said was sensible, and she wondered if he was right. This was Gregorio's drama to deal with, not hers, at least not now. First, he had to see if the babies would survive. Afterward, they'd figure out the rest, and what would happen to their marriage.

'I think you're right,' she said sadly. 'The whole thing has been so awful. And everybody knows. It's been all over the papers in Italy. The paparazzi have taken pictures of her every day since she moved to Rome. He's never gotten as deeply involved as this before, and as publicly,' she said, trying to be loyal to Gregorio, although she could no longer figure out why. 'I think I'll go back to Milan.'

'Do you have people to support you there?' he asked, worried about her, and she nodded.

'My family, and his. Everyone is angry at him for being in this mess. And so am I.' She looked at Dharam with all the sorrows of the world in her eyes and he nodded, relieved to hear that she wouldn't be alone when she got home.

'That's hardly surprising. It sounds as though you've been very patient about it, if you're here with him.'

'I thought it would blow over, but it hasn't. At least not yet, and now with all the drama of the babies being premature, and gravely at risk, I don't see it getting better anytime soon. I feel sorry for him, but I feel sorry for me too,' she said honestly, and he nodded again.

'It sounds like things are going to be rough for a while,' Dharam agreed with her. 'May I call you to see how you are, just as a friend? I want to know that you're all right.'

'Thank you.' She was mortally embarrassed to tell him her troubles, but he was a compassionate person. 'I'm sorry to tell you all this awful stuff. It's not a pretty story.'

'No, but it's real life,' he said, sympathetic but not shocked. 'People get themselves into terrible situations sometimes. My wife left me for another man fifteen years ago, it was all over the press. He was a well-known Indian actor. Everyone was horrified, and I hated having my private life in the papers. Eventually it all calms down and people forget. We all lived through it. My children stayed with me, and we were fine. At the time, I thought it would kill me, but it didn't.' He smiled at her. 'You'd be surprised what you can endure. This will sort itself out in time. You'll survive it. Does he say he's going to marry her?'

'He says not,' Benedetta answered quietly, feeling better after talking to him. She was glad she had run into him in the lobby, although it was humiliating telling a stranger her problems, but he was very kind and reassuring about it. It helped her get perspective. 'I think it was just a casual affair that got out of hand. And now he's in deep waters.'

'I'd say so,' Dharam said wryly, and Benedetta smiled. An hour before, she couldn't have imagined smiling, but it was better than sobbing in her hotel room. Dharam had a calm, protective presence as he thought about her situation. She was an innocent victim in the story, as he had been in his divorce. And he wondered if it would come to that for her, or if she'd forgive Gregorio. She had obviously put up with his other infidelities, from what she said. But the current drama was extreme.

They walked slowly back to the hotel then,

and he said he was leaving for London the next morning, and going back to Delhi a few days later. 'Let me know what you do,' he said when they were back in the lobby of the George V, with a profusion of pink and purple orchids around them. The hotel was known for its spectacular floral displays by their famous American designer. 'I'd like to know if you go back to Milan.' She nodded and thanked him for his kindness and apologized again for burdening him with her troubles.

'That's what friends are for, even new ones,' he said with a warm look in his eyes. 'Call me if I can do anything to help you.' He handed her his card with all his contact numbers on it, and she thanked him again and slipped it into her pocket. He had dinner plans that night or he would have offered to take her to dinner, but he suspected she was too distraught to eat or go to a restaurant. He gave her a gentle hug a few minutes later when he left her, and she went back upstairs, and he went outside to the car waiting to take him to dinner. He thought about her all the way to the restaurant. He felt desperately sorry for her. She was a nice woman and didn't deserve what was happening to her. He hoped it would all work out the way she wanted. And he was very glad to have met her the night before.

When Benedetta got back to her room, she lay down on the bed, and Gregorio called her a few minutes later. He sounded anxious and rushed and said he couldn't talk long. He told her the babies were still in distress but alive, and Anya

38

was hysterical. He said there was no way he could come back to the hotel that night. He was in a life-and-death situation, with the babies hanging on by a thread. Benedetta closed her eyes as she listened. She had never heard him sound that way before. All he could talk about or think of now were the babies, he had no time or compassion for her.

'I think I'll go back to Milan in the morning. There's no point in my sitting here waiting to hear from you.' She sounded sad but calmer than he had expected. He couldn't have dealt with her losing control too. At least she was being sensible, which was how he interpreted what she said to him, and her tone. He had no idea how panicked she was feeling too when Gregorio said he didn't know how he could leave Anya and the babies in Paris, and for now he didn't want to. It was out of the question. And Benedetta realized that he might be there for a long time, given what was happening. The doctors had said that if the twins survived, they would be in the hospital for at least three months, until their due date. And she didn't want to ask him now if he intended to stay there too.

'I'll call you and tell you what's happening here,' he said in a somber tone. He was relieved to know that she was going home. It was too stressful to have her waiting for him at the hotel. He didn't want to have to worry about her too. 'I'm sorry, Benedetta, I never expected it to turn out like this.' She didn't know how to answer him. It shouldn't have been happening at all, but now that it was, they just had to ride the wave and see where it took them. It was hard to believe that things would ever be the same again between them, but she wasn't sure he understood that yet. All he could think of was Anya and their two babies in their incubators. He wasn't thinking of Benedetta at all.

After they hung up, Benedetta packed her suitcase and finally ordered something to eat from room service. She hadn't eaten all day, and she ordered a salad, and made her reservation for her flight back to Milan the next day. The concierge asked if Mr. Mariani would be flying with her, and she told him he wasn't.

She was up at six o'clock the next morning, and left the hotel by eight. She thought about calling Dharam to tell him, but it was too early. She sent him a text message instead, and thanked him again for his kindness to her the day before. And as the car and driver took her to the airport, she thought of Gregorio at the hospital, and wondered what was happening. She knew she couldn't call.

★   ★   ★

The babies survived the night, and Gregorio had slept in a chair next to their incubators. He had fallen instantly in love with two tiny beings, and all he could do now was pray that they would live. He was suddenly a father, and his heart had never been so full of love and pain at the same time. Their well-being was all that mattered to him now. And as he watched them, tears of joy and sorrow rolled down his cheeks. He and Anya sat with them for hours, holding hands, and for the first time, he realized he was in love with her, and he hadn't felt that way before. She had given him the greatest gift of all. It was something he and Benedetta had never shared. She was suddenly part of another life. His heart and children were here now. And Anya had been transformed into a new role in his life, a sacred one to him. She was the mother of his children. It transformed her from a young woman he had been involved with casually to one of dignity and vital importance. And as he looked at her, he saw someone completely different than the girl she had been before. Overnight they had become bonded to each other, as devastated parents praying for the survival of their children. Anya fell asleep that night sitting next to him, in the hum of the incubators and the beeping of the monitors, and with Anya's head on his shoulder, the last thing on his mind was Benedetta. For now at least, in the universe of love and terror he had been catapulted into, his wife had ceased to exist. Anya was his partner now, the mother of his twins.

3

As he had promised he would, Jean-Philippe
called Chantal the morning after the White
Dinner. He had been busy with his guests the
night before, and had had very little time to talk
to her. As always, he had wanted to make sure
everyone was having fun and the evening was
going well for them, and he had been concerned
about Benedetta as soon as he realized that
Gregorio had left, which he thought rude of
him. But fortunately, Dharam had taken her
under his wing and even danced with her, and
she seemed to have a good time anyway.
Jean-Philippe always worried about his guests,
and wanted to be sure they were all well taken
care of. And he had seen Chantal greet several
people she knew at the other tables, and others
had dropped by to see her. He had hoped that
Dharam would be attracted to her since he was
such an interesting, kind person and he thought
they'd like each other, but his Indian friend
seemed far more drawn to Benedetta. Chantal
didn't seem to mind, and had no romantic
interest in him. Those things were always hard
to predict, but Jean-Philippe had set the stage
for them as best he could. The electricity that
happened between men and women was
ephemeral and elusive, and either it happened
or it didn't.

'What a *wonderful* evening,' Chantal said

enthusiastically the moment she heard him on the phone. 'Thank you for including me. I thought it was the best one ever. The lanterns at the end made it even more special, they were magical. It was nice of those people to share them with us.' He heartily agreed, and then commented on Gregorio's early disappearance.

'It must have been something about that girl he's involved with. I didn't want to ask Benedetta about it. She's crazy to put up with it. Valerie says there's been a lot of talk about it in the fashion press. It sounds like this time he's really done it.'

'Do you suppose he'll leave Benedetta for her?' Chantal asked, feeling sorry for her.

'I would think it would be rather the reverse. Maybe she'll leave him. He's hardly been exemplary before this. He's so damn charming, she puts up with it, and they have a major empire they've built together. But one of these days she may get tired of his affairs. I felt sorry for her last night. It's embarrassing for her to have him run off even before dinner. It was good of Dharam to step in.'

'He's a nice man,' Chantal agreed. She had enjoyed talking to him. He seemed brilliant, and very modest about his accomplishments. He had gone to MIT in the States and was a legend in his own country, according to Jean-Philippe.

'But he's not for you?' he asked her, getting straight to the point. He always hoped she would meet someone who would protect and take care of her. Her work was so solitary, and he knew how lonely she was at times now without her

43

children. He would have loved to introduce her to the right man.

'I don't think either of us had any sparks for the other,' she said honestly, 'but I'd love to see him again, as a friend. I'm probably too old for him.' He was strikingly handsome, and exotically elegant, as well as intelligent, and only a few years younger than she was. But no current had passed between them, and she had sensed that he felt that way too. He had seemed much more interested in Benedetta, or maybe he just felt sorry for her and was being chivalrous. Chantal wasn't sure. But he definitely hadn't been drawn to her as a woman, and he hadn't made her heart beat any faster either. But that had been Jean-Philippe's fantasy, not her own, so she wasn't disappointed. She didn't really expect to meet a man anymore. She was beginning to feel past that, and all the good men she knew were married. French men rarely divorced, even if they were unhappily married. In that case, they had discreet 'arrangements' on the side, which didn't appeal to Chantal. She didn't particularly want a husband, and she emphatically didn't want someone else's. It was one of the reasons why other women liked her, she was a straightforward, honest, decent person.

'That's too bad about Dharam. He's such a great guy. If you ever go to India, he will introduce you to everyone. Valerie and I visited him in Delhi last year, and we had a fabulous time. Everybody loves him. He even has nice children the same ages as yours.' It was why he had thought they would be a good match, but fate had decided otherwise. There was obviously no chemistry between them. And they both knew that those things couldn't be planned or dictated. 'So, are we on for lunch today? I need your advice.'

'About a new color for the living room, or something serious?' she teased him. They consulted each other about everything, and he valued her opinions. He had bounced many things off her over the dozen years of their friendship, even about marrying Valerie seven years before. Chantal had approved of her wholeheartedly, and still did. She thought they were a perfect couple, and they were very happily married. It had been the right decision.

'Serious,' he answered cryptically.

'Business or personal?' she inquired.

'I'll tell you at lunch. Same time, same place?' They had lunch together regularly, at least once a week, in the same simple bistro in the seventh arrondissement on the Left Bank, not far from her apartment. They had tried other restaurants over the years, but preferred this one.

'Perfect. See you there,' she confirmed.

He was already seated at their usual table on the terrace when she got there in a red sweater and jeans and the flat shoes the French called 'ballerines,' inspired by ballet shoes. She looked pretty and fresh with her long blond hair pulled back in a ponytail with a red ribbon. He had come from the office, wearing a business suit, and had slipped his tie in his pocket. He ordered a steak and she a salad, and he ordered a glass of wine for each of them. He didn't always drink

45

wine at lunch, and it telegraphed to her that he was worried and tense. She could see it in his eyes as they wended their way through small talk about Valerie and the children and the dinner the night before.

'So what's up?' she finally asked him, unable to stand the suspense. Sometimes he was very French and took a long time to get to the point, taking a circuitous route rather than a direct one. She had had lunch with him only five days before, and he had said nothing about needing her advice on a serious subject, so whatever had come up must have been very recent. He hesitated for a moment before he answered.

'I have a problem, or I'm about to. Business isn't going well, the economy is terrible. Half the countries in Europe are shaky, and no one is making big investments here. The French have been afraid to show wealth for years, because of the tax on large fortunes and personal wealth. They're investing abroad as much as possible, and hiding their net worth wherever they can. The last thing the French want to do is invest in France and expose themselves to higher taxes. They don't trust the government.'

'Are you getting fired?' She looked instantly worried for him. She knew that he did well at the investment firm where he worked, but he had no large personal fortune, and he had a wife and three children to support, and a very comfortable lifestyle. And she knew how generous he was with Valerie, and loved to buy her pretty things, live well, and take her on great vacations. The children were starting to go to private schools, and they had a beautiful apartment in the sixteenth arrondissement, the fanciest part of Paris. Losing his job now would be a major challenge and represent a serious change for them. Valerie had a great job at *Vogue*, but she made far less than he did, since magazines didn't pay nearly as well. They relied on his income to live. At thirty-nine and thirty-five, they had to make their own money to support their lifestyle, and he had.

'No, I'm not getting fired. But realistically, I'm never going to make more than I do right now, unless there is a major upturn in the economy, and that's not going to happen. Not for at least a decade. I can't complain, I make a very decent salary, but I'm never going to be able to put aside real money for my family, and everything is expensive. And let's face it, with three children, and a pleasant life, it all adds up. I just can't see myself ever getting ahead here. If anything, it will get more expensive as the kids grow up, but I don't see more coming in in the future unless I make a drastic change of some kind. I've been thinking about it for the past year, but I couldn't see a solution. Until now. Beware of what you wish for. I was offered an incredible job three days ago, with a fantastic chance to make some real money. The kind of money I can only dream of here.'

'What's the catch?' Chantal knew there always was one. And there had to be for him, or he wouldn't have looked as worried or wanted her advice. If it was a straight-across move to another firm offering him significantly more, they would have been celebrating, and he would have told her.

'I've had an offer from a very important venture capital firm. They have American partners, and they have been making a fortune. They'll give me an opportunity to participate, and there is some very major money to be made. The starting salary is fabulous, but the participation they're offering is even more attractive. It's just what I need, if I'm ever going to make real money to support my family into the future. It's a golden opportunity.' But he was tense as the waiter set their food down and walked away, as Chantal waited to hear what was stopping him.

'Why are we not ordering champagne to celebrate this?' she asked him, as he glanced at her miserably.

'It's in China. That's where the big money is being made these days. They want me to move to Beijing for three to five years. It's not an easy place to live. I can't see Valerie wanting to take the children there. She's in love with Paris, and she loves her job here. It's a career for her, and she'll probably end up editor of French *Vogue* one day, but her job is never going to support us, and she knows that. A chance like this one doesn't come along every day, and if I turn this down, there may never be another. I may be pounding along for the next twenty years, trying to make ends meet and put money aside. If we go to Beijing, I could make money and secure our future. I think she'll hate me if we go, and she'd have to give up her career. And I'm going to have a hard time swallowing it if she deprives me, and us, of this opportunity. It's a terrible situation,' he said, looking mournful. Chantal thought carefully about what he'd said. It was not going to be an easy decision, and she agreed with him that Valerie would be upset. She would have to give up her career for his. And she couldn't put it on hold for three to five years. Someone else would take her place. Competition at fashion magazines was stiff.

'Have you asked her?' Chantal inquired quietly, trying to weigh all the pros and cons in her head. But if he was trying to make money, and needed to for his family, the pros in favor of China won out hands down.

'They just called me three days ago, and I met with them yesterday. Their American partners were in town, and last night was the White Dinner. I didn't have time to sit down and talk to her about it before last night. But I have to tell her very quickly. They want to know in the next few weeks, and they want me there by September.' He told Chantal the name of the firm, and she was impressed, and by the Americans they were allied with. It was a bona-fide offer from an important group.

'When are you going to tell her?'

'Tonight. Tomorrow. Soon. Chantal, what do you think I should do?'

'Wow,' she said softly, meeting his eyes as she sat back in her chair and stopped eating. 'That's a tough one. Someone is going to lose here, or it's going to look that way. You or her in the immediate, or all of you in the long run if you

49

turn down the offer.'

'I don't see how I can,' he said honestly, 'but what if she won't do it? What if she leaves me?' He looked panicked as he said it, and Chantal felt sorry for him. Why was there always a downside to a golden opportunity? Nothing was ever simple, not when there were big bucks attached. And Beijing was going to be the rub here. Chantal couldn't see Valerie making the move easily, or even willingly. He would have to drag her kicking and screaming to Beijing, or she might refuse to go and give up her own career, even if it was less lucrative than his. It meant a lot to her, and she had worked in fashion, and for *Vogue*, in two countries for more than a dozen years, ever since college. That was a great deal for her to give up. But so was the job he'd been offered.

'She's not going to leave you. She loves you.' Chantal tried to reassure him. 'But she'll be upset.' She couldn't deny that, and they both knew it. 'And you can't blame her. She works hard at *Vogue*, and the big job she wants is in sight now, when the Paris editor-in-chief retires. Could you go to Beijing for a shorter time? A year or two maybe, not three to five?' That was a long time to commit for, and he shook his head in answer.

'I might be able to limit it to three, initially at least, but no less than that. They want me to head up the Beijing office. The guy they have there now is leaving. He's been there for four years and opened the office for them.'

'Do you know why he's leaving?'

50

'His wife hates it there. She moved back to the States a year ago,' Jean-Philippe said ruefully, and then they both laughed.

'Well, that tells us what we need to know, doesn't it?' Chantal said, smiling at him. 'I think if you do it, you just have to know it won't be easy, but it's worth it for a limited amount of time, to achieve your goals. Sometimes we have to do something unpleasant to get where we want to go. It's a good career move for you. Valerie will understand that too.' But she also knew, as he did, that Valerie couldn't walk out on her job and come back to it three or four years later. By then, another senior editor would be in place, and she wouldn't be it. And she had waited a long time for that.

'I'm not sure what Valerie will understand, or want to. All she's going to hear is that it will impact her career and she'll have to leave *Vogue*, to move to a miserable place everyone says is a difficult city to live in, with three young children. I'm not at all sure how reasonable she's going to be. Maybe not at all.'

'Have more faith in her than that. She's a smart woman, and the realities are pretty clear here, economically. If she wants a secure lifestyle in the future, this is it. And in any case, you have to tell her and work it out together, even if she doesn't take the news well at first. She'll come around, and maybe you can come up with some kind of reasonable compromise.' But she couldn't see one, and neither could he. He would either have to accept their offer or not. And Valerie had to go with him or not. It was

51

painfully simple, *painful* being the operative word.

They talked about it all through lunch, and she left him on the sidewalk in front of the restaurant.

'Call me after you talk to her, and tell me how it goes.' Valerie was a sensible woman, and she loved Jean-Philippe. Whatever happened, Chantal was sure their relationship would survive it, even if it was turbulent at first, which she thought it might be. 'I'll be here for the next week, and next weekend I'm going to see Eric in Berlin,' her younger son. 'I haven't seen him since February, he's been producing a new body of work, and he didn't want to be interrupted. He's getting ready for a show.' He was doing well, although his conceptual installations were too edgy for her, but he was one of the more respected emerging artists, and his pieces were selling well. She was proud of him, and enjoyed visiting him. He had been living in Berlin for three years, and the art scene there had been great for him. And he had a new girlfriend he wanted her to meet too. Eric included her in his life more than his brother and sister did, and they lived farther away. But even with him living in Berlin, she only saw him a few times a year. He was too busy with his art to see her very often, and only came back to Paris now for Christmas every year, when the others did.

She had raised very independent children, none of whom wanted to live in France. It was bad luck for her, as she said to Jean-Philippe. All three of them had an excellent work ethic, as she did, and were doing well, but they had found other countries better suited to them. Charlotte had been living in Hong Kong since getting her master's at Columbia five years before and spoke fluent Mandarin.

And her older son, Paul, loved living in the States and had become more American than hot dogs and apple pie, with an American girlfriend there, whom Chantal didn't like, but he had lived with her for seven years. Her youngest, Eric, was the last to leave the nest three years before, and they had been lonely years for her, a fact she confessed to no one but Jean-Philippe. Her children were talented and productive but had no time for her.

Chantal went back to her apartment after lunch with Jean-Philippe and didn't hear from him for several days, which was unusual, since he called her frequently to check in. He had become her self-appointed family since her children had left. She had no siblings or parents, so her children and friends were all she had. She plunged into her writing for days and weeks at a time, and was currently writing a very serious script about a group of women in a concentration camp in World War II and their ultimate survival.

She suspected that the announcement of Jean-Philippe's job offer had not gone over well with his wife, and she didn't want to call him and intrude. She worked all weekend and was pleased with her progress, and he called her on Monday afternoon.

'How did it go?' she asked, as soon as she heard his voice.

'The way you'd expect,' he said, sounding tired. It had been a long, stressful weekend, and Chantal could hear it in his tone. 'She was shocked, upset, angry that I'm considering it. She cried all of Sunday afternoon. The good news is she didn't ask for a divorce.' He was kidding, but Chantal was sure that it had thrown a live bomb into their well-run life that had gone smoothly for seven years. They had been luckier than most, with happy children, easy times, good health, good friends, jobs they loved, and a lovely home in a city they adored. Now, overnight, they had to make a tough choice where one of them was going to lose and have to sacrifice. She didn't envy them, although they loved each other, and their marriage was solid, which would help, whatever decision they made.

'Do you think she'll agree to move to Beijing?' Chantal inquired.

'Right now, no, I don't. But that could change. She's thinking about it, and I have three weeks to decide.' It was going to be a long three weeks for him.

They had lunch on Wednesday that week, and he seemed very tense. There was nothing more to say on the subject, until Valerie made up her mind. For Jean-Philippe the decision was clear. He thought they should go, for all the reasons he had outlined to Chantal the week before. They talked of other things, and he told her that Valerie said that news of Gregorio's twins was all over the press, and that they were in a Paris

54

hospital, dangerously premature.

'Poor Benedetta,' Chantal said with feeling. They had realized by then that they were born the night of the White Dinner, which was why he had left early. 'I wonder how that's going to turn out. I'm not sure I'd be as forgiving as she is.'

'Maybe she won't be this time either. It must be a hell of a shock to know that he now has two children with someone else, when she can't have kids.' She had always been open about it, and shared her regrets, although she had made peace with it over the years. But now he had children, and she didn't, and they both wondered if it would give the Russian girl more importance in his life. He had brushed aside his affairs before, and they had never lasted long, but this added a whole new dimension to it. Chantal felt sorry for Benedetta, and Jean-Philippe thought Gregorio had been an idiot and finally gone too far. He didn't approve of his affairs, and Jean-Philippe had always been faithful to his wife, which Gregorio seemed to be incapable of.

After lunch Chantal went to the food hall at the Bon Marché, to get some favorite items that Eric loved. She always tried to bring him the French foods he missed, since he said he lived on sausages and schnitzel in Germany. So she filled a basket with tinned foie gras and assorted delicacies, his favorite cookies, French coffee, and everything she knew he liked to eat. It was a motherly gesture he always appreciated, when she arrived in Berlin with a bag full of French gourmet treats, and the Bon Marché was the perfect place to find them all. She had just dropped a box of his favorite cookies into the basket on her arm, when she saw a man staring at her from across the aisle, where he was selecting several brands of tea. He looked familiar to her, but she couldn't place him and walked on.

They met again in line at the checkout, where his face haunted her. She couldn't decide if he was just a stranger she had seen before, possibly at the Bon Marché, had a familiar generic look, or if they had actually met somewhere, which seemed unlikely or she would have remembered him. He was good-looking and somewhere in his late thirties. He was wearing jeans and suede loafers and a black sweater. He was behind her in the checkout line, and after she forgot about him and dismissed him from her mind, she heard a male voice in her ear.

'Did you get your wish yet?' She turned to stare at him when he said it, and this time she realized who he was. He was the man who had brought the beautiful paper lanterns to the White Dinner and held one for her and told her to make a wish. She smiled when she recognized him, and where they had met before.

'Not yet. It might take a little while,' she said easily, and he was smiling too.

'Oh, one of *those* wishes. It sounds like it's worth waiting for.' She nodded, and he glanced into her basket, impressed by the assortment of delicacies she'd chosen. The basket was heavy on her arm. 'It looks like you're having quite a party.' She had added two bottles of red wine, which added to the weight and the festive look.

'I'm taking it all to my son in Berlin.'

'Lucky boy. He has good taste, and a nice mom,' he said, noticing the foie gras and the wine.

'He's a starving artist, he gets tired of sausages and beer.' He laughed at what she said, and then it was her turn at the checkout. When she finished signing the receipt, she turned to the man behind her as she left. 'Thank you again for the wish, and the pretty lantern. You made the night for all of us.' She smiled at him and noticed that he had deep brown eyes, and he looked straight at her. There was something very powerful about his gaze, and it felt like an electric current running through her. She remembered that she had noticed his eyes at the White Dinner too, when he held out the lantern for her and told her to make a wish. There had been urgency in his tone then, before the lantern floated away, and he looked just as intense now. He had a serious, handsome face.

'I'm glad you enjoyed it. So did I. I hope you get your wish. And have fun with your son.'

'Thank you,' she said, and left. She thought about him for a minute, and how attractive he was, and then forgot about him, and went back to her apartment, and packed the food for Eric in her valise. She couldn't wait to see him. It had been too long. Waiting four months to see her youngest child felt like an eternity to her. It always did. The long time span between when she saw them was one of the reasons why she worked so much. She enjoyed her writing, but it also populated her life with the fictional people

57

she wrote about, who became real to her while she was creating them. Writing screenplays, and scripts for occasional documentaries about subjects that were meaningful to her, filled her life, and the results were excellent. She put her heart and soul into everything she did, her writing, her friendships, and her children, when they let her. She was excited at the prospect of seeing Eric in Berlin.

4

When Valerie came home from work at night now, she could cut the tension in the apartment with a knife. She had hardly spoken to Jean-Philippe since he had told her about Beijing. They had dinner together after they put the children to bed, and unlike the conversations they usually enjoyed at the end of their workday, these days she said not a word. He felt like she was punishing him, but she said she just needed time to think. And in the meantime she didn't want to discuss it with him. She knew all the pros and cons. But her mulling over the decision had precluded all other subjects or exchange.

Their children were too young to understand the unpleasant atmosphere, but they were instinctively aware of the tension between their parents. And inevitably their ultimate decision would impact the children as well. For Western children, to grow up in Beijing didn't sound ideal to her. If nothing else, the pollution was terrible, living conditions difficult, and most Westerners did not take their young children to Beijing with them. Their children were five, three, and two. She was even worried about medical care for them there, and the risk of disease. For Valerie, it was not just about giving up her job and impacting her career, maybe permanently, but also about her children. Jean-Philippe insisted that other families moved there, and it would expand their children's horizons at an early age, which could be good for them.

But for Valerie, it was also true that fashion was an unforgiving milieu, and she wouldn't have an easy time stepping back into it in three to five years. It might be over for her, and she wasn't ready to give that up. At times, she wondered how Jean-Philippe could even consider it. And although she tried not to be she was angry at him for wanting to turn their life upside down.

He tried to talk to her about it several times after their first conversation, and she refused.

'Why can't we at least discuss it?' he asked, pleading with her.

'Because I don't want to. I don't want you pressuring me, or trying to influence me either way. I need to think about it without your pushing me.' She had been short-tempered with him since the subject came up, which was unlike her.

'I'm not going to push you or force you to go,' he said reasonably, but she didn't want to hear it, and she didn't believe him. She knew what he wanted. He wanted to take the offer in Beijing. He had made that clear. 'It's your decision too.'

'Is it?' She turned to him halfway through dinner with her eyes blazing, and she set her fork down. 'Or do you just want me to say it's all right, so I can't blame you for destroying my career? This isn't my decision, Jean-Philippe. You've given me an impossible choice. Go with you to a place we're all going to hate, and screw

60

up my career, or stay and have you hate me forever for the opportunity I robbed you of. You make more money than I do, so I guess in the end, you have the bigger vote. I just don't think it's fair to put it all on me. And what happens when we hate it there, or the kids get sick, or I never get another job, or you don't make the money you think you will? Then what?'

'Then we come home,' he said quietly.

'It may be too late for me by then. It's taken me almost thirteen years to get where I am at *Vogue*. Why do I have to give that up? Just because you make more money than I do, or because you're a man?'

'We'd be doing this for the family, Valerie. For our future. I can't make that kind of money here, and it's a big step up for me.' It was the truth, and she knew it too. 'The time is now, the market there is hot. There are fortunes to be made.'

'We don't need a fortune,' she said seriously. 'We're fine with what we have.'

'Then maybe that will be our decision in the end. I'd just like a chance to make more and put some aside. We may be happy to have it one day. And I can't make that kind of money in France or even in the States,' although he had never thought of working there. They were totally entrenched in France, and loved it.

'Why does money have to rule our life? You've never been that way before. That's one of the reasons I love it here. It's not just about running after money, it's about quality of life. And what kind of quality of life will we have in Beijing?

We're not Chinese. It's a completely different culture for all of us, and not an easy city. Everyone says so. Are you willing to sacrifice all of that for the money you'll make? I'm not sure I am.'

'Then we won't go,' he said, looking depressed. He felt beaten down by their arguments, and he was well aware of the downsides himself, especially relating to their kids, and couldn't deny them to her. He didn't want to lie to her. He realized there was a good chance they would hate it there, and even three years at a minimum was a long time.

She was still at her computer, working, when he went to bed, and she barely said goodnight to him. She hadn't kissed him in days, and overnight she had turned into an angry woman, ready to blame him for everything. She had never been that way before. But she felt as though their whole life was on the line, and she was worried about their marriage too. What would happen if they were miserable there and fighting over it all the time? Nothing about his Beijing offer appealed to her, but Jean-Philippe wanted it desperately. She knew that. And it had started a war between them that was poisoning everything. They both felt like their world was falling apart. They had gone from being allies and best friends to enemies instantly, which was unfamiliar to both of them after seven easy, happy years. And whichever way they turned now, whatever they decided, one of them would lose, or even the whole family.

When Chantal boarded the plane to Berlin on Friday afternoon, all she could think of was the thrill of seeing her youngest child again. She was bringing him the food he loved, two new sweaters she was sure he could use, since everything he owned had holes in it when she last saw him, and several books she thought he'd like to read. And once she was there, she always noticed things in his apartment that needed replacing. She'd even brought her tool kit with her to do small repairs. Eric never paid attention to them or bothered to do them himself. She was the full-service mother, and her children always teased her about it. Eric was the only one who appreciated it, and loved it when she fussed over him. It was just bad luck that the art scene in Berlin was more avant-garde than in Paris, and professionally he was happier there. He felt that for his art he needed to be in Berlin, which was a loss for her.

Her relationship with Charlotte, her second child, had always been more difficult, and Charlotte liked living halfway around the world from her mother. And Paul had fallen in love with the States when he went to film school at USC, and decided to stay, which didn't surprise her. At thirty-one, he seemed far more American now than French, after thirteen years there. Eric was her baby, a sweet boy who enjoyed her company, and was totally open with her. They always had fun together. He was only three when his father died, and she had raised him alone.

And he was the one she missed most. He had retained the same sweetness even as a man of twenty-six, and he still seemed like a boy to her.

He put his arms around her in a giant bear hug when he met her at baggage claim, and had borrowed a friend's truck to drive her to his apartment, where he always insisted that she stay. Eric loved her staying with him and having breakfast in the morning with her when they both got up. He actually made enough money from his art to survive, although she helped him occasionally, but he didn't need much. He lived in the Friedrichshain district and paid a tiny rent for an apartment that looked like a hovel, but he loved it, and he rented a studio in the same building, where he built his installations. They still made no sense to her, but there was a market for his work, and he was represented by one of the best avant-garde conceptual galleries in Berlin. She was proud of him, although she didn't understand his work. But she admired how dedicated he was, and how much it meant to him. And she loved meeting his friends, and seeing his milieu while she was there. It was always an adventure visiting him.

When they got to his apartment, she gave him the food she'd bought him at the Bon Marché, and he was delighted. He opened the foie gras immediately, and she made toast for him in the decrepit oven he never used. She felt like a mother again just being with him, listening to his stories, laughing at things together, and talking about the World War II script she was working on. He was always interested in what she was writing. It made her realize again how much she missed him, and how empty her life was now without all of them at home. But there was no turning back time to when they were children. Those days were over, and all she could do now was enjoy them when she saw them, when they had time to spend with her, however infrequently, or however far away they lived.

It was an art being the mother of adult children, and it hadn't come easily to her. They had left a tremendous void in her life when they moved away, which she never said to them. There was no reason to make them feel guilty for growing up, however challenging it was for her. It was up to her to make her peace with it, and she had, as best she could. And seeing her younger son always gave her a boost for weeks. He made her feel so welcome while she was there, and seemed so genuinely happy to spend time with her. She was always careful not to work when she was with her children, so they had her full attention.

They took his new girlfriend, Annaliese, to dinner that night. She was a sweet girl from Stuttgart, an art student, and she worshipped Eric. She clearly thought he was a genius, and Eric was mildly embarrassed by her unbridled adoration, but he was happy that Chantal liked her and seemed to approve, in spite of her many tattoos and facial pierces. Chantal was used to that look by now, on so many of his friends. His mother was just grateful that he had none himself.

It always amused her how different her

children were from each other. Charlotte was the most conservative of the flock, and had always objected to her younger brother's disreputable-looking Beaux-Arts friends and his lifestyle. She even accused her mother of being bohemian and expected her to dress for dinner when she came to Hong Kong to see her. And Paul had adopted every aspect of life in the States, including some serious bodybuilding and heavy workouts, and he had been a vegan for years. He always lectured his mother about her diet and took her to the gym with him to do cardio and Pilates when she was in L.A. She told Jean-Philippe that it had nearly killed her the last time, and she had warned him of the crazy fads his children might engage in when they grew up. But she was a good sport about it, and always heaved a sigh of relief when she got home and could do what she wanted again, eat what she wanted, dress as she pleased, and even smoke occasionally if she felt like it. The one advantage to living alone was that she could do whatever she chose to do, but it was small compensation for seeing so little of her children.

By the time Chantal left Berlin on Sunday night, she had stocked Eric's refrigerator with the food he liked, changed all the burnt-out light bulbs in his apartment, cleaned it as best she could, repaired two shelves in his studio with her tool kit, replaced a broken lamp, taken him out for hearty meals at his favorite restaurants, and spent enough time with his new girlfriend to get to know her, at least superficially. They all went to the Hamburger Bahnhof museum on

Saturday, which was one of Chantal's favorites, and Eric and Annaliese enjoyed it too.

She held him close and hugged him when she left him at the airport, and fought back tears, so he wouldn't realize how much she was going to miss him in the days ahead. Their time together had been precious, as it always was, and she boarded the plane to Paris with a heavy heart.

When the plane took off, she sat staring out the window mournfully as Berlin shrank beneath them, and she was still feeling sad to have left him when she landed in Paris and went to get her bag at baggage claim. It weighed a ton with her tool kit in it, but she was glad she'd brought it. She always put it to good use when she visited him. And she had taken dozens of photos of him with her cellphone, which she would print out and frame and put around her living room when she got home. She always did after visiting one of her children, as though to prove to herself that they still existed, even if she no longer saw them every day.

She was dragging her bag off the conveyor belt at the airport when she bumped into someone behind her, turned to apologize, and found herself looking into the face of the man who had done the lanterns and whom she'd seen at the Bon Marché when she bought the food to take to Eric in Berlin. He looked equally surprised to see her, and offered to carry her suitcase for her, at least until she found a cart.

'No, really, I'm fine. I can manage it.' He could barely lift it himself, it was so heavy, and she didn't want to tell him there was a tool kit in it. 'Thank you, though.'

'No worries. I'll get it outside to the curb for you. I have no luggage.' All he had was a briefcase, and he was wearing a suit and looked quite respectable. She was traveling in jeans and a sweater, which was all she needed when visiting Eric in Berlin. 'Did you see your son?' he asked conversationally as he carried the bag for her, and she apologized again for how heavy it was.

'Yes, I did. I'm just coming back.'

'Was he happy with all the food you brought him?' He smiled, remembering the foie gras. 'My mother never brought me things like that. He's a lucky kid.' He imagined her son to be a student, since she didn't look very old. 'What did you bring back with you,' he asked, with mischief in his eye, 'a bowling set?' She laughed at the question and looked sheepish.

'My tool kit. He always needs things fixed in his apartment.' He looked suddenly touched as she said it. It gave him an insight into what kind of mother she was, and how much she must miss the boy who lived in Berlin.

'You can stop by my place anytime. Are you good at it?'

'Very,' she said proudly.

'I'm Xavier Thomas, by the way,' he said, introducing himself as he stuck out his hand, when he reached the curb and set her bag down.

'Chantal Giverny,' she said as they shook hands.

'Where do you live?' he asked politely.

'Rue Bonaparte, in the sixth.'

'I don't live far from you. Why don't we share

a cab?' She hesitated for a second and then nodded. It was strange the way she kept running into him. He had an explanation for it in the cab.

'I think destiny is involved here. When you meet someone by accident three times, it means something. First at the White Dinner. There were seven thousand, four hundred people there that night. You could have been seated at any table, and we'd never have met. Instead you were at the one next to mine. Then in the food hall at Bon Marché, and now at the airport. My flight from Madrid was two hours late. If it had been on time, we would have missed each other. Instead here we are, which is damn lucky for you, because I don't know how you would have carried that ridiculously heavy bag yourself.' She laughed at what he said. 'So clearly, we were meant to meet again. Out of respect for that and the forces that brought us together, will you have dinner with me tonight? There's a bistro I like, which I use as my canteen.' He named the one where she met Jean-Philippe for lunch regularly. It was their canteen too. Their world seemed to be full of coincidences, and she was about to tell him she was tired and wanted to go home, and then decided what the hell. He seemed nice. Why not have dinner with him? He looked young and was obviously not trying to seduce her; just being friendly. And she had a lonely night ahead, without Eric. It always depressed her to come home to her silent empty apartment after she saw her kids.

'All right.' He smiled and looked pleased.

'Let's drop off your bag first, though. I'd hate

to walk that back from the restaurant after dinner, although it would be good exercise. I hope your son carried it for you in Berlin.'

'He did. He's a good boy.' She smiled proudly.

They got to her building a short time later, and she took the bag up in the elevator while he waited for her downstairs, and she was back a moment later, having stopped long enough to comb her hair and put on lipstick. She felt like a mess compared to his proper business suit. On the way to the restaurant, he explained that he had been visiting a client in Madrid and had only gone for the day. He said that he was an attorney, specializing in international copyrights and intellectual property. He had gone to see a French writer who lived in Spain and was a longtime client. And Chantal volunteered that she was a screenwriter, and wrote scripts for documentaries, and fictional screenplays for movies.

'I thought your name rang a bell,' he said as they got to the restaurant and he asked for a table on the terrace. It was next to the one where she and Jean-Philippe usually sat, and the owner recognized her, and then Xavier. 'Do you come here often?' he asked her as they sat down, and he slipped his briefcase under the table as she nodded. 'So do I. Maybe we've seen each other here before.' It was possible, and she wondered if he was right, and their paths were meant to cross. It seemed like a pleasant coincidence to her.

He asked about her children at dinner, and she told him about them, and then he inquired about her work in detail. He was familiar with her movies and had seen several of them and her two prize-winning documentaries, which had impressed him a great deal. He seemed like a relaxed, interesting person who wasn't full of himself and enjoyed her company. And she inquired about his work too. He asked if she was married, and she said she had been widowed when her children were small and had never remarried. And he said he had never been married. He volunteered that he had lived with a woman for seven years, and they had split up the year before.

'Nothing dramatic happened, there's no tragic story. She didn't run off with my best friend. We both worked too hard, and had drifted apart. When we started to bore each other, we both agreed that it was time for a change. We're still on very good terms. The relationship just played itself out.'

'You were smart to recognize it, a lot of people don't. They stay together, hating each other for years.'

'I didn't want to get to that point,' he said quietly. 'This way we stayed friends. It worked out for the best. She's madly in love right now, with a guy she met six months ago. I think they're going to get married. She's thirty-seven and desperate to have kids. That was always a major difference between us. I'm not sure I believe in marriage, and I'm fairly certain I don't want kids.'

'You might change your mind about that one day,' she said in a motherly tone, and he smiled.

'I'm thirty-eight years old, and I figure that if I've never wanted them till now, I probably never will. I told her in the beginning. I think she thought she'd change my mind. She never did. And her biological clock was ticking loudly by the time she left, which was another good reason to end it when we did. I didn't want to blow her chances to have kids, if that's what she really wanted.' He sounded like a fair person, and a sensible, practical one. 'I've never wanted to be a father. I'd rather put the time and effort into my relationship with a woman I love. Kids don't stick around forever anyway. So you put all that love and time into them, and then they fly away. Hopefully, the right woman will stay.'

'That's very sensible of you,' Chantal said, smiling. 'No one ever explained that to me, and I've wound up with children living all over the world. They're having a great time, but I hardly ever see them, which isn't a lot of fun for me. They live in Berlin, Hong Kong, and L.A.'

'You must have done a good job with them for them to have enough confidence to spread their wings like that.' It was an interesting comment for him to make. Jean-Philippe always said the same thing.

'Or chased them as far away as they could get,' she said, laughing, but he doubted it was that. She seemed like a good person, and he could tell she loved her kids, just from the way she spoke about them. She seemed to accept them for who they were, not who she hoped they would become, which impressed him.

'My grandfather and father were lawyers, so

72

they expected my brother and me to be too. My brother became a musician, so I felt even more obligated to carry on tradition, and now here I am, flying to Madrid on a Sunday to see a client. But at least I like the work I do. I wanted to be a criminal attorney, but except for the rare important crime, it was tedious and not very interesting, so I got into intellectual property, and I really like my clients. I never joined my father's firm. They did tax law, and closed when he retired. That would have bored me to tears. It sounds like your kids have interesting jobs.'

'They do. I told them to follow their dreams when they were growing up. They believed me, so they all did. Banker, filmmaker, and artist.' She smiled as she said it, and he could see how proud of them she was.

'That's a great gift you gave them, instead of obliging them to take jobs they hate.'

'Life is too long to do something you don't enjoy doing.' It was an interesting point of view. 'I was a journalist first, and I hated it. It took me a while to discover what I love to write. It was particularly hard when I lost my husband and I had to make a living with my writing. It was frightening for a while, but it worked out well. I have fun doing it.'

'And you're good at it,' he commented.

They talked animatedly all through dinner, and it was after eleven when he finally walked her home the short distance to her apartment. 'I'd love to have lunch with you sometime, or dinner again, if that sounds all right to you,' he said hopefully, and she couldn't tell if he was just being friendly, or was interested in her as a woman, which seemed unlikely given the difference in their ages. He hadn't asked her, but it was obvious from the ages of her children. And she was clearly considerably older than he was. In fact, there were seventeen years between them, even if she didn't look it. But she didn't flatter herself that he was trying to date her, and there was no reason why they couldn't be friends. She didn't usually have dinner with strangers, but their paths had crossed often enough that she had felt comfortable doing so, especially after meeting at the White Dinner.

'I'd like that.' She smiled easily at him. He handed her his business card then, and told her to call or text him so he'd have her number.

'Let's do it again soon,' he said, smiling at her, 'so we don't have to keep meeting in grocery stores or airports.' She laughed, it had been a pleasant, easy evening. 'And I definitely don't want to wait until the White Dinner next year.'

'I don't either,' she confirmed, 'although I hope you'll come and bring more lanterns and sit near us again. You made the evening for the rest of us.'

'You made it for me too,' he said, suddenly looking intently into her eyes with his intriguing dark brown ones. There was more than friendship there. She suddenly felt a current pass through her, and then told herself she had imagined it. He had very expressive eyes, and a very masculine attitude. The look he had given her had nothing to do with their age difference, or the kind of warm, friendly, brotherly looks she got from Jean-Philippe. Xavier Thomas was a man talking to a woman, no matter what age she was. She wondered if he was a womanizer, but he didn't look it. There was nothing of Gregorio's frivolous ways about him. Xavier just seemed direct and straightforward, and made it clear that he liked her, and that appealed to her about him. He seemed very sincere, and she had a feeling Jean-Philippe would like him, which was important to her, since she respected his opinion. Maybe they could have lunch together one day, the three of them.

She thanked him for dinner again when he left her at her building, and she waved as she pressed the door code, then let herself in through the outer door and disappeared. Xavier was smiling as he walked away, all the way back to his apartment.

5

The days after the White Dinner in Paris, once Benedetta got back to Milan, were worse than she had feared. Someone had notified the press that Gregorio's babies had been born, and the paparazzi camped out at the hospital, hoping to catch a glimpse of him, Anya, or the infants fighting for their lives in incubators. And when the hospital stonewalled them and gave them no information, they hounded Benedetta in Milan, photographing her as she came and went from work and at her home. So far all they had gotten was a photograph of Gregorio entering the George V with a somber expression, when he had gone to pick up some clothes. He hadn't left Anya or the hospital otherwise. The hospital had given them a room in the maternity ward, where they were essentially living, spending every hour in the neonatal ICU with their babies, observing the procedures they underwent, and watching their tiny hands open and close and their fingers unfurl. Both twins still had inadequate lung capacity and heart problems, and were constantly at risk. And facing the possible loss of either or both of them, Anya had grown up overnight, sitting solemnly, holding vigil, and praying for her infants in the hospital chapel late at night after visiting hours, with Gregorio constantly at her side. He had become the loving father he had never been before, and the devoted spouse he should have been to his wife. And the agony they were living enmeshed him more with Anya every day. He still planned to return to Benedetta, but he had no idea when, and he never mentioned it to Anya, given the constant terror they were dealing with.

He tried to call Benedetta more frequently than he had at first, but every day there was a new problem to contend with, another obstacle for the babies to overcome. They had named the twins Claudia and Antonio, and Gregorio had insisted on having them christened by the hospital priest, which the press discovered as well. Benedetta felt sick when she read it. Gregorio had a whole life now separate from her, with two children and a woman who should never have happened at all. And whenever he called her, all he could talk about were Anya and the babies, since they were the only people in his universe, sequestered in the hospital in Paris. Benedetta came to dread his calls, and yet he promised constantly to come back to her as soon as he could, which was now in the distant future, probably months away. He was being responsible to Anya and the babies, which some thought was noble of him, but he had a wife in Milan, whom he claimed to love and said he didn't want to lose.

And all the while Benedetta was left to cope with their business and their families and the paparazzi who besieged her in Milan. Weeks after the twins were born, the press was still chasing after her, and ran photos of her looking distraught, since they could get none of

Gregorio, Anya, or the babies.

Gregorio's family was as upset as her own when they read the stories. His father was furious with him, and his mother called Benedetta every day, wanting to know when he was coming home, and all Benedetta could say was that she had no idea. The babies were in slightly better condition than they had been in when they were born, but it was too soon to know if they would live, or how damaged they might be if they did. His mother cried constantly on the phone, about the disgrace to all of them, and the shame, and Benedetta had to console her too. Her own mother said she never wanted to lay eyes on him again, and said he had betrayed them all.

Benedetta was so busy dealing with all of them that she hardly had time to think. And they had one business crisis after another to deal with. They had a problem at the mills with a run of silk, which impacted hundreds of garments they had to produce. One of their main suppliers had a fire in China that destroyed three factories, which meant they could not fill a major order for the States. And there was a dock strike in Italy, and they had goods trapped offshore.

Benedetta's life had become a constant round of agonies and problems she couldn't solve. She was the head of their design team, but with Gregorio out of touch in Paris, she had to shoulder his workload as well, and make all the difficult business decisions that he usually handled. Until now, they had been a team. One of his brothers tried to help her, but he had to handle issues at the mills, and couldn't take over Gregorio's role either. For all his lack of responsibility in his private life, Gregorio had a keen sense of business and could always turn a disaster around before it happened. But not this time. Benedetta felt as if she'd been hit by a tsunami when Valerie called her at the end of June. She didn't ask her for any of the details, all she wanted was to let Benedetta know she was thinking of her, and was sorry all of it had happened. And she had heard echoes of their problems at the mills, but she didn't mention that either. She could imagine that Benedetta had enough on her plate without inquiries from friends.

'I just wanted to tell you that we love you, and at some point the worst of this will be behind you, and it will seem like a bad dream.' It was all she could think to say to support her friend.

'It's a nightmare,' Benedetta admitted in a breaking voice on a particularly bad day. A container ship carrying goods they needed desperately had sunk in a storm off the coast of China. It was turning into a litany of disasters, and all of them landed on her. 'Everything that could possibly go wrong has, and meanwhile he's sitting in Paris with that girl and their babies, and we can't even call him. He doesn't want to be disturbed. It's insane.' The whole situation was surreal, and Benedetta sounded as if she were reaching her breaking point. For the first time in twenty years, she felt that she no longer had a husband. He had cheated on her before, and they had lived through it, but it had never reached these epic proportions. The babies had changed everything, particularly given the crisis circumstances in which they were born.

'Has he said anything,' Valerie asked cautiously, 'about when he can come home?' She assumed he was still planning to. He couldn't be stupid enough to leave his wife for a twenty-three-year-old Russian model, with or without twins. Gregorio was badly behaved, but he was no one's fool, and their respective family businesses were so intertwined that there would be no way of dissolving an alliance that had been in existence for more than a century. Doing so could destroy their business and their families', and none of them wanted that.

'All he says is that he can't leave Anya all alone in Paris, and she has no one to be with her. They still don't know if the babies will survive. There are problems with their hearts and lungs because they were so premature. It's all he talks about when he calls me. He acts like they're our babies, and he doesn't give a damn about the business.'

'I wish I could help you. You just have to hang in. Sooner or later he'll come back and return to his senses, and you can sort it out then.'

'That's what I keep telling myself. But who knows how crazy he is now? He's not making sense.' Benedetta sounded overwhelmed.

'Try to stay as calm as you can,' Valerie said gently.

'I'm trying,' she said with a sigh, 'but it's not easy. I haven't slept in weeks. I just lie awake and worry about it every night.' And aside from the business she was running in his absence, she had

80

the same worries as any woman whose husband has just had twins with a girl almost twenty years younger than his wife. She was beginning to think he might stay with her, and not come home at all. 'What about you? Is everything all right in Paris?' She assumed it was. Valerie and Jean-Philippe had such an orderly life. They were the ideal couple, with three beautiful children, good jobs, wonderful friends, and a perfect home. They were everybody's role model, and Benedetta envied them. She didn't expect the response she got.

'Not exactly. We're having something of a crisis ourselves. Jean-Philippe has a big business decision to make, and it's going to impact my career as well. Or our marriage. I'm not sure which one yet. Maybe both.' Benedetta was shocked to hear it.

'I'm sorry. Is there anything I can do to help?'

'No, we have to work this out ourselves. It's the first really big problem we've ever had.' Benedetta had lived through many bad times with Gregorio, and she was sorry for Valerie, but she had faith in Jean-Philippe to keep a level head.

'He's a good man. He'll do the right thing in the end. I have confidence in you both,' Benedetta said warmly.

'I wish I could say the same. I'm not sure which way the wind is going to blow on this one. And it's already taking a toll. But I didn't call to complain about my problems. I just wanted you to know that I'm thinking about you, and Jean-Philippe and I both send our love.'

'It's so humiliating to have the whole world know about this. I feel like such a fool,' she said, near tears again.

'You're not the fool, Benedetta. He is, for getting himself into this mess in the first place.'

'I look like an idiot for putting up with it. I just want things back the way they were. I don't even know when I'll see him again or when he's coming home.'

'It won't go on forever. It'll settle down, and eventually everyone will forget.' Valerie wasn't entirely sure that was true, in a situation this scandalous, but it seemed like the right thing to say.

'Thank you for calling me. It means a lot to me, and I'm sorry you and Jean-Philippe are having problems too. I'll say a prayer for both of you.'

'Thank you,' Valerie said with tears in her eyes. And when they hung up, both women wiped away tears. The men in their lives were causing them considerable grief. Even Jean-Philippe, who was usually a perfect father and husband, had destabilized their life and was upsetting Valerie.

And at the beginning of July, Benedetta had a less important decision to make. They were supposed to go to Sardinia with friends the following week, and she didn't know whether to go. She asked Gregorio when he called.

'How can you expect me to think of a holiday at a time like this? How can you even ask me? My son's heart stopped for several seconds today, and they had to massage his heart to revive him. Do you think I give a damn about our holiday in Sardinia on Flavia and Francesco's boat?' He sounded outraged and pushed over the edge. Benedetta burst into tears at the other end of the line.

'Are you serious? I've been living this nightmare with you. I'm running the business and dealing with dock strikes and disasters at the mills, a fire in the factories in China, the goddamn paparazzi who won't leave me alone because of you and your whore, and you act like an indignant father when I ask about our vacation? Why don't you just stay there with her? You are anyway. Never mind, don't worry about Sardinia. I'll decide for myself.' And with that, she hung up on him, and he called her back instantly and apologized for what he'd said.

'It's just such an upsetting situation here. You should see them, they're so tiny, they look as though they couldn't possibly survive, and Anya just isn't equal to dealing with it. I have to be here for her.' And he expected his wife to understand and sympathize.

'Of course,' Benedetta said in a dead voice. She couldn't listen to him anymore. On the one hand, he had instantly become the responsible devoted father, and on the other, he wanted her to understand how worried he was about the babies and their mother, which had nothing to do with her, except that all of them were ruining her life.

'I think you should go to Porto Cervo with Flavia and Francesco and relax. And hopefully by the time you come back, I'll be able to come home, at least for a while.'

'Are you planning to commute now between her house and mine?' Benedetta asked in an icy voice.

'Of course not. And Anya and the babies won't be able to leave Paris for months. It will be September or October before they can go home.'

'And where are you planning to be until then?' Benedetta asked him, and he said the same thing he always did now.

'I don't know. I'm just living from day to day.'

'So am I. And I can't run a business that way, or my life. You're going to have to figure out what you're doing soon.' She was tired of listening to him tell her that the babies were at death's door, as though that absolved him from what he was doing to her. And if he was going to stay with Anya, she wanted to know.

It was the first time she had said that to him, and Gregorio was shocked. 'Is that a threat?'

'No, it's a reality,' she said quietly, but there was steel in her voice. 'We can't go on like this forever. It's not fair to anyone. This was all going to be over when she had your babies, and you wrote her a big check and came home. It's very different now. Your babies may be damaged and may need your help for a long time. You don't seem to want to let go of her, and you're dignifying her as the mother of your children. There's no room for me in this story anymore.' She hadn't expected it to turn out like that, and neither had he. But he hadn't anticipated what might happen to the twins, or the bond it would form between him and Anya once it did.

84

Somewhere between their birth and the weeks of sitting by their incubators, he had begun to have deep feelings for her that he'd never had before. He had fallen in love with her. But he loved Benedetta too and had so much history with her. He didn't want to let either woman go. He didn't say it to Benedetta, but she had sensed it for weeks. He was attached to Anya now in a way he hadn't expected to happen. He and Anya were partners now, while he still pretended to Benedetta and himself that he was coming home to her. He was making promises to both of them that he couldn't keep. He could only be with one or the other, not both. He was assuring Anya all would be fine, and telling Benedetta that he'd come home, and their marriage would survive, and resume as before.

'Of course there is room for you,' he said to Benedetta in a raw voice. 'You're my wife.'

'That can be changed,' she said coldly. 'I'm not going to live like this for long.'

'You won't have to. I'm just asking for your compassion until we know what will happen with the twins.'

'That could take months.' And he knew it too. She had been reading about premature babies on the Internet, and knew a lot more than she had previously, about the risks and what they faced once they were born. And she knew just how damaged they might be if they lived. And how was he going to leave them and Anya then?

'I'll come home as soon as I can. I promise,' he said, sounding sobered by what she had said. 'Go to Sardinia. I'll come home after that, even if I can't stay long.'

She stunned herself by what she said next. 'If you can't stay, or don't intend to, don't come home.' And then she surprised him again by hanging up. The pass she had given him till then was over. It was time to clean up his act. In Paris, Gregorio sat staring at the phone, and then he went back to intensive care where Anya was watching their babies. She turned to look at Gregorio when he walked in.

'Did you call her?' He knew who she meant, and he nodded. 'How was it?' Anya treated Benedetta like the enemy now. She was a threat to her life with him, and the future she wanted for their twins. And she knew that Benedetta had a powerful hold on him.

'The same as always. She's very upset. And she's running the business alone.' Anya had no concept of how vast their empire was, and he had no desire to share that information with her. He looked nervous when he talked about his wife, and even more so when Anya did. Neither woman was willing to tolerate the other for much longer, and he was caught in the middle and being torn in two.

'Did you tell her?' Anya asked with a hard look in her eyes.

'Not yet.' Anya wanted Gregorio to leave Benedetta for good. 'I can't tell her something like that over the phone. I have to go to Milan.' And Anya didn't want him to leave her for five minutes. She was terrified that something terrible would happen while he was gone. And they both knew it could, so he stayed. In some ways, she was like a child and had become totally dependent on him.

'You should go as soon as the babies are stronger. I want her to know that you're not hers anymore. You belong to us.' He didn't answer. He might be falling more in love with her every day, but he didn't want to belong to her either. He wasn't ready to make that kind of commitment to her yet, and he wasn't sure he wanted to leave Benedetta, which was why he hadn't mentioned it to her. He was on the fence, pulled by agonizing decisions, with both women making demands of him and thinking they had that right. The only people he was ready to fully commit to at this point were the two infants struggling for their lives. What he felt for them was overwhelming and had come as a surprise.

Benedetta called their friends in Rome the next morning and told them she would come to visit them in Porto Cervo as planned, but alone.

'Gregorio can't come?' Flavia asked her in a solemn voice.

'No, he can't.' They both knew why, and Flavia didn't question her further. 'Unless you'd rather not have me alone. I don't have to come.' She offered to let them off the hook.

'Don't be silly, we'd love to have you. I'm just sorry . . . you know . . . I know this is a hard time. It must be difficult for him too.' She felt sorry for both of them. They had been friends for twenty years.

'I'm sure it is,' Benedetta said coldly, annoyed by the sympathy for Gregorio, who was ruining so many lives, particularly hers. They agreed that she would come in a week and stay for ten days. They had a beautiful yacht and went out on it every day, and a lovely home where she and Gregorio stayed every year. This would be the first time she would go alone.

Dharam called her two days later, and told her he had business in Rome. He was hoping to come to Milan, and he was disappointed when she said she wouldn't be there, and that she was going to Sardinia to visit friends. He hesitated for a moment and then made a suggestion.

'Could I come to see you there? I could stay at a hotel. It seems a shame to be so close and not see you, but of course if it would be awkward, I'll see you another time.' And as she thought about it, it sounded like fun. As long as he stayed in a hotel, it wouldn't inconvenience Flavia and Francesco, and he could come out on the boat with them in the daytime. He said he could only stay a few days.

'If you don't mind, I think it would be great. They have a wonderful sailboat, you could come sailing with us in the daytime, and we usually go out in the port at night. They're very nice people and old friends.' Francesco was from an important family of bankers and about Dharam's age, and she thought the two men would get along. And Flavia was a well-known jeweler. They both had a lot of style.

She gave Dharam her dates for Sardinia, and he sent her an email the next day, confirming that he would come to Porto Cervo for a weekend, and he had gotten a room at a hotel, the Cala di Volpe. He had asked her how things were going with Gregorio, and she told him nothing had changed. She didn't really want to talk about it. The situation between them was too depressing, and there was no resolution yet.

★   ★   ★

As she had hoped, the time in Sardinia did her a lot of good. Flavia and Francesco were wonderful to her, and she loved staying at their home and going out on the boat every day. It didn't change the situation with Gregorio, but it gave her some respite and perspective, and when Dharam came, they had a terrific time together. He and Francesco got along just as she thought they would, and it was only on the last night of his stay, sitting on the terrace of her friends' home after Francesco and Flavia went to bed, that Dharam asked her what she thought she was going to do about Gregorio. She could sense his attraction to her, but he had done nothing to put their friendship in jeopardy, or to create an awkward situation for her. He could tell how fragile she still was.

'I don't know,' she told him honestly. 'I haven't seen him in over a month. I don't know what he feels for that girl. I suspect more than he did in the beginning. I can hear it in his voice. And he seems to be taking his fatherhood seriously. Maybe he'll stay with her, and perhaps he should,' she said sadly, trying to be philosophical about it.

'What do you want?' Dharam asked her gently.

'I wish none of it had ever happened, but it

89

did. I'm not sure we can recover from it this time, or if either of us will want to. I'll know more when I see him. At least I hope I will. He said he'd come home after I get back from Sardinia. I'm not sure if our marriage is still salvageable. I don't even know if I love him the way I did. I love him, but everything is changed.'

'My wife wanted to come back to me after her romance fell apart with the actor, but it was too late for me,' he said quietly. 'Only you can know how you feel. And maybe it's still too soon. This has been quite a shock.' He felt deep compassion for her.

'Yes, it has,' she agreed as their eyes met, and he held a hand out and took hers.

'I would love to spend time with you, if things don't work out between the two of you. I don't wish that on you, if you want to stay married to him. I just want you to know that I have strong feelings for you. But if you stay with him, I will be happy to be your friend.' He made no move to kiss her, and had the utmost respect for her.

'Thank you,' she said softly, and they sat in silence for a while in the moonlight as he held her hand. They had had a lovely time together with her friends, and he was leaving the next morning, flying back to Rome, and then to Delhi on his plane.

'You can always call me if you need me,' he said before he went back to his hotel, and she thought about him that night. They had breakfast together the next day with Francesco and Flavia, and then he gave Benedetta a chaste kiss on the cheek and left, after he thanked

Francesco and Flavia for hosting him so generously on their boat. They had been enormously impressed with him, and said as much to Benedetta after he left.

'What a terrific person.' It was clear to them that Dharam would have liked to be more than a friend to Benedetta, but he was a gentleman and never stepped over the line, which they admired him for. He didn't want to complicate her already difficult situation, which was noble of him. And she had to face Gregorio when she went home. Benedetta was relieved that Dharam had put no pressure on her.

Gregorio came to Milan two days after she returned, and after they talked for a while, he promised her that as soon as he could decently leave Anya, he would. He was hoping that the twins would be stable in another month, if they improved, and by the end of the summer, he wanted to be home in Milan.

'Has she agreed to that?' Benedetta asked him pointedly. 'I don't want any more drama after you come home.'

'She'll have to agree,' Gregorio said seriously, although this was not what he had promised Anya before he came home. But being in Milan and seeing Benedetta, in their home, had told him what he needed to know, and brought him to his senses. Despite his very emotional tie to Anya, and new feelings for her, he wanted to come back to his wife. And when they were older, he would want visitation with the twins. But he realized that no matter what he and Anya had just been through together, their relationship couldn't last, she was too young, and didn't have Benedetta's depth. Seeing Benedetta, in all her dignity and grace, he knew that this was where he belonged.

He stayed for two days, and then he went back to Paris. He didn't tell Anya what he had decided, there was time for that, and then the night he got back to the hospital, the worst happened. Their baby boy, who had fought so valiantly to live, had a cerebral hemorrhage, and there was nothing they could do to stop it. He was brain dead after the hemorrhage. Gregorio and Anya stood next to his incubator sobbing and bereft when he died. The nurses let them hold him one last time, and then they took him away. And now they had to plan a funeral for him. It was unthinkable. Gregorio sent Benedetta a text that night. He couldn't have told her on the phone. She closed her eyes and cried when she read it, wondering if the nightmare would ever end.

Gregorio made the arrangements for the funeral himself at the crematorium at Père Lachaise cemetery. It was the worst moment of his life, with the tiny casket with Antonio's body in it, and Anya sobbing hysterically in his arms. And then she made him promise he would never leave her again. He didn't have the heart to tell her that he had promised Benedetta he would return. He couldn't do that to Anya. Instead they sat watching their infant daughter all night, praying that the same thing wouldn't happen to her. She was just as fragile as her brother had been. Gregorio doubted now that she would survive. And Anya was inconsolable over the loss of their son. It would have been impossible and too cruel to tell her he was leaving her too. He had to wait for the right time.

Anya clung to him constantly after that, and he realized that she wasn't strong enough to survive his leaving her. She talked of suicide if their baby daughter died, and it finally dawned on him that his irresponsible lark of the year before had turned into a tragedy of such proportions that there was no escaping it now. He had to stay with her, and Benedetta would have to understand. Perhaps he could go back to her one day, but not now. He couldn't have Anya's blood on his hands. She had all the drama of her fellow countrymen and a very dark side. Benedetta was clearly the stronger of the two, and Anya needed him more.

And with a heavy heart, Gregorio flew to Milan again, this time to tell Benedetta what she had feared, and exactly the opposite of what he had promised two weeks before. He felt like a madman and a monster. He was leaving Benedetta and felt he had no choice after the death of his son, and the condition Anya was in. He didn't want to be responsible for her death too. And he knew Benedetta was powerful and stable enough to survive. Anya wasn't.

Benedetta looked at him in shock when he told her. He was agonized and deathly pale. He tried to put his arms around her, and she pulled away from him as though he were a snake about to strike. In fact, he was. She had waited all this time to hear him say he couldn't come back, only weeks after he had promised her he would. His promises meant nothing, he was like a ball bouncing between two women, and changing his mind every day, but no longer.

'I'll stay involved in the business, of course,' he said sympathetically. 'You can't run it alone.' He had already thought it out and made the decision.

'I have been running it since you left. And no, you won't stay involved. I've considered it a lot, in case you made this decision. I want our partnership dissolved. I will buy your shares from you, but you can't keep an interest in our business. You are leaving that too.' She said it with an iron resolve.

'That's ridiculous,' he said, staring at her in disbelief. 'Our families have collaborated for generations — you can't simply dissolve that. Why would you punish them for this unfortunate mistake?' He was still calling it that instead of the disaster it had become.

'Why should I be punished? I've spoken to our lawyers, and the partnership can be dissolved as part of our divorce.' Her face was set in stone as she announced it to him, and he looked horrified.

'What divorce? I said I was leaving you, not divorcing you. We don't need to get divorced.'

'You may not, Gregorio, but I do. I'm not going to have one of those marriages where you live with your mistress and her child, and I'm the wife you abandoned but stay married to, and run our business on top of it. What kind of life is that for me? And when you get rid of her, you come back to me for a while, and then find someone else? No.' She smiled at him icily. She was better prepared than he was for what came next, and had braced herself for it. 'If you want out, then you need to be out completely, of our marriage and our business. It's over, Gregorio. You've made your decision. Now go back to her. I wish you luck with her and your little girl.' She stood up then as a signal for him to leave. He was in shock.

'You can't mean this.' He was panicked.

'Yes, I can. I do.' She opened the door to her office to show him out.

'What am I going to tell my family?'

'That's up to you. It will take a while to extricate our families from the business and separate the parts they were involved in. Our lawyers can work it out. I'll have papers drawn up to remove you from the partnership immediately.'

'You can't do that,' he said, incensed.

'Yes, I can, and I will. I was a fool to wait this long. I only did it out of love for you, to give you a chance to come back if you wanted to. At least now everything is clear.'

'We don't need a divorce, Benedetta,' he insisted again. 'Everything can be agreed privately between us, informally.'

'No, it can't. I need a divorce, even if you don't. I want everything clear between us. And that way if you want to marry her, you can. You're a free man.' He walked out of her office looking dazed, and the last thing she said to him was that she would have his things sent to Anya's

95

apartment in Rome. She assumed they'd be going back there, and there was too much to send to a hotel. He turned one last time to look at her before she closed her office door.

'I thought you loved me,' he said with tears in his eyes. 'That's why I was willing to come back to you a few weeks ago.' But that had changed when their boy twin died and Anya fell apart, and he decided to stay with her. But he'd still been sure of Benedetta only weeks ago.

'I do love you,' Benedetta said quietly. 'I still love you very much. Enough to have been willing to stay with you. I hope one day I won't love you. That's all I wish for now.' And after she said it, she silently closed her office door. And Gregorio walked away in tears. He had never thought that Benedetta could be so cruel.

6

Gregorio flew back to Paris that night, and called Anya from the airport to ask how the baby was. Anya said she was the same, there was no news.

'Could you meet me at the hotel?' he asked, sounding jagged. Other than their son's death, it had been one of the hardest days of his life. He felt as though he had lost everything in a matter of hours. Benedetta wanted him out of their business. He had lost his job, his history, and his wife of twenty years. He had wanted to leave her to be with Anya, but he was shocked that she wanted a divorce. He had thought they would stay married, while he lived with Anya and the baby. That was what most people he knew did. Mistresses were still more common than divorces in Europe, particularly in Italy and even France. Gregorio was appalled at the idea of a divorce, even more than at the idea of his having twins with someone, other than his wife.

'What's wrong?' Anya was startled by how he sounded. 'How did it go with her? Did you tell her?' She had been waiting for his call all day, but he had never called her. He had gone to see his older brother to tell him about the business, and his brother told him he was a fool and had ruined the family and their business.

'I told her I was leaving her. I didn't ask for a divorce.' He was still in shock. Benedetta was going to play hardball with him, and his brother

97

warned him that the divorce would cost him and the family a fortune. He didn't blame his sister-in-law for what she was planning to do. He said his own wife would have killed him. Gregorio was lucky.

'What did she say?' Anya sounded happy at the news that he had told her, but he hadn't explained the rest yet.

'It's too complicated to tell you on the phone. I need a break. Why don't we spend a night at the hotel? Claudia will be all right without us for one night.' He didn't have an ounce left to give anyone. He needed to recharge his batteries, with room service, a hot bath, and a comfortable bed. His quick trip to Milan had been far worse than he'd expected.

'We can celebrate.' Anya sounded fifteen years old and hadn't picked up on the tone of his voice. He had lost everything. He suddenly wondered if his brother was right and he'd gone crazy. He had done it for the mother of his child, and she had no idea what any of it meant to him. To her, the divorce would be good news, though he didn't intend to tell her about it yet. She didn't need to know, and in Italy it would take two years. He had a long dark road ahead of him, while Benedetta destroyed what was left of his life.

'Meet me at the hotel,' he said, sounding exhausted.

He took a cab to the George V, and Anya arrived five minutes later, looking fresh and beautiful in a T-shirt and jeans, which was all they had at the hospital, and all they needed to sit in the neonatal ICU ward every day and night. They had been there now for over a month. It seemed a lifetime since the night of the White Dinner.

Anya ordered champagne almost as soon as she walked into the room, and Gregorio went to take a shower. He barely said hello to her, and she was lying on the bed watching TV when he came back into the room wearing one of the robes of the hotel. It was thick and luxurious, and he lay on the bed next to her, not even knowing what to say. Everything that had happened that day had been so awful, and he would never forget the look on Benedetta's face and the hardness of her eyes when she told him she was divorcing him. She had always been so understanding before. But he had never left her for another woman, nor had a baby with her, and humiliated her so publicly.

'So what did she say?' Anya asked him again, as she snuggled up next to him on the bed. They hadn't made love in months, but he knew he couldn't have now. He had nothing left in him. He felt as if Benedetta had killed him. He lay there feeling he was the victim, wondering how she could be so vicious, enough to take away their business and divorce him. To him, it was even worse than what he'd done, and punishment beyond measure.

'She's kicking me out of our business' was all he was willing to tell Anya. 'Our families have worked together for more than a century, and she's willing to break with tradition.' Anya didn't appear to be impressed, nor to understand the

99

magnitude of his wife's reaction. And then for an instant, she looked worried.

'Does that mean she's taking all your money?'

'No, but she'll probably go after that too.' He was morbidly depressed, and then she kissed him, and he smiled at her, hoping that somehow it would turn out all right, and maybe Benedetta would calm down and forget about the divorce. He couldn't believe she would do that to him, but seeing Anya lying next to him made the horror of a divorce seem less immediate and less real. She wrapped her arms around him, and slipped a hand into his robe. In spite of everything that had happened, she managed to arouse him, and a moment later they were making love passionately, and all that he'd been through that day and in the past month faded away as they clung to each other until they lay spent. He had forgotten how incredible she was to make love to. She was his now, and he needed her as desperately as she needed him.

They finished the bottle of champagne and ordered room service at midnight. It was a night of respite for both of them. And when he woke up lying next to her the next morning, he made love to her again.

He tried not to think of Benedetta as they showered together and dressed to go back to the hospital. But it was comforting to know that their baby and their future were waiting for them. And maybe when Benedetta calmed, she would change her mind about the business and the divorce. She was normally so reasonable, and he hoped she would be again.

Jean-Philippe had always loved having breakfast with his wife and children, while they waited for the nanny to arrive, so they could leave for work together. When he had time, he dropped Valerie off at her office. But ever since he had told her about Beijing, she was constantly late, the children cried, she burned their breakfast, and she took so long getting ready that he couldn't wait for her, and she took a cab to work. Their life seemed to be unraveling with the pressure of having to make a decision, and that morning even the nanny was late. And their two-year-old son, Damien, had been crying since four A.M. with an earache. Valerie was going to take him to the pediatrician before she went to work.

'Doesn't anything go smoothly here anymore?' he snapped at her, looking exasperated. Their five-year-old son, Jean-Louis, had hit his sister at breakfast, and she was crying too.

'How would you like to deal with all that in Beijing?' she threw back at him. 'With a pediatrician who doesn't speak French or English?' She had spoken to several friends in the past few weeks who knew the city and said almost no one spoke English. You needed a translator everywhere if you didn't speak Chinese. The firm that had made Jean-Philippe the offer had told him he would have his own.

'I'm sure there must be Western doctors there. We can find one through the embassy. It's not a third-world country, for God's sake.'

'No, it's China,' she said tartly.

101

'Is that your answer, then?' He'd been pressing her for days. He had already told his potential future employers that he needed more time to make the decision. It was a big career change for his wife too, and they said they understood.

'If you want an answer now,' she barked back at him, as their children stared at them, shocked by the unfamiliar tone, 'if you want an answer today,' Valerie said, lowering her voice when she saw her children's faces, 'the answer is no. I'm not ready to walk into *Vogue* and quit today. I need more time to think about it.'

'I'm not doing this for myself,' he said, frustrated, 'I'm doing it for us, for the long term.' They were both beginning to wonder if there would be a long term, the way things were going. In seven years they had never faced anything so divisive, that had shaken them this badly. And each of them blamed the other for the unbearable tension that engulfed them every day. Damien started to cry again then, and the young girl who worked for them arrived and took him to his bedroom to get him dressed. He was pulling on his ear, and when Jean-Louis spilled his orange juice all over the table, Valerie mopped it up.

'You're making the children nervous,' she accused her husband in a taut voice, as he shook his head in despair, and left without saying goodbye. That had never happened before.

'Where is Papa going?' three-year-old Isabelle asked, visibly worried. 'He didn't kiss me.'

'He was in a hurry to go to work,' she said, kissing the chubby cheeks instead, as Valerie realized that if Jean-Philippe went anyway, and they didn't go with him, she would have three children to manage on her own.

'What's Pay-ching?' Jean-Louis asked her as she helped him out of his pajamas and into jeans with a red-checked shirt.

'It's a city in China,' Valerie tried to sound calm when she answered, as she put red sandals on his feet.

'Why don't they speak French or English?' He had heard every word of their conversation, and probably listened to their arguments at night, even if he didn't understand what they were about. The tension in the air between Jean-Philippe and Valerie was palpable.

'Because they speak Chinese, silly. Now I want you to be gentle with Isabelle today. It wasn't nice of you to hit her at breakfast. She's smaller than you are.'

'She said I was stupid. That's a bad word.'

'Yes, it is,' Valerie agreed with him, and then went to check on the baby. She still had to get to the pediatrician, and she was going to be hours late for work. They always made her wait.

She was in her car with Damien half an hour later, and it was nearly eleven when she brought him home and left him with the nanny, and then dashed off to work.

'Bad morning?' her assistant asked her sympathetically when she finally got to her office at *Vogue*. She didn't want to tell her that every morning was bad now, and her job was on the line because her husband wanted to move them all to Beijing. She tried to force it from her mind

103

as she glanced at her messages and emails, and they had an editorial meeting on Skype with the New York office at noon, about the September issue, which was their biggest edition of the year, and the Paris office contributed to it too.

And she knew that by the end of a busy day at the office, she would be no closer to knowing what to do. Every fiber of her being told her to stay in Paris, where their life worked. Why did he want to drag them halfway around the world? It made no sense to her for any amount of money or career move. And why was his career more important than hers?

She was distracted through most of the meeting, and had a crushing headache by the end of the day. But at least when she got home the children had been bathed and fed, and Damien wasn't crying anymore. The antibiotics the pediatrician had given him had kicked in. And she was reading them a bedtime story when Jean-Philippe came home, and the children were all wearing matching pajamas with little teddy bears.

'You forgot to kiss me this morning, Daddy,' Isabelle reminded him, with her long dark hair like her mother's still damp from her bath.

'Then I'll just have to kiss you twice tonight when you go to bed.' As he said it, Valerie smiled at him, wishing their life were still as simple as it had been before. 'How was your day?' he asked her over the children's heads. She shrugged in answer, there was nothing she could say. All she could hear now was the constant drum roll of the decision that had to be made. He let her finish the bedtime story, and came in to each of their bedrooms when she put them to bed. The nanny had gone home by then. And a few minutes later, their children were all tucked in.

She and Jean-Philippe walked into the kitchen together a few minutes later, but neither of them was hungry. Valerie pulled some leftover chicken out of the fridge and made a salad for them to share. They didn't say anything to each other. They were both too afraid to start an argument again. They ate at the kitchen table in silence, which was unusual for them. She did the dishes after they ate, while Jean-Philippe went over some papers in his office, and by the time he got to their bedroom, Valerie was in bed, and her headache was worse.

In the past several weeks, everything about their marriage seemed to have gone sour. It was hard to believe how quickly it had happened. And suddenly they had nothing to say to each other except to fight about the job in Beijing. Jean-Philippe went to get ready for bed then, and climbed into his side of the bed. Valerie lay with her back to him, and when he turned off the light, all she said was 'Goodnight.' And as they lay there in the dark, neither of them had ever felt as lonely in their lives. It was as though the people they loved had disappeared and left strangers in their place. And the strangers they had left were destroying the marriage it had taken them seven years to build. It was beginning to feel like there was nothing left.

★　★　★

Xavier called Chantal a week after they'd met at the airport and had dinner. She had texted him her phone number when she thanked him for dinner, and forgot all about him while she went back to work on her script, with renewed energy after her trip to Berlin. Seeing her children always fueled her.

'I meant to call you sooner,' Xavier explained, 'but I've been in Zurich all week. I just got back last night.'

'You travel a lot,' she commented. She was happy to hear from him.

'Yes, I do travel a lot. I've got clients all over the place. Are you free tomorrow night? I'd ask you for tonight, but it's short notice, and I'm still in the office.' It was eight o'clock by then.

'Tomorrow would be great.' She smiled at the prospect of dinner with him.

'Perfect. What kind of food do you like?'

'Anything, I'm easy. Just not too spicy.'

'I don't like spicy food,' he concurred. 'I'll figure it out. I'll pick you up at eight-thirty, and you don't have to get too dressed up. I love bistro food.'

'So do I.' She was pleased. She hated wearing fancy dresses and high heels. She loved casual evenings with friends.

He picked her up as promised, at eight-thirty, and she had compromised. She wore jeans and high heels, and a cashmere sweater the color of her eyes, with a blazer in case it got chilly. And he was wearing jeans too, with brown suede shoes, which she always liked. She thought they looked sexy on men.

They drove to the restaurant in his car, which was an old MG he loved, with the steering wheel on the British side. She admired his car, and he was pleased, as they drove with the top down on the warm night. He headed for the Right Bank to a restaurant she didn't know, with a pretty garden and a terrace. And when they ordered, the food was good. It was typical French bistro fare, and the atmosphere was friendly and relaxed.

He told her what he'd been doing in Zurich, without revealing any of his client's secrets, and he asked if she'd ever been to the Basel Art Fair. When she said she hadn't, he said they'd have to go sometime. 'It's an amazing event, with some fabulous art. Mostly work by major artists, but a few unknowns. I have several clients who show there, although one of them only designs for video games now.' His work sounded like fun to her, and he asked about the script she was working on, and she explained it to him in detail, as she thought about how nice it was to have someone to talk to about her work and have dinner with. He was impressed by the subjects she wrote about, both for her dramatic screenplays and documentaries. And he liked the sound of her current story about the female survivors in the concentration camp. She was nearly halfway through, and had been working on it for months. And when he suggested they go to the FIAC art fair in Paris in the fall, she couldn't resist asking him what he was doing with a woman her age. She was mystified by that, unless he wanted to be friends. It made no sense to her that a man as interesting and attractive as he was would want to hang out with someone seventeen years older, when any girl his age would have been thrilled to go out with him, as lover or friend. She and Jean-Philippe had a friendship that spanned sixteen years, but there was a very different feeling to the way Xavier spoke to her, and he made it seem as though he liked her as a woman, not just as a friend.

'What does age have to do with anything?' He looked puzzled when she asked. 'You're beautiful and interesting and fun to talk to, and intelligent.' He smiled at her. 'That's all I care about. And with any luck, you won't be hounding me about babies. You've already got three.'

'There's a plus.' She laughed at what he said. 'And they've already left home, so you don't have to deal with them.'

'Neither do you, another plus. You have time for me, I hope.' She had plenty of time, and room in her life for a man, although she had stopped hoping to meet someone, and had never dated anyone his age.

'Are you serious about going out with me? You really don't care how old I am?' She found it hard to believe.

'You're not geriatric, for God's sake. Age is just a number to me. You could be thirty and bore the hell out of me, or twenty-five. You're a fantastic, sexy, talented woman, Chantal. I'm lucky you're willing to have dinner with me.' And she could see that he really felt that way. It boosted her ego immeasurably as they laughed

108

their way through dinner and had a great time together. They drove back to her apartment after that. And he took her out again that weekend. They walked through the Tuileries, had dinner in the garden at Costes, and went to a movie afterward. It was another terrific evening, and she told Jean-Philippe about him when they had lunch. She explained that he was the man who had provided them all with the Chinese lanterns at the White Dinner.

'I remember him, he seemed like a cool guy. Well, aren't you a sneaky devil.' He smiled at her. 'When did that start? That night? You never said anything about it when we had lunch the next day.'

'I ran into him a couple times, at the Bon Marché and at the airport when I came back from Berlin. He helped me with my bag, and then told me we were destined to get to know each other since we had met three times.'

'Who knows? Maybe he's right.' He was pleased for her — she seemed to be having fun with him.

'I'm nervous about him,' she confessed to her friend. 'He's seventeen years younger than I am. That seems like a lot. He doesn't seem to care, but if I ever take him seriously, sooner or later he'll run into some girl his age or younger, and I'll be out on my ear.'

'Maybe not,' Jean-Philippe said seriously. 'Who can tell what relationships work? My marriage appears to be falling apart at the moment, and look at the mess Gregorio made of his life after twenty years. Valerie heard that

Benedetta is filing for divorce.'

'I don't blame her,' Chantal said honestly. 'I think he crossed too many lines too often, particularly this last time.'

'The rumor is she's kicking him out of the business. I think she's right on that too. You can't run a business with a guy who left you for another woman and who you divorced. That would be crazy. But as far as relationships go, no one can predict what will happen in the end. Maybe this is the right guy for you, Chantal. Why not?'

'I can't compete with women his age.'

'You don't have to. He's dating you, not someone else.'

'For now,' she said cautiously. 'What about you? Has Valerie made up her mind yet about Beijing?' He sighed when she asked, and Chantal could see he was strained. He seemed tired and unhappy and had lost weight.

'She said if I need an answer now, it's no. But she's not sure. I don't think she'll agree to go, though. I may have to do this on my own.' He was resigning himself to it, and she looked shocked.

'And leave Valerie and the children here?' He nodded. 'That doesn't sound like a good idea to me. You're both too young to be separated for that long. One or both of you could get into mischief when you get lonely.' He had thought of that too, but he trusted Valerie, and he had never been unfaithful to her.

'I could come back every couple of months. We could try it for a year and see how it works. I don't want to give up this chance. It's the most important move of my career.'

'And she'll have a hard time alone here with three kids. Believe me, I've done it, but I had no other choice. She does.' And Jean-Philippe was a great father and very hands-on with their kids.

'I don't think she realizes yet how hard that would be. There are no good solutions to this if she won't come. And I don't think she'll give up her job at *Vogue*. She put too much into where she is now to just throw that away.'

'She may wind up throwing your marriage away if she doesn't.'

'I guess this is where we find out what her priorities are,' he said sadly, 'and I don't think I'm top of that list. I'm public enemy number one right now, for risking her career. And I can't sacrifice mine for hers.' It was a terrible situation for both of them, and Chantal felt sorry for them. She hoped their marriage would survive, but it didn't sound like a sure thing by any means at the moment.

They talked about other things after that, and then Jean-Philippe had to go back to work, and she walked back to her apartment. She had to deliver several scenes of her screenplay to the producer the next day, and wanted to check them one last time before she scanned and sent them.

She had dinner with Xavier that night and thought about what Jean-Philippe had said about not worrying about the years between them. She wondered if he was right, and Xavier was certainly convincing. And that night he surprised her at dinner.

111

'I'm going to visit my brother in Corsica next week. He has a very pleasant house there, with several guest rooms. Could I talk you into coming with me? It's very relaxing, all we do is swim and fish and eat and lie in the sun. He's got two great kids and a terrific wife. You could have your own bedroom,' he said to entice her, and she smiled. They hadn't even kissed yet, and she wasn't sure they were going to. In her mind, the jury was still out as to whether she would sleep with him, or they would stay friends. And she didn't want to be pressured into a decision, so she was glad to know about the separate bedroom if she went to Corsica with him. And much to her surprise, it sounded very tempting.

'Would they mind having a stranger there?'

'Not at all,' Xavier said easily. 'They're very easygoing people. I've brought friends before, and I think you'd like them, and they'd be crazy about you. Can I talk you into it?' She thought about it for a minute, remembering what Jean-Philippe had said, and decided to throw caution to the wind. She had nothing else to do, except finish the second half of her script, and she was well ahead of her deadline.

'I'd love it,' she said, smiling at him, and he leaned across the table and kissed her, which surprised her too. He was unpredictable, and she liked that. She never quite knew what to expect from him, and he was so bright he never bored her.

'Thank you,' he said, pleased, as he held her hand across the table.

'What for?' she said, startled.

'For trusting me. We'll have fun there,' he promised, and she knew they would. And whatever happened, she was looking forward to the vacation with him. Suddenly being on her own, and able to do whatever she wanted, didn't seem so bad. It gave her the chance to go to Corsica with him. She wondered what her children would think. But for once, she didn't care. She was a free woman, and he was a free man.

7

Chantal and Xavier flew to Ajaccio Airport in Corsica and rented a car when they arrived. She offered to pay half of it, and he wouldn't let her. He was always chivalrous about paying when they went out. It was nice of him, and she smiled to herself as they put their suitcases in the trunk, and got into the small Peugeot. It had been years since she'd gone on holiday with a man, ten years since her last serious affair. Time had just slipped by her when no one had captivated her heart. And what surprised her most was that she hardly knew him. They had had dinner a few times, they had a good time together, and they had compatible philosophies about life. But a vacation? That was a big deal to her. It meant involvement and commitment, and in the past it had meant love. And now it was just a good time with a new friend, who one day might become more, or might not. She felt very carefree as they took off toward his brother's house.

'What are you smiling about?' he asked her as they left the airport. He had noticed the Cheshire cat grin on her face.

'Nothing. Everything. Us. It's been years since I went away with a man. I always went on vacations with my kids, and I never included the men I was dating at whatever time when I was. It never felt right to combine my romances with my children. They were used to having me by

114

myself, and I was never sure enough about anyone to want to make an issue of it with my children.'

'And now?' He was interested in what she said. It was already obvious to him how much she loved her children, and how dedicated she had been to them, and still was. They lived somewhere else now, but they were still important to her. He wondered if she was as important to them, but he didn't want to ask.

'Now they think I'm a hundred years old,' she said, smiling at him, 'and it never occurs to them that there might be a man in my life, or that I'd want one.'

'Do you?' he asked, turning to her as they stopped at a light.

'I don't know,' she said honestly. 'I stopped thinking about it a while back. I just figured I'd always be alone. It's not what I wanted, but I accepted it. I stopped waiting for Prince Charming to come along. I stay busy with my work, and see my kids when I can. It's only two or three times a year for each of them, which isn't much, but they have full lives, and I don't want to intrude or impose on them.'

'And now here I am,' Xavier said, smiling at her, and she laughed. 'I'm beginning to wonder what you wished on that lantern that night that conjured me up.' He hadn't expected to meet her either, and they seemed to have been thrown together by fate, an unexpected pairing, but one that appealed to both of them, and seemed to work so far, regardless of age. She blushed when he made the comment about the lantern. 'Aha!

115

Then I'm right. Maybe I was your wish!'

'Don't be silly.' She brushed it off, but he was closer to the truth than he knew. She had wished for someone to love, and who would love her, to share her life with. It had seemed like a silly wish at the time, but she figured she'd try it, it couldn't hurt. And then he'd appeared. In fact, he had been standing right next to her when she made the wish, and she hadn't meant him.

'Beware of what you wish for!' He teased her again as they rolled through the beautiful Corsican countryside, with its rugged natural landscape and vacation homes. It took them an hour to get to his brother's home, and they drove past orchards and a farm, with the sea in the distance, and then they stopped at a big rambling old house that looked like it had been added on to several times and needed a coat of paint. But the feeling it exuded was of welcome and warmth, and there were horses in a nearby pasture, which Xavier said belonged to the neighbor. It was a lovely place, and looked ideal for a relaxing vacation.

They walked in through the back door and found his brother Mathieu and sister-in-law Annick at the kitchen table. They were both wearing shorts since the weather was warm. The kids were out, and they were enjoying some quiet time together before heading to the beach. It was just after lunch, and there was evidence of a hearty French meal on the table. Mathieu rose to his feet immediately with a broad smile of welcome and hugged his brother and then shook hands with Chantal when they were introduced.

Mathieu looked a good ten years older than his brother and was closer to Chantal's age, and Annick appeared to be somewhere in her late forties. Mathieu had been a jazz musician in his youth, and had gone into real estate finally and done well, and Annick worked for a publishing house, doing translations. Their home looked well worn and much loved, but was spacious and inviting. It was the kind of place that made you want to stay forever. Xavier had warned Chantal that the kids' friends would be there in great profusion. Mathieu and Annick enjoyed having people around them, and they offered Xavier and Chantal the remains of lunch when they sat down. They helped themselves to cold chicken, a Mediterranean salad, some bread and cheese, and a glass of wine. The vacation had begun.

'I'm going fishing. Do you want to come?' Mathieu asked him, hoping he would.

'Not yet. I want to show Chantal around first.'

'Have you been to Corsica before?' Mathieu asked her as Annick cleared some of the used plates off the table. They had obviously fed a dozen people at lunch at the long refectory table.

'Not in a long time.' She smiled at him as they ate the delicious lunch. 'I came here with my kids when they were little. We chartered a small sailboat and had a great time.'

'Are you a sailor?' She nodded, and Xavier groaned.

'Don't tell my brother that. He'll have you out on his boat all day long. He uses guests as galley slaves. For every hour you spend on the boat, he has you swabbing the decks afterward for five.

That boat is his mistress.'

'It's an old wooden boat from the forties,' he said proudly, 'with teak decks. We use it a lot here.' Annick rolled her eyes at what he said, and they all laughed.

After lunch, Annick showed them to their rooms. She had given them rooms side by side, since Xavier had said Chantal would want her own, and she didn't know what the arrangement was between them and didn't ask. Her brother-in-law had brought assorted women to the house in Corsica before, some he was in love with, some not, some lovers, some friends. And neither Mathieu nor Annick seemed surprised that she was older than Xavier, they were just happy to meet her and have her in their midst. Annick knew her movies too, and said she was a big fan.

They put their bags in their respective rooms, and Xavier gave her the bigger one with the prettier view. Then he drove her around the area that afternoon. And by the time they came back to the house at six o'clock, his niece and nephew were returning from the beach with their friends. They were a lively, wholesome group, a few years younger than her own children, but not much. Their daughter was nineteen and their son twenty-two. She was studying in Lille to be a lawyer like her uncle, and he was in pre-med in Grenoble. It was the kind of relaxed family vacation that most people dreamed of. There was lots of bantering and joking, easy exchanges with their parents, and they teased their uncle mercilessly, which he returned in kind. The whole atmosphere made Chantal miss her own children, which she didn't say to Xavier. And that night they had a big communal dinner in the kitchen, which everyone helped prepare, and Chantal did too. There were nearly twenty people at the table when they sat down, including the neighbor's son.

'Are you all right?' Xavier whispered to her halfway through the meal. She seemed to be enjoying herself, talking to his nephew, but Xavier wanted to be sure. He knew that his family could be a little overwhelming at times.

'I'm loving it,' she said, beaming at him. 'This is what families are about.' It was just what she had had when her kids were younger, but now they had all flown the coop and had lives of their own, which made her miss them all the more. They came home at Christmas, but not for long, only a few days. Hers had followed their dreams halfway around the world, except for Eric, but he was too enmeshed in Berlin to come home often either. She envied Mathieu and Annick with their family still near at hand, and since their children were still students, they would be there all summer. She had spent summers with her kids at those ages too. She had rented houses in Normandy, Brittany, and the South of France, near Ramatuelle in the Var, but now it would no longer make sense since no one would come, and she didn't want to be in a summer house alone.

'This is why I don't want kids.' Xavier smiled at her and said in an undertone, 'I can enjoy theirs. And then I go home.' And they liked him. Uncle Xavier was a big hit with the kids, and by the end of the evening, he and Chantal sat outside and looked up at the star-filled sky. It was a peaceful moment after a fun, lively evening.

'I love it here,' Chantal said happily, 'it makes me feel like a kid too.' It was all so easy, and there was a strong sense of community among them.

'Me too. I'll come back again in August. You're welcome, if you'd like to come. I stay for two or three weeks then, and I try to get here for weekends when I can.' He looked relaxed and happy as he smiled at Chantal. She fitted in perfectly, just as he had suspected she would. He loved that about her — she wasn't grand or pretentious, despite her success. She was a talented woman, but at the same time very modest. And Xavier was too. He couldn't stand women who liked to impress and show off. Chantal had the credentials to do so, but it wasn't her style.

'I'm going to visit my daughter in Hong Kong in August,' she said regretfully. 'I go every year. I only stay a week. She can't tolerate me for much longer, I get on her nerves. We're very different. She's much more formal than I am, and traditional. She thinks I'm a hopeless bohemian. I love her, but as the Brits say, we're like chalk and cheese. She's actually very British, she's lived there since business school, and she speaks fluent Mandarin now.' Xavier could hear the pride in Chantal's voice, and the regret. It sounded as though somehow they were like two ships passing in the night. He guessed right.

'And at the end of the month, I'm going to L.A. to visit my older son, the filmmaker. He's a whole different story. We usually have fun, although he's become totally American. I don't know what went wrong, but no one in my family seems to want to be French, except my younger son, but he doesn't want to live in Paris. He says the art scene here is dead, and he could be right.' She didn't sound critical of them, but it was clear that their lives were very separate from hers, and their choices and personalities very different. She seemed to respect it, which he admired.

'I'd like to meet them sometime. They sound interesting.' She laughed at what he said. 'That they are, and very different. From each other, and from me.'

'Are they close to each other?' He was curious about them, and about her. He was enjoying getting to know her, and was struck by what a solitary person she was, by trade and by force of circumstance. And he could see sadness and loneliness in her eyes at times. It pained him for her. She seemed to have no quarrel with her children, but they spent very little time with her. And she had soaked up the joy of the young people around them that day, and had fun with them, as she had had with her own.

She thought about his question about her kids. 'They're close when they're together. But they're all very individual and with their own divergent interests. Charlotte is the most conservative. Paul is very engaged with his life in L.A. and has an American girlfriend, and Eric is the most far out.

121

He's very avant-garde. If you see him with his sister Charlotte, it's hard to believe they're related.' She laughed at the thought. 'It gets complicated once they have significant others, who magnify the extremes and create friction sometimes. It was easier before they had partners. I'm very tolerant about who they live with, but they're not always that open-minded with each other, and they're critical of their siblings' choices of partners. I figure they're grown up and have a right to love who they want.' He liked what she said, and she sounded like the ideal parent.

'Are they as understanding about you?' he asked seriously.

She laughed in answer. 'Probably not. They were pretty horrible to the people I dated, when they met them, which wasn't often. And now they just figure I'm alone and it suits me.'

'And does it?'

'Not as well as they think,' she said honestly. 'I stopped introducing them to the men I went out with a long time ago. It wasn't worth the trouble since there was no one I was serious about. I actually think that they don't see me in that way, as someone who would have a partner. Their father died when they were so young, and they think of me as a mother, a service industry, not as a woman or a human being with needs. I was a slave to them for a long time,' she said, looking mildly embarrassed, 'so I created my own monster. I don't think they ever think about me as someone who gets lonely or sick or sad.' He remembered the tool kit in her suitcase and could easily imagine the kind of hands-on mother she was.

'That's not good,' he said quietly, 'if they don't think of you as having needs too. Why should you be lonely or alone? You're still young.'

'No, it's not good,' she admitted. 'I need to work on that. I never wanted them to see my weak side, or my frailties, when they were younger. Now they think I don't have any.'

'It sounds like you need your own life. They have theirs.' She didn't disagree with him. But she had to have a life worth fighting for to make the point with them. She didn't want to ride into battle for nothing, although she had thought about it often, especially with Charlotte, who was singularly uninterested in her mother's problems, and hardly ever called her, except when she wanted something. She never called just to ask how Chantal was or to chat. Eric was the one who did that, and was more sensitive to his mother's feelings. He was a sweet boy, and had been the closest to her growing up too. Charlotte was essentially a cold person. It was amazing how different they all were, from each other and from her, but it was also what made having children interesting. There were no two alike.

They went upstairs to their rooms then, after they had talked for a while, and he stood looking at her warmly for a minute outside her bedroom door. He would have liked to come in, but didn't want to ask. It was too soon. Instead he kissed her, tenderly, and with real passion for the first time. And as they embraced and he held her, he

123

heard a door open and his nephew walk past them on his way to the bathroom in the hall.

'Way to go, Uncle Xavier!' he murmured, and then closed the bathroom door as Xavier burst out laughing and so did Chantal.

'Welcome to my family,' he said, grinning.

'I love it!' she said, beaming at him, and they kissed again.

★　★　★

In spite of the presence of many young people coming and going in the house, Mathieu's insistence on his brother fishing with him at dawn, and relatively thin walls, by the third day they were there, Chantal was so happy and relaxed that she and Xavier wound up in bed together late one night, and became lovers. It had been the perfect place to start their romance in earnest, in an atmosphere that was loving, warm, and safe. They slept together every night after that, and liked to think that no one had noticed, but it was an open secret by the end of the week, and they gave up his room for the last two nights so the kids could use it for one of their friends. Chantal felt like part of the family by the end of the week, and she even put in her time scrubbing down Mathieu's boat after an afternoon at sea on his pretty sailboat. She looked at Xavier on the last night, grateful for every moment they had shared. She was so happy she had come, and hated to leave.

'It was perfect,' she said softly as they kissed, sitting in two chairs outside as falling stars filled the sky. They held hands, and she couldn't remember ever being as happy in her life, and Xavier looked just as pleased.

'Will you come back?' he asked hopefully.

'Anytime you ask me,' she assured him, and they kissed again. 'I wish I weren't going to Hong Kong next week. I hate to leave you.' They had grown very used to each other in the past week, and she hadn't thought of the difference in their ages since they arrived. He was right, it didn't matter at all, to them or anyone else. No one commented on it or seemed to care.

And then she had an idea. She couldn't invite him to Hong Kong to reciprocate the week she had just spent with him. Charlotte was much too uptight and formal, and needed some preparation before her mother showed up with a man, particularly a younger man, which she wouldn't understand. And Chantal wanted no headaches with her, or to have to justify her relationship with Xavier. But she could much more readily see taking Xavier with her when she went to visit Paul in L.A. He was more open-minded than his sister, and more relaxed. And she suggested it to Xavier as they went to bed.

'Would you come with me?' she asked him, hoping he would agree.

'I was planning to be here for my holiday, but I haven't been to the States in a few years. Maybe we could drive down the coast, and then visit your son in L.A. Do you suppose he'll object to me?' She thought about it for a minute before she answered.

'He'll be surprised, but I think you'll get

125

along. He's very relaxed about his own standards and view of life, though not always about me. We'll need to stretch his mind a bit, but I think he'll live through it.' She smiled at Xavier. 'I'd love for you to come.'

'Then I will. I'll have had two weeks in Corsica by then.' She was planning to spend a week with Paul in L.A., and they could add on a few days for the driving trip Xavier had suggested. It sounded like a wonderful idea to both of them, and she was going to warn Paul that she was bringing a friend, which would give him a heads-up. And knowing Paul, he wouldn't even ask who it was, and it would never occur to him it might be a man. He would see for himself when they arrived. Chantal always stayed at a hotel when she visited Paul, so Xavier would be no imposition on Paul and his girlfriend. Only Eric loved it when she camped out at one of his grungy apartments. And Charlotte hated houseguests of all kinds, but tolerated her mother staying there, under duress. Chantal knew them well.

When they left Corsica the next day, all the kids came out to wave goodbye. Mathieu and Annick kissed her, and they felt like old friends by then. She was sad to leave, and they all told her to come back soon. They checked in at the airport, and couldn't help smiling at each other on the flight back to Paris. It had been the best vacation she'd had in years, and she thanked him again as he kissed her before they landed at Charles de Gaulle Airport. And now they had another vacation together to look forward to, to visit Paul in L.A. They could both hardly wait.

8

Xavier stayed at Chantal's apartment every night until she left for Hong Kong. She talked to Jean-Philippe once before she left, but they were both busy, and he said nothing had changed. He and Valerie were barely speaking, and he hoped things would improve between them when they went to her family home in Maine as they did every summer. Chantal told him about the trip to Corsica, and he was happy for her. He said he wanted to meet Xavier when they all came back from their summer vacations, which wouldn't be till he returned from Maine. And he wished her a good trip to Hong Kong to see Charlotte.

Xavier took her to the airport when she left. She had taken two suitcases with her. As a banker, Charlotte led a more serious life and expected her mother to be well dressed while she was there. No blue jeans or casual clothes or what she referred to rather harshly as 'hippie' outfits. There was nothing bohemian about Charlotte's life in Hong Kong, and as a young, up-and-coming bank executive, she looked the part.

Xavier kissed Chantal when he said goodbye to her at the airport, and went back to his own apartment. They had loved staying at her place and waking up together every day as they had in Corsica. He was leaving the next day for London to meet with clients, and going to Geneva after that. He was going to be busy while she was gone, and then back to Corsica at the end of the week for a few more days. She envied him that, but was excited to see Charlotte. She hadn't seen her since Christmas, and regretted the fact that they only saw each other twice a year. Chantal visited her every summer in Hong Kong, and Charlotte came home for Christmas. Despite the little they had in common, Chantal was still her mother and loved her deeply, although Charlotte was not a demonstrative person, and hadn't been as a child either. She was far cooler and more reserved than her brothers, and always reminded Chantal of her maternal grandmother, who was a strong, austere woman of few words. Charlotte was a great deal like her, which told the story of just how strong genes were, and traveled through the generations.

She landed at Hong Kong International Airport after the twelve-and-a-half-hour flight, and she had slept on the plane. Charlotte had told her she would be in a meeting, and had left her keys to the apartment with her doorman so Chantal could let herself in, and the daily maid Charlotte hired would come in to help her. She had a new apartment, which her mother hadn't seen yet, and Chantal was stunned by how beautiful it was, on the fortieth floor of a brand-new building in the Victoria Peak District, a short drive from the business section, with a view of the modern buildings of Hong Kong. The apartment had been expensive, but she could afford it. Charlotte had filled it with English antiques she had found there. It looked more like a London or New York apartment than one in Hong Kong, but the British influence was still felt strongly. The apartment wasn't warm or cozy, but formal and traditional, like Charlotte herself.

Chantal was waiting for her when she got home from work, and Charlotte looked genuinely happy to see her and poured her a glass of wine. She had been in an important meeting all afternoon, and she said she was due for a promotion and a raise. She was all about her work, and her dream was to be head of the bank one day. She was the most ambitious of Chantal's children, and willing to work hard to get there.

They cooked dinner in the kitchen that night, and Charlotte had big news for her mother while they ate. Oddly, she looked like her mother, with the same blue eyes and blond hair, but the energy she expressed was different in every way. But it warmed Chantal's heart to see her nonetheless. She was her only daughter, and always tried to find points in common with her.

'So what's the big news?' Chantal asked, smiling at her, happy to be there with her.

'I'm engaged.' Chantal's heart did a little double flip when Charlotte said it. On the one hand she was happy for her, but on the other she knew that if she married in Hong Kong, she would never move back to France again. Now it was for sure. 'He's British, from London, but he's lived here longer than I have. He's an investment banker at a rival firm.' She smiled at her mother. 'He's thirty-four, he went to Eton

129

and Oxford. He's *very* British. His name is Rupert MacDonald, and we're getting married here in May.' It was all the pertinent information her mother needed, and she could already imagine him, British to the tips of his toes. 'And I want you to come to the wedding, of course. I want you to plan it, although we want to keep it very small. The tradition is huge weddings here, in the Chinese community. We only want a hundred people. And I need to find a dress. We want to hold the reception at the Hong Kong Club. He asked me two weeks ago, but I didn't want to tell you till you were here.' She held out her hand to show her mother a very pretty sapphire ring, circled with small diamonds, that looked like something a British royal would wear. It was perfect for Charlotte, and Chantal admired it. It looked nice on her hand. Chantal knew they had been dating for just under a year, but Charlotte looked totally sure.

'Are you planning to stay here, or go back to England with him one day?' At least they would be closer then, if they had children. Hong Kong was so far away, but Charlotte shook her head.

'We love it here. Neither of us can imagine living in Europe again. I wouldn't mind living in Shanghai, but we're happy in Hong Kong, especially if I get the promotion I'm in line for, and Rupert is a partner in his firm.' So they weren't going anywhere.

'When am I going to meet him?' Chantal asked calmly.

'Tomorrow night. He's taking us to dinner at Caprice in the Four Seasons. It's a three-star restaurant.' It was one of the finest restaurants in Hong Kong. 'He wanted to give us the first night to catch up.' And then she smiled at her mother, and looked gentler than Chantal had ever seen her. 'I really love him, Maman. He's so good to me.' Chantal smiled at her daughter and put her arms around her.

'That's how it should be. I'm so happy for you.' And in a single instant, Chantal felt as though she had lost her forever, but if she was happy with a man she loved, then it was for a good cause. And Charlotte was more open with her than she had been in years, talking about the wedding and her plans. She was hoping to find a dress in Paris when she came home for Christmas, and wanted her mother to go shopping with her. Chantal said she'd be delighted and could hardly wait.

She went to bed early and called Xavier from her room and told him about the engagement and the wedding. She wondered if they would still be dating by then. If so, she would bring him to the wedding, if her daughter didn't object, or maybe even if she did, depending on how involved she was with Xavier at the time. It was a long way away, nearly a year. And a lot could happen in a year or less. Chantal didn't like counting her chickens before they hatched. They chatted for a while, and then she went to sleep.

Charlotte had already left for work when Chantal got up the next day. She went to the Hong Kong Museum of Art, and then went shopping in the Causeway Bay shopping area. It was full of the same stores she knew from

Europe. Prada, Gucci, Burberry, Hermès, Chanel. And there were streets full of jewelers and smaller stores that specialized in copying designer goods at bargain prices that delighted visitors to Hong Kong, looking for great deals. One of Chantal's favorite places was the Temple Street Night Market, which opened at four P.M. In every way, Hong Kong was the shopping mecca of the world. She had fallen prey to it the first time she visited, but she no longer did, or tried not to go crazy in the shops, but it was always fun. And she went back to her daughter's apartment at the end of the day. It was still very hot — it always was in August.

They were meeting Rupert at the restaurant at eight o'clock. Charlotte came home at seven, and Chantal was already dressed in a simple black silk dress that made her feel like her own grandmother, but she knew that it was what her daughter expected of her, and she didn't want to embarrass her with her future husband. And Rupert was so classically British that Chantal could hardly keep from laughing when she saw him. Upper class, conservative, stuffy, old beyond his years, incredibly uptight, and the epitome of a British banker. It disappointed her in a way for Charlotte to be with a man with so little levity and imagination, but Charlotte was absolutely beaming and looked at him adoringly. He was everything her daughter wanted. Chantal couldn't imagine spending a lifetime with him, but he was Charlotte's dream and vision of a handsome prince, even though his humor was so stilted and trite that it was painful listening to his jokes. It was a relief when dinner was over. Later that night Charlotte came to her mother's room in her nightgown.

'Isn't he wonderful, Maman?' she asked her with stars in her eyes. 'He's perfect.' Chantal nodded. She just wanted her to be happy, whatever that meant to her. She was willing to set her own feelings aside and respect Charlotte's.

Her daughter rhapsodized about him for half an hour and then drifted off to bed, and then Chantal called Xavier and told him about the evening more honestly, about how painfully stuffy she found her future son-in-law, how humorless and dreary. 'There's no accounting for people's tastes,' she said with a sigh, as Xavier questioned her.

'Did you tell her what you thought of him honestly?'

'Of course not,' she said quietly. 'He's not a bank robber, he's not a drug addict, he's never been in jail, he's not a wife beater that we know of, he doesn't have ten illegitimate children, he's not a pedophile. What would I object to? That he's boring, stuffy, or too conservative? That's what she's looking for in a husband, and what right do I have to impose my value system and dreams on her? To each her own Prince Charming. I'm not marrying him, she is. There's nothing objectionable about him. He's just very dull and not my cup of tea. But Charlotte is nothing like me.'

'You're an amazing mother, Chantal,' he said admiringly. 'I wish mine had been more like you. She kept telling me who I should marry, so I

133

decided I never wanted to marry anyone, because she wanted them all to be like her, and I didn't want to marry my mother, or someone she picked for me. More parents should be like you and accept their children's choices. My parents expected Mathieu and me to marry people just like them, and they were very rigid, cold people. Mathieu did what he wanted and married Annick, who is warm and fun and perfect for him. And I decided to stay clear, and that marriage wasn't for me.'

'I just want her to be happy, whatever that means to her. It's going to be a very boring wedding!' she commented ruefully. 'I hope you'll be there,' she said warmly.

'So do I,' he said, and meant it.

And for the next week, every night, mother and daughter talked about the wedding, and discussed the details. They had dinner with Rupert again, at Amber at the Mandarin Oriental, and Chantal bought them a beautiful engagement present at a store she happened on by accident, and Charlotte was very touched by it. The gift was two lovely silver swans like the ones by Asprey, which were particularly meaningful since swans mated for life, and they were the perfect gift for the very traditional couple. They agreed to leave them in Charlotte's apartment until they moved in together the following year. They spent most of their nights together, but Rupert had kept his own apartment, which he felt was more proper, and Charlotte preferred that too.

The week flew by, and Charlotte actually looked

regretful when she took her mother to the airport. They talked about the wedding dress on the way there, and Chantal promised to look at Dior and Nina Ricci. At no time during the week had she mentioned Xavier to her. They had only talked about Charlotte and the wedding, and she hadn't asked her mother a single question about her life. It didn't seem appropriate to just drop it into the conversation, 'Oh, by the way, I have a new boyfriend and he's nearly twenty years younger than I am, I'm sure you'll love him,' so she kept the information to herself. And Paul was going to meet Xavier shortly, and undoubtedly he would tell his sister about him. Chantal didn't want to give it undue importance by making an announcement, so she said nothing, but it always struck her how little her daughter knew about her life. She never asked. She was a very self-centered person, and with the wedding coming up it would get worse. Brides were not known for their sensitivity about others, it was always about them, and Charlotte would be no different, she was already that way now.

The two women kissed and hugged at the airport, and the affection expressed was sincere. It just didn't encompass who Chantal really was as a person. Charlotte loved the mother she wanted Chantal to be, but not the human being in the role. Chantal had to fit the job description perfectly, there was no room for her to be herself, and who she really was Charlotte had never known, and didn't want to. Xavier was part of that. One of the unknown details of her mother's life.

Xavier met Chantal at the apartment after the long flight from Hong Kong. He could hardly wait to see her. He had missed her for the week she was away, and he had come back from Corsica the night before, and was rested and tanned, and looked very handsome. Chantal had showered and changed the moment she got home, and was wearing jeans when she saw him. She was thrilled to be back, and as much as she loved her daughter, and it had been a good visit this time, it was exhausting playing a role, the role of the perfect mother who never let her hair down, never did anything silly, never wore anything inappropriate, had no boyfriends, and lived alone. Chantal was tired of being that person, and after all these years of measuring up for all of them, and meeting their high standards for her, Chantal had begun to feel that she had earned the right to be herself, make mistakes, and be whoever she chose to be, just the way they did. She was tired of motherhood being a one-way street, and until now it had been. Falling in love with Xavier had freed her, and she felt more relaxed, whole, and at ease than she had in years.

★ ★ ★

Xavier and Chantal spent that week in Paris together, catching up on work, projects, and each other. Chantal was doing research for her script so she could finish it, and Xavier had to see clients at the law firm. On Thursday night, they packed their bags, and on Friday, they left. They flew to San Francisco and spent two days in Yosemite National Park, taking long walks and looking at waterfalls, and then they drove back to San Francisco, picked up the Coast Road, and headed south, and stopped in several places along the way, a night in Big Sur at the Post Ranch, another in Santa Barbara at the Biltmore. They drove through Malibu, and watched a sunset and then arrived in L.A. Chantal had booked a bungalow at the Beverly Hills Hotel in all its 1950s Hollywood glamour. Their bungalow had its own pool, and Xavier dove into it with delight while she called her son. He was shooting on location that day for one of his movies, in the Valley, and he said that he and Rachel would meet her at the Polo Lounge at her hotel for dinner at nine o'clock. It was where all the Hollywood types, actors and producers and studio heads, met to make deals and be seen.

She reminded Paul that she had a friend with her, and he sounded startled.

'I forgot. Who is it again?' He never paid close attention to what his mother said.

'A friend from Paris. We've had fun driving down from the north.' Chantal bringing a friend seemed odd to him, and for some reason, he assumed it was a woman, and he never asked. And she knew he'd be surprised at dinner.

She and Xavier lounged at their pool for a while, and then walked around Beverly Hills. Xavier loved it, and Chantal was enjoying it with him.

'I've always wanted to live here,' he confessed to her. 'It's so decadent, and innocent at the same time, like Disneyland for grown-ups with a twist.' She liked it there too, although she always thought that living there full time would be too much. But her son never tired of it. After thirteen years, he loved L.A. more than ever. And Rachel was from L.A. She had grown up in the Valley, moved to Beverly Hills as a teenager, and gone to Beverly Hills High, and then to UCLA. She was the classic Valley Girl. It always surprised Chantal that her son didn't want someone more sophisticated, but they had been together for seven years, since she was twenty-one and he was twenty-four. And they had lived together for all that time. Rachel wasn't the girl she would have chosen for him, but she had long since given up hoping that he would find a better one. Rachel suited him and the new person he had become when he moved to L.A. He was like a Valley Boy himself, and no one would have guessed that he had grown up in Paris and was French.

Xavier and Chantal got to the Polo Lounge before Paul and Rachel and were shown to a table in the garden. She had added high heels and a sparkly top to her jeans, which was the perfect costume for L.A. Charlotte would have fainted if she had worn it in Hong Kong. Chantal still had a lithe, trim figure and looked great in a bikini, and she looked sexy in her well-cut jeans. Xavier was wearing white jeans and a white shirt, loafers, and no socks, which was de rigueur here and looked great on him. And no matter what he wore, he always looked French to Chantal.

And then the young couple arrived, and Chantal almost laughed at the surprise in her son's eyes when he saw Xavier. She introduced them, and Rachel said 'Bonjour' in painful French, and Chantal hugged her. By now, they were old friends. And Chantal and her son exchanged a warm hug, as she looked him over and was pleased. He looked happy, healthy, and fit, and his hair was longer than it had been six months before.

Conversation was awkward at first with the addition of Xavier, while Paul tried to figure out who he was.

'So, you two are working on a film together?' he asked, thinking he looked like a director or a cameraman, and Chantal laughed.

'No, Xavier is a lawyer, specializing in international copyrights. We met at a dinner in June.' It had only been two months, and one could sense the intimacy between them in a relatively short time.

'You're friends?' Paul asked, groping for a reason for their being together, and Xavier stepped in.

'Yes, we are. Your mother was referring to the White Dinner. Have you been to it?' he asked them, and both young people shook their heads. It struck Chantal that Xavier was only seven years older than her son, but was so much more mature. He was a grown-up, and Paul seemed like a kid. It was the high-top Converse he wore, the long hair, the T-shirt he had worn to dinner with a famous band name on it. And he still had a baby face. And Rachel could have passed for

139

sixteen at twenty-eight, in a little baby-doll top that left her midriff exposed, and sparkly Mary Janes, with long Alice in Wonderland blond hair. She looked like a little girl.

Xavier described the White Dinner to them then, and they were fascinated.

'They ought to do it here,' Rachel said. And Chantal told them about the Chinese lanterns Xavier had provided, which was how they met.

'I think they've tried to copy it in other cities, but they modify it and it's not the same,' Chantal explained.

'I didn't know you went to stuff like that, Mom.' Paul looked surprised. And after they ordered, she told him that his sister was engaged and was getting married in May. Neither Rachel nor Paul looked old enough to drink and were carded when they ordered wine. Paul looked younger than all her children, even his baby brother.

'May?' he asked pointedly about Charlotte's wedding, and Chantal nodded as Paul glanced at Rachel and they exchanged a smile. She wondered if they were getting engaged too, after all these years, but the secret didn't come out till dessert.

'We're having a baby, Mom,' Paul said proudly, beaming at Rachel. 'In March.' He said that Rachel was two months pregnant and they had just found out. Rachel explained that they had already decided to have a water birth at home with a midwife, which made Chantal nervous just hearing about it. Childbirth was not always as easy and trouble free as people hoped.

She had had her share of scares herself.

'You might want to rethink that, in case some problem comes up. Rachel and the baby will be safer in a hospital, even with a midwife and a natural birth. You were born with the cord wrapped around your neck six times. Those things happen, and that can be a tragedy at home. But congratulations to you both.' It took her a minute to absorb the full impact of the news and all that they had just shared with her. And it shocked her to realize that she was going to be a grandmother, which she found embarrassing vis-à-vis Xavier. But the word was out now. She tried to look happy for them, but she was more than a little stunned. 'Are you planning to get married?' she asked as an afterthought, trying not to sound judgmental, and realized that Rachel had taken only a sip of her wine to be polite. Chantal was wishing she could drink the whole bottle at the prospect of being a grandmother in seven months. Xavier had seen the look on her face when she heard the news and had to make an effort not to laugh, and keep a straight face when he congratulated the young couple.

'We don't need to get married, Mom,' Paul answered her question, and Rachel nodded. 'That's so old school. No one gets married anymore.' Except his sister, who was as old school as it got, with an equally uptight groom. 'It's just not necessary, it's all window dressing,' he said dismissively.

'Do you think you'll go to Charlotte's wedding? I think she wants you to walk her down

141

the aisle,' Chantal said in response to his comments.

'Sure, the baby will be two months old by then. We can travel with him to Hong Kong, that'll be fun.' Chantal was not convinced it was the word she would have chosen for traveling that far with a two-month-old, and she wasn't at all certain how Charlotte would react to their having a child without being married, with her very conservative in-laws present. Chantal started getting nervous thinking about it, and asked Rachel how she was feeling. She said she felt great and had had no problems. She was still going to Pilates and spinning class and intended to keep it up throughout the pregnancy, and take Lamaze classes once she was further along. It made Chantal feel ancient as she listened to her and all the do's and don'ts they were mindful of, and they were going to talk to the baby in her womb and play their special music for it, and they were going to see it in a 3D Technicolor sonogram in two months and would know what sex it was. Chantal's head was spinning by the time she and Xavier got back to the bungalow, and he burst out laughing the moment they closed the door. Chantal looked like she was in shock.

'Oh, my God,' she said as she collapsed into a chair. 'How did I end up with such crazy children? I'm feeling schizophrenic. Charlotte is marrying a man who looks like the headmaster of an English school in a movie, and they think everything has to be ultraconservative. Paul is having a baby out of wedlock, with a water birth at home. Am I crazy or are they? And if you stick around, you'll be sleeping with a grandmother in March, for God's sake.'

'I think I'll survive it,' he said, smiling at her. 'You just brought up very individual freethinkers, and each one wants to be who they are.'

'Maybe I taught them to be a little too independent.' She looked dazed.

'Do you really care if they're married or not?' He was curious about that.

'Not really,' she said thoughtfully. 'I've never liked Rachel enough to want him to marry her, and now she's going to be the mother of my first grandchild, if they don't drown it at the water birth. How ridiculous is that? I smoked, and drank a moderate amount of wine, and did whatever I wanted when I was pregnant, and they survived it. Things are different now, but they sound so crazy with all their modern ideas, and playing their favorite music, hopefully not rap, for a baby in the womb.' Xavier laughed at the whole idea, but it had kept them from asking too many questions about him. Until the next morning, when Paul called her to make plans for dinner that night.

'So what's with Xavier, Mom? Is he your boyfriend or just a friend?' She hesitated for an instant and decided to be honest with him. Why not?

'A bit of both. We've been having a good time,' she said casually.

'Isn't he about my age?' Paul asked, sounding shocked.

'No, he's older. He's thirty-eight.'

'You could be his mother,' he said disapprovingly, which seemed strange coming from him. From Charlotte maybe, but not Paul.

'True, but I'm not. He doesn't seem to care.'

'What's he after?' her son asked suspiciously, and fortunately Xavier was in the pool when he called, so he didn't hear the conversation from her end.

'Nothing, as it happens. We're just enjoying each other. I'm surprised you're upset about it. You and Rachel are having a baby out of wedlock, which is fairly untraditional, so I can't imagine who I'm dating is a big concern. And if he's younger, so what? As long as he doesn't mind, why should you?' She hit him with it right between the eyes. Turnabout was fair play.

'I'm not upset, I'm just surprised, that's all.' He was a little huffy as he said it. 'Are you planning to marry him?'

'Of course not. I'm not pregnant.'

'Oh, my God.' Paul was horrified. 'Could you be? ... I mean could you still ... ' The possibility of that sent him into orbit.

'That's none of your business,' Chantal said bluntly. 'But if so, at my age I'm smart enough not to do that.'

'Are you upset about the baby?' He suddenly seemed worried, and she sighed. They were such children leading grown-up lives.

'Babies are serious business, Paul. They last forever, and they don't stay babies. Having kids is a messy business. It can get complicated. It's a big commitment. Do you feel ready for that?'

144

She wanted to be honest with him and share her thoughts.

'Of course I do,' he said without hesitating.

'Young people these days don't want the commitment of marriage, but they leap into the commitment of kids without marriage. Marriage is a lot easier — you can get out of it if you make a mistake. Kids are forever. The commitment doesn't get any bigger. And you'll be tied to Rachel for the rest of your life. Every decision you make for that child will have to be made with her consultation and consent, so you'd better be sure you like each other, or your life will be hell later, fighting with her about it.'

'We agree on everything for our child,' he said, trying to sound adult to his mother, but she wasn't convinced.

'You won't always agree, and you don't have to, but you'll have to come to reasonable compromises for the benefit of the child.'

'I know that. And you're not planning to marry Xavier?'

'No, I'm not.'

'Why didn't you tell me about him?'

'There's not much to tell. We're going out, we're having a good time, for as long as it lasts. If it gets serious, I'll let you know.' He still sounded shocked, he had never thought about her in that context. 'You guys are all adults now. You're having a baby, Charlotte's getting married. There's no reason why I can't have a life of my own too.'

'Why do you need to be with a guy? Why do you need that?' It made no sense to him.

145

'Why do you need Rachel?'

'That's not the same, Mother. Of course I need Rachel.' He was incensed at the question.

'That's right. And Charlotte needs Rupert, and Eric has Annaliese. Why do I have to be alone just because I'm your mother? I don't comment on your choices, to get married or not married, have a baby, or who you're with. Why don't the same rules apply to me?' The question was stunningly reasonable, and an eye-opener for him.

'Because you're our mother,' he responded immediately.

'Maybe you need to think about that, and what that job entails for people your age. I'm always there for you, I love you, I'll always be here to help you. But why do I have to be alone while you lead your own lives in other countries and cities? What am I supposed to do?' He had never thought of it that way and the concept shocked him. Enough that he called his sister a few hours later and told her about Xavier. Charlotte called her mother immediately.

'You have a *boyfriend?*' she shrieked into the phone.

'News travels fast.' She sounded calm. 'I'm dating someone. I'm not marrying him.'

'Paul says he's young enough to be your son.'

'Not quite, but close. Is that a problem?' She took the bull by the horns, and was ready to do so. 'What business is it of yours or your brother's who I go out with, and how old he is? He's intelligent, employed, and treats me well. I don't see the problem.'

'You could at least tell us.' Charlotte sounded hurt that her mother hadn't.

'Who knows if I'll be dating him a month from now? Why worry about it?'

'You should have told me while you were in Hong Kong, Mom.' She still sounded hurt.

'You never asked me anything about me. We talked about your wedding.'

'Why didn't you bring him?'

'I wanted to be alone with you.'

'Are you bringing him to the wedding?'

'I have no idea if I'll be dating him nine months from now. That's a long way ahead. Let's not worry about it now. And if I do decide to bring him, I'll talk to you about it. I'm not going to do anything to upset you and embarrass you.' Charlotte was relieved to hear it. But Xavier was too young to be presentable as her mother's date, in her opinion.

'Paul made it sound like he's fourteen years old.' Charlotte chuckled, and so did Chantal.

'That would be your brother and his girlfriend. They look like kids at camp. Xavier is a grown-up, and an attorney. I hope you'll like him if you meet him.' It was the most adult conversation they'd had, and Chantal found it refreshing to put her cards on the table with her and be direct.

'I was just shocked when Paul called,' Charlotte admitted.

'I understand, but you don't need to worry about it.' Their mother sounded sensible, and Charlotte was still surprised. It was just a whole new concept to them. And she was right, they never did ask her questions about her life. It never occurred to them to do so. From now on they would, to avoid surprises like this one. But at least Paul said he was a nice guy.

'What do you think of Paul and Rachel's baby?' Charlotte asked her then, and Chantal hesitated.

'I think it's fine if they can handle it. Your brother has an irregular income and I help him, and Rachel is supported by her parents. That doesn't sound like an ideal way to bring up a child, while you're dependent on people other than yourselves. I'm not sure either of them thought of that.' Although Chantal had the night before. She was still subsidizing him, so now she'd have to support their child? That didn't sound grown-up to her, but she hadn't wanted to embarrass him in front of Rachel and ask him. But the subject would have to come up before the child was born. Children having children. She was twenty-eight, and Paul was thirty-one. It was a little odd, and irresponsible, to be dependent on your parents and then get pregnant without thinking it through.

'I'm sure her parents will support them. They have a ton of money.' Rachel was an only child and they spoiled her rotten. But Chantal didn't want her son and grandchild to be supported by Rachel's parents. She would have to talk to him about getting a job other than his indie films, to make a salary they could live on. That would come as a shock to them too. 'Rupert and I don't want children for a few years,' Charlotte added, and Chantal was relieved to hear it, although they could afford it. And it was a more sensible plan than a water birth at home, a baby out of wedlock, and two people with unstable incomes.

'That sounds reasonable,' Chantal said about Charlotte and Rupert's plan. She had heard from Eric earlier, Paul had texted him about the baby, and Eric had texted her that they were crazy.

They talked for a few more minutes and then hung up, and the subject of Xavier was no longer an issue. A surprise, but not an issue. She wasn't marrying him, and she sounded so relaxed about it that Charlotte calmed down, and Paul decided that he really liked him by the end of the trip. They went out to dinner almost every night, at Paul and Rachel's favorite restaurants, and barbecued at their house in West Hollywood one night. They would have to move to bigger quarters when the baby came. Rachel was trying to talk him into the Valley, and Paul wanted to stay in town. They had a whole lot of decisions ahead of them, more than they could imagine.

By the time Chantal and Xavier flew back to Paris, she had almost made peace with the fact that she was having a grandchild. Almost, but not quite. But the visit with Paul had been great. They invited her to be at the water birth with them, and she told them she'd wait until afterward, or meet the baby in Hong Kong at Charlotte's wedding in May, when he or she would be two months old. The whole idea was still shocking to her. Her son was having a baby. And just as surprising to them, their mother had a thirty-eight-year-old boyfriend. It was a brave new world for them all. But at least now it was a two-way street for the first time.

9

While Chantal was in Hong Kong visiting Charlotte, Jean-Philippe, Valerie, and their children left for Maine to share the vacation home that she and her brother had inherited from their parents after their mother died two years after their father. They had spent their childhood summers there. They coordinated their vacations every summer so that her brother's two children and their three could spend their summer holiday together and the cousins could enjoy each other. They stayed for the month, and for Valerie and her brother, it always brought back happy memories of their childhood and the vacations they had spent there growing up. The house had deep meaning to them, and they loved that their spouses enjoyed it too and were willing to spend time there.

Valerie's brother was five years older, a banker, and his wife was a pediatrician in Boston, and she and Valerie had always gotten along well. Their children were slightly older, but not enough to make a difference, and Jean-Louis, Isabelle, and Damien loved their cousins.

This year Valerie was hoping she'd find peace there, as she always did. There had been so much tension between her and Jean-Philippe recently that she longed for the nights of fireflies and crickets chirping and falling stars in a summer sky, and sailing on the little sailboat they kept at the house to use in the summer.

It was an idyllic place where normally they could forget their cares and disengage from the world, except this year Valerie felt as though their problems were attached to them like a trail of tin cans rattling behind them. And once they got there, the tension with Jean-Philippe was as acute as it had been in Paris, and a sense of well-being was as elusive as it had been there.

'What's happening with you two?' her sister-in-law Kate finally asked her, and Valerie told her the whole saga of the decision they had to make about Beijing.

'Wow! That's a bitch,' Kate said sympathetically. 'Your career or his. I'd hate to be dealing with that one. We went through something like that during my residency, but your brother worked it out. He got a job at a bank in Chicago, and we made it through my residency and then came back to Boston. But this sounds a lot more complicated.'

'Yeah, and I'm not a doctor,' Valerie said mournfully. 'My job means a lot to me, and I've worked hard to get there. I'm in line for editor-in-chief in a couple of years, but it's a great career move for Jean-Philippe, and I will never make the kind of money he can make in China. If money is the deciding factor, I lose hands down. But I'm not ready to give up my career to move to Beijing. And I won't have a career by the time we come back if I go with him.'

'I wouldn't want to move to China either,' Kate said honestly. 'I had a chance to teach in

152

Scotland for a year, and we turned it down. The weather is too depressing. And living in Beijing with three small children would be damn hard. I'm sure some people do it, but I wouldn't want to.' It reinforced how Valerie was feeling about it, and she managed to avoid the subject with her husband for the first two weeks, but they couldn't dodge it any longer. He was getting insistent emails from the firm making the offer, and the deal was going to come off the table shortly. And he didn't want that to happen and lose his chance to make the decision.

He and Valerie were sitting on the dock while their children were down for naps, her brother had gone fishing, and her sister-in-law had driven into the small town with her children to buy groceries. Jean-Philippe looked at his wife unhappily. It hadn't been their best vacation.

'I don't want to pressure you, Valerie, but we have to make a decision.'

'I know we do,' she said sadly. 'I've just been stalling. I didn't know what to say to you. I don't want to lose you, or our marriage, but I just can't go to Beijing. It's too much for me, the kids are too young, and my career will be finished when we get back. Once I get out of the lineup at *Vogue*, they'll pass me over. That's how it works. And I know there are other magazines, but I've worked so damn hard at this one. This has been my dream since I was in high school.' He nodded, as sad as she was. He had expected her to say that, and he wasn't surprised.

'I've thought about it a lot too. I think it would be wrong for all of us as a family if I gave up on

153

this. I'm going to take it, and make a deal with them to send me home every two months for a week or two so I can see you. We can't do it forever, but I'll try it for a year. Maybe that'll work, and if I make serious money there, maybe you'll reconsider.' In the meantime, he was buying them a year of her continuing her work at *Vogue*, while he seized the opportunity to make fabulous investments in Beijing. It was going to be the best of both worlds, or the worst, but he was willing to try it, and so was she. It was the only solution they could come up with.

'Do you hate me for not going with you?' she asked solemnly, and he shook his head and put his arms around her.

'I love you, Valerie. I don't hate you. I wish I could come up with a better solution that works for both of us.' But this was the best he could do. And not having his family in Beijing would give him time to work harder. He would have no distractions and not have to worry about them in an unfamiliar country and how they were adjusting. In some ways, this might be better, if his bosses would let him do it. He still had to negotiate the deal with them. And he sent them an email that night outlining his plan, and much to his relief, they sent their approval the next day. Jean-Philippe was smiling when he told Valerie.

'They agreed. That's something at least.' It wasn't cause for celebration, but it was a valid compromise, and took a lot of the pressure off him.

'When do you leave?' Valerie asked, feeling

nervous. She was sad to think that her husband would be living in China, while she and the children lived in Paris, and she couldn't help wondering how heavily it would impact their marriage. But it was only for a year, and after that they would examine the issues again.

'Sometime in September. I have a lot of prep work to do before I leave.' And he had to give notice at his current job. He wanted to give them four weeks to replace him, as soon as he got back to Paris.

They left Maine earlier than usual, so he could get all his ducks in order, and his brother-in-law and sister-in-law wished him luck in China.

In the plan he had outlined, he would be coming home for Thanksgiving, which was important to her, though not a holiday in France, and Christmas, and in February, April, June, and August, as long as there was nothing crucial that required his presence in China to close a deal, but it was something for Valerie and the children to look forward to.

Jean-Philippe told Chantal about it when they had lunch after she and Xavier got back from L.A., and she warned him that being gone so much for a year could have a disastrous effect on their marriage.

'If that happens, she says she'll quit her job and come over.'

'She says that now, but what if she doesn't want to?' Chantal was worried about him. He was making a tough decision.

'Then it's up to me at that point if I want to quit and come home.' Their life had been so easy

155

until then, for seven years, and now it was so complicated. Chantal hated to see that happen to them. And it was impossible to predict the toll it would take on either or both of them. 'What about you?' he asked her then. 'How did the vacation in California go? Did the romance with Xavier survive it?' He smiled as he asked her, and so did she.

'Yes, it did. I went to Hong Kong alone to see Charlotte. But he came to L.A. with me to visit Paul. He and his girlfriend are having a baby, unmarried of course. I'm going to be a grandmother,' she said, making a terrible face, which expressed how she felt about it. 'That's just what I need, a grandchild when I have a twelve-year-old boyfriend.'

'What does he say about it?' Jean-Philippe asked her.

'He doesn't seem to care,' she said, still surprised.

'He sounds like a good man.'

'He seems to be.' And Jean-Philippe could see easily how happy she looked. 'I'm still worried he'll run off with someone younger. But there's no sign of it yet. And you'd better Skype me when you're in China!'

'I promise.' He smiled at her. He was going to miss her, and his family.

'When are you going?' she asked, sad about it already.

'In about three weeks. I have a lot to do before that.'

Chantal thought about him all afternoon after their lunch. She wondered if commuting from

Beijing every two months was really going to work. But like everything else in life, only time would tell.

* * *

Benedetta had spent most of the summer unraveling her business, restructuring it, and disengaging Gregorio's interests from hers. It was a complicated process, and she had spent hours every day with lawyers, but by the beginning of September she had made progress. Gregorio's lawyers were working closely with them, and he was shocked by how cutthroat she had been. All she cared about was salvaging their business while removing him. She wanted him to have no toehold in her business and wanted nothing to do with him. She communicated with him only through attorneys, and she was forming an entity that she felt she could run efficiently on her own. She had eliminated certain departments, streamlined the staff, and shut down all use of his family's textiles. It had been a severe blow to their business, and his brothers weren't happy with him. His oldest brother had come to see her to try to reason with her, but she was merciless. She wanted all ties severed between the two family empires. She wanted no link to her ex-husband, neither personally nor through the business.

'You can't do this to him, Benedetta, and to us,' his brother implored her. 'Gregorio made a mistake. You know how he is. He's childish.' Her face was set in stone when she answered.

'He's more than childish. He abandoned me with a business to run, and left me with all the responsibility and decisions, while he ran off with that girl and had their babies. He told me he wanted out of our marriage after I waited for him and made excuses for him. Now I want him out of my business. He doesn't belong in it anymore. And I'm sorry if it hurts you and your brothers, but he should have thought of that before. He hurt all of us, he made a fool of me, now he has what he wanted. That girl and their baby. Give him a job at one of your factories. I won't work with him anymore, or with you,' she said as she stood up. 'The bond between our two families has been severed, and you can thank Gregorio for it.' All of Gregorio's brothers were livid with him for pushing Benedetta to this point. Separating the two entities and canceling her orders from their mills had already cost them millions, not to mention what she wanted in the divorce. She didn't need the money, but she wanted to punish him for what he had done to her, and not just this time but all the times before. He had humiliated her publicly repeatedly, and it was going to cost him.

'You don't need to divorce him,' his older brother pleaded with her. 'You can stay married and lead your own life.'

'Why would I stay married to a man like him? This isn't the old days where people stayed married, while the men lived with their mistresses. He lives with her, they have a child, he should do her the honor of marrying her. I

158

won't be his wife. I want nothing to do with him anymore.'

His brother left her office on the verge of tears, and Benedetta was proud of everything she was doing. And no one on her side disagreed with her. Gregorio deserved it.

Dharam had called her several times in August, to see how she was. He was busy working in Delhi. And at the beginning of September, he called and invited her to what sounded like a fabulous event in London. It was very tempting, but there was no way she could get away. She still had things to work out for the divorce, the rest of the division to implement, and she was getting ready for Fashion Week, and to show their new line at the end of the month. She couldn't leave Milan for a minute.

'I'm so sorry,' she said apologetically. 'I've spent the whole summer restructuring my business.'

'I completely understand. I just want you to promise me that when things settle down, you'll have dinner with me.' He was as warm and understanding as ever.

'Just let me get through Fashion Week, and then I'll have time, I promise.'

'I'll be back in Europe in October. I'll call you then.'

'That will be perfect.' She had barely had time to think of him since she filed the divorce and took apart the business. It had been a mammoth undertaking, and she wasn't finished yet. And at the same time she was getting ready for their fashion show. Her plate was overflowing.

★ ★ ★

Gregorio called Jean-Philippe in Paris a few days later. It was the first time anyone had heard from him since June, it had been three months, and he told his friend that the last months had been rugged.

'Benedetta is divorcing me,' he said, sounding sorry for himself.

'I've heard that,' Jean-Philippe said, trying to appear neutral, although he was far from it. His sympathy was for Benedetta and all she'd been through.

'She kicked me out of the business. I'm fighting it legally, but my lawyers say we won't be able to stop her. My brothers are ready to kill me. I've been in the hospital with Anya and the baby for the last three months, I haven't seen anyone. We're going back to Rome next week, with the baby. Would you like to have lunch before I leave?' He seemed lonely when he asked him. He had been out of touch and isolated for so long. Jean-Philippe had taken the call out of politeness, but he disapproved of everything he'd done, and how he'd done it.

'I wish I could, but I'm moving to Beijing next week. It's been a crazy three months for me too since the White Dinner,' which was the last time they had seen each other.

Gregorio was shocked by the news. 'Is Valerie going with you, and you're taking the children?'

'No, they're all staying here. I'm going to commute for a year. We'll see how it works.'

'That sounds difficult,' Gregorio said seriously.

160

'I'm sure it will be,' Jean-Philippe said, while trying to maintain an upbeat attitude.

'I have a baby girl now, you know,' Gregorio said proudly. 'We almost lost her. She's very small, but she's going to be all right.' At least he hoped so, and it might be years before they knew for sure. 'She had a brother, and we lost him.' He sounded shaken by all he'd been through, and not the carefree Gregorio of the past.

'I know. I'm sorry,' Jean-Philippe said sympathetically, but he needed to get back to work, and Gregorio appeared to have nothing to do and wanted to talk.

'Email me sometime. I'd love to hear from you,' Gregorio said, reaching out as though Jean-Philippe were his last friend, which might be true. 'Let me know when you're back in Europe. We'd love to see you.' Except the 'we' he was talking about included Anya, and Jean-Philippe had no intention of seeing her. His loyalties were to Gregorio's ex-wife, not to his girlfriend.

They hung up a few minutes later, and all Jean-Philippe could think of was what a loser Gregorio was, and what a fool and bastard he had been. And he didn't blame Benedetta a bit for what she'd done. No one did.

★ ★ ★

The following week Anya and Gregorio left the hospital with the baby, three months to the day from when she'd been born, and a week after Anya's original due date. As they walked into the

161

September sunshine, Gregorio's heart ached remembering the baby boy who should have been going home with them too. Dressed in a little white dress, a pink sweater, and a knit cap, and wrapped in a matching blanket, Claudia looked perfect, and they went back to the George V with the nurse. They had taken an additional suite for them, and planned to spend a few days there before they went back to Rome.

Anya called three or four of her modeling friends that afternoon, and asked if they wanted to come to the hotel to visit. They were all going to a party at Le Baron that night, which was Anya's favorite discothèque. She was disappointed that they were busy, and she looked mournful when they ordered room service and Gregorio turned on the TV. This was not how she had envisioned their first night of liberty. They were free at last, and Gregorio didn't even want to go out to dinner. He just wanted to stay at the hotel with the baby. He fell asleep in front of the TV, and Anya stood at the window, looking at people outside and feeling like she was in prison. She wanted to start modeling again soon, and to have some fun.

Her friends never had time to come to see her while they were there, and Gregorio's Parisian friends didn't return his calls. And three days later they left for Rome, feeling like outcasts, with their baby. Once they were back, he wanted to contact his friends in Milan and go to visit them. He missed his old life, his work, his home, his city, even his brothers. But as soon as he started calling people, he found that no one in

Rome or Milan would return his calls either. After what he had done to Benedetta, he had become a social pariah. Feeling panicked, he flew to Milan to see his brothers and begged them to let him work with them. They reluctantly agreed, although they weren't happy with him, and his youngest brother wouldn't speak to him at all. But working with his family gave him an excuse to move back to Milan. He rented a beautiful apartment for them and told Anya when he went back to Rome.

Anya was excited at the prospect of getting runway work in Milan during Fashion Week. She hadn't worked in months and wanted to now, but two days after they got to Milan, her agent called to tell her that she had been canceled everywhere in Italy, and no designer would hire her for any show. Her agent had booked her instead for three shows during Fashion Week in Paris, and Anya was thrilled. She reported it to Gregorio immediately, and he looked shocked. He assumed that Benedetta's numerous supporters had blackballed Anya in Milan.

'You're going to Paris to work? What about me and the baby?' He had had no idea she would go away so soon.

'I'll only be gone a week or two.' She was nearly dancing around the room, she was so pleased to go to work again and see her friends.

Having the baby had changed both of them. All Gregorio wanted to do was stay home and spend time with her and the baby. But Anya was young, and now that the baby was out of danger, she wanted to get out and live again. And to her, that meant modeling in Paris or anywhere she could. She had told her agent to start booking her fully again, anywhere in the world.

The days before Fashion Week in Milan were painful for Gregorio. His brothers were still angry at him, his friends wouldn't see him. All he kept hearing about were Benedetta's victories with her new line, and Anya kept complaining that he didn't want to go out. She wanted to go to parties, and Gregorio told her they couldn't unless they wanted to make fools of themselves. And no one invited them anyway, which he didn't explain to her. Anya loved the baby, but she wasn't ready to give up living and become a recluse with him. She was relieved, and so was he, when she finally left for Paris. She was too young to stay locked up at home at night with him.

Shortly after his return to Milan, his brothers wanted him to talk to Benedetta to ask her to renew her contracts with their mills. But she wouldn't take his calls and only communicated with him through attorneys, about the divorce, and the dissolution of their business partnership. His brothers were upset because she was buying all her fabrics now from their competitors in France. It was costing her a fortune, but she refused to give Gregorio's family her business. And Gregorio's first assignment, once they brought him in to work with them, was to change her mind and convince her to use their mills again.

'I can't,' Gregorio told them miserably. 'You don't understand. She wants nothing to do with any of us.' They had lost half the volume of their business from Benedetta canceling her account with them.

But despite the anger of his brothers, Gregorio was happy to be back in the fold, working with them, and living in Milan, even without friends. He had Anya and the baby now to console him for all he'd lost, and he would sit for hours at night with his infant daughter in his arms. Having her made up for everything.

He missed Anya while she was in Paris. She called him every day, but he was shocked when he saw paparazzi shots of her in nightclubs and at parties with other models and her friends. She was making up for lost time, after months of being trapped in the hospital with the babies and him. She needed to have fun again. And although Gregorio was happy being back in Milan, she found it oppressive, since she couldn't work there, and depressing being at home with him every night while he held the baby and took care of her. Paris was much more exciting, as she began leading her old life again.

Gregorio had a major argument with her on the phone one night. He'd seen her in the fashion press and on the Internet that morning, after she'd been at a big party the night before. She looked beautiful in the photographs, and as though she was having a great time. She looked half naked in what she was wearing, and there was a ring of men around her, as she danced wildly at Le Baron. And he assumed that she was drunk.

He had fallen in love with her in the hospital,

when she had been serious and subdued, watching over their babies with him. But now the girl she had been when he met her had emerged again. He had been transformed into a father by all they'd been through, but Anya was just a beautiful young girl who wanted to have fun. He wanted to maintain and strengthen the bond they had formed in the hospital. He had left his wife for her, and lost his business. But the girl he had fallen in love with had disappeared. She was Anya the supermodel and party girl again. There was no sign of her being a mother. Tragedy and his love for her had not transformed her after all.

★   ★   ★

The day after Gregorio's argument with Anya on the phone, Benedetta had her big show in Milan to introduce her new line. She was nervous about it. She was showing stronger shapes, exciting colors, bolder designs, and innovative fabrics in the spring collection, and she had developed a whole new look, to mark the change in the company she had stripped to the ground and put back together again. And she had no idea how it would be received, or if it would be successful, and well reviewed by the critics.

She was backstage herself before the show just as she always was. And usually Gregorio was with her to support her. This was the first time he wasn't, and it felt strange doing it without him, but she kept telling herself she could. She just prayed that it would work. She had taken a major risk, by restructuring the company without Gregorio in a very short time.

Her cellphone rang backstage as she looked over the models for a last time. They were still sewing on some of the buttons and trims, which she had gotten from new sources as well, and the seamstresses were shortening several hems. A number of the models were pinned into their dresses. She answered her phone as she looked over the hair, makeup, and shoes. She had used a new shoe designer as well, since their old one was Gregorio's cousin.

'Yes?' she said, sounding distracted. It was Dharam, calling to wish her luck.

'Your show is going to be wonderful, Benedetta,' he said warmly. 'I know it will.' He was calling from Delhi, and it was three and a half hours later for him. He had waited to call her at the last minute to give her a final boost, right before the models went out on the runway. He knew she had no time to talk. 'I want to come to your next one,' he said hastily.

'You will. And thank you,' she said, grateful for his call. 'I'll call you later.' And then she hung up. The music came up, the lights came on in the room, and the models strutted down the runway as Benedetta stood backstage, holding her breath. They went out one after the other, in a pounding rhythm, wearing her beautiful clothes, and twenty-five minutes later it was over. She had shown fifty-five looks and the applause was thunderous when it was over. She had orchestrated it all herself, and seen to every detail. Her talent was on full display, to the delight of everyone watching.

There was a pause, and then one of the stage managers signaled to her to go out on the runway too. This was the part she always hated, when she nearly ran to the end of the runway, took a quick bow, and went backstage again. But she knew that more than ever, this time she had to do it. The audience was waiting for her, buyers and journalists and the fashion press from around the world. She was wearing black jeans and a black sweater and ballerina flats, her work clothes at times like these, with her long straight dark hair loose down her back.

And as she came from behind the curtain onto the runway, everyone stood up, the entire room. She hadn't been prepared for that, as tears filled her eyes. A cheer rose from the crowd, applause and whistles, as they stamped their feet and called her name. They gave her a standing ovation, to celebrate what she'd done, but also to show their support. Everyone in the room knew what she'd been through, how hard she'd fought to survive and save her business from what could have been a deadly blow. Instead, she had stolen victory from the jaws of defeat. She had done it. She had won. Gregorio hadn't destroyed her. She reached the end of the runway with tears rolling down her cheeks, and a broad smile for all her supporters. They were there for her, and she wanted to kiss each one of them and thank them, as she waved and ran behind the curtain again. It was a total win for her, and the line. It had been a perfect night.

There were parties that night all over Milan to celebrate Fashion Week, but Benedetta went home. She wanted to savor the moment, and Dharam called her again to congratulate her. He had seen it on the Internet in video.

'The clothes were spectacular, Benedetta. I was so proud of you!' She had been proud of herself too. She hadn't let Gregorio crush her business or her spirit. She had fought back with all the strength she had.

'I can't wait till you see it live next time,' she said, walking around her living room, unwinding from the tension of the past few weeks.

'Neither can I. You have to come to India for inspiration. There is so much beauty here, you would love it.'

'I'd like to see it sometime.'

'You will,' he promised her. 'I'll see you in a few weeks.' They hung up then, and Benedetta grinned as she walked into her bedroom, lay on the bed, and stared at the ceiling. What a fabulous night it had been!

10

Paris Fashion Week was even crazier than Milan. It always was. It was bigger, there were more French designers, and it was the lineup everyone waited for. Valerie and her editor-in-chief were in the front row at every show, as well as the principal editors of American *Vogue*, who flew over just for that. The pressure was huge on the designers, and Valerie had to run from one show to the next, observing them all. But she remembered to send Benedetta flowers to congratulate her on her spectacular show in Milan. People were still talking about it and what a victory it was.

As usual, Valerie hardly saw Jean-Philippe that week. She left the house at eight in the morning, and rarely came home before two A.M. And the hardship about it this time was that he was leaving at the end of the week, and she didn't have a minute to spend with him. But he understood. This was her job. And this very craziness, and her part in it, was why she wasn't moving to Beijing.

Jean-Philippe was leaving on Saturday, and had lots to do that week, getting ready. He had video conferences and a dozen meetings by Skype to prepare for his new job. And he had mountains of files and research to read before he arrived. He was hoping to do some of it on the long flight.

Just before noon on Friday, Valerie got a call from Beaumont-Sevigny, a major investor in mid-priced clothing companies with a golden reputation, and they wanted a meeting with her before their top executives flew back to the States that night. She canceled her lunch date with the editors of American *Vogue*, and managed to spend an hour with the CEO of the company and their whole creative team. They offered her a sizable retainer to consult with them, on a regular basis, which was something she was allowed to do at *Vogue*. Usually only senior editors got these offers, which were very lucrative, and supplemented their salaries from the magazine. She was in shock when she left the meeting, after she heard their offer. They wanted her to commit three days a month to them, along with giving them her advice on the direction of clothing lines, her expertise about silhouette, proportion, color, fabrics, trends, and putting on presentations. They wanted to pay her twice her annual salary at *Vogue*, and it suddenly helped to justify not going to Beijing with Jean-Philippe. Clearly, she was destined to stay in Paris, at the hub of the world of fashion design. She told Jean-Philippe about it that night. Even he was impressed, and very proud of her.

'That's fantastic,' he said, genuinely thrilled. She explained what they wanted her to do, and she knew she could do it for them with ease.

'When do you start?' he asked her.

'Next week.' It was like a dream come true, and she chattered to him about it that night until they both fell asleep. And when they woke up in

171

the morning, Valerie suddenly felt as though a wrecking ball had fallen on her heart. She remembered what the day was. Jean-Philippe was leaving for Beijing. It had finally come, after months of talking about it and struggling with the decision. And now she felt sick at the thought of his going, but she knew more than ever that it was right for her to stay, especially with the offer she'd gotten the day before. She had serious, valid professional reasons for being here, and she was being paid well. Her husband couldn't argue with that.

She and the children had lunch with Jean-Philippe at home. The children had helped make a cake for him, and sang a song about how much they loved him. And Valerie took a video of it with his phone, so he would have it with him. There were tears in his eyes when he kissed them and his wife. With all she had done that week, she had managed to practice the song with them.

At four o'clock they left for the airport, and the children went with them. They could only take him as far as security. And they lingered after he checked in, and then walked him to the security lines. He kissed Valerie hard on the mouth and held her tight.

'I'll be home soon,' he whispered to her, while his daughter complained.

'You're squeezing Mommy too hard. You're not supposed to do that.' They were always scolding Jean-Louis for doing that to her.

They all kissed him and hugged him, they'd had a nice day together, and then the moment came when he couldn't wait any longer and he had to leave them so as not to miss his plane. He kissed Valerie one last time, hugged the kids again, and then entered the security area, and waved at them until he went through to the other side and disappeared. The children all looked sad when they couldn't see him anymore.

'I want him to come back,' Isabelle said, crying.

'He can't, silly, he'll miss his plane,' Jean-Louis scolded her, and Damien just sat in his stroller, sucking his thumb and looking sad. Valerie got them all to the garage, and put the stroller in the trunk with some difficulty, got Isabelle and Damien into their car seats, and Jean-Louis between them in his seat belt. She tried to get them to sing on the way home, but none of them were in the mood, and neither was she. It felt like a day of mourning once he left, and she wondered now with a wave of panic if she had done the right thing, not going with him. What if her staying in Paris destroyed their marriage? It was a distinct possibility. But giving up her career and moving to Beijing might have destroyed it too, and was too big a sacrifice for her.

He called her on her cellphone before they left the garage, and she pulled over to talk to him, then passed the phone to each of the kids. He was in the first-class lounge waiting to board. And then she talked to him again.

'I love you . . . I'm sorry I'm not going.' He could hear that she was crying and was touched.

'It's the right thing for you,' he said, trying to reassure her. 'We'll make this work.' He hoped he was telling her the truth.

'Thank you for being understanding about it,' she said softly.

'You too, for letting me try it in Beijing.' They were both doing what they needed to do, but sadly not with each other. Their respective needs were in conflict, and there had been no other way to resolve it. He had to get off the phone then to board, and she drove the children back to the city, and made dinner for them, gave them their baths, and put them to bed. And then lay on the bed she had shared with him only that morning, and felt a wave of sadness overwhelm her. The next two months without him were going to seem endless. And she had done something she had never thought herself capable of. She had sacrificed her marriage for her work. It was a painful realization, and she cried herself to sleep that night.

* * *

When Jean-Philippe arrived at Beijing Capital International Airport eleven hours later, the translator who had been hired for him was waiting to take him to his apartment. It was a temporary apartment for arriving employees until they got settled, and since he was alone, he had said it was good enough for him. It was on Financial Street in Haidian in West Beijing, where many foreigners lived, in a modern building that reminded him of some of the uglier high-rises in other cities. But the apartment was neat, sparsely furnished, and clean, and someone

174

had left a modest amount of food in the refrigerator. He had the odd feeling of suddenly being hurled back into his bachelor days, or a flat he'd shared with three other men when he was in graduate school and did an exchange program for several months at NYU.

Nothing about the apartment, the building, or the neighborhood was pretty, and he had been aware of a heavy fog of pollution hanging over the city. And between the polluted air and the depressing surroundings, it suddenly hit him how dreary it was going to be being there without his family or anything even remotely familiar. He had brought photographs of Valerie and the children and set them on his desk immediately, as though that would instantly improve the unattractive apartment. But all it did was make him feel lonelier and wonder why he had thought that it would be a good idea to come here. The main reason he had done it was as a career move that would benefit all of them. He could see why his predecessor's wife had gone home, and he was suddenly glad he hadn't brought Valerie with him. She would have hated it even more than he did.

He called her that night, after settling in and unpacking. His translator had gone home when he decided not to go out. Instead he hard-boiled some eggs and made toast, drank a glass of orange juice, and decided to go to bed early. Valerie asked him what the apartment was like, and he didn't have the heart to tell her so he said it was all right, but she could tell from his tone that he wasn't happy, and by the end of the

175

conversation how glad he was, for her, that she hadn't come. 'It's pretty basic,' he said about the apartment, which was a vast understatement. What it was most of all was ugly. Everything was poorly made and purely functional, like a cheap motel, and the bed was desperately uncomfortable when he lay down, but he finally fell asleep from sheer exhaustion.

He got up at six o'clock the next morning, and went to his office at nine after reading several newspapers online. A driver picked him up and drove him through highly populated areas, and then to what looked like a business district, with cars cluttering the streets like cockroaches, belching exhaust fumes as they stalled in traffic.

There was nothing lovely about the city, from what he had seen so far, but he wanted to see the famous tourist attractions: the Forbidden City, the Great Wall, and the Terracotta Warriors and horses, when he had time to take the train there. It was a two-day train trip to Xian in Shaanxi Province and back. But first he had to familiarize himself with the office and the people in it. But the year loomed ahead of him like an obstacle course, as he longed for his first trip home to see Valerie and the children. He felt like a homesick kid at camp. But by midmorning he was engrossed in what he was doing. They had several major deal proposals on the table, and some very interesting mergers and acquisitions. It was why he had come, and he was relieved to plunge into his work, to distract himself from the loneliness he was feeling. And by eight o'clock that night, he was back in his apartment, eating a bowl of rice his cleaning person had left him, with something else he didn't recognize and was afraid to eat. Everything he touched, saw, heard, smelled, or dealt with was unfamiliar, and he wondered if he would ever feel at home here, or even at ease.

By the end of the first week, he had developed a routine of rising early, exercising, and working at home for two hours before he left for the office. And on Saturday he hired a tour guide to take him to the Forbidden City, and it was well worth it. It was as spectacular as he had been told it would be. He described it to Valerie on the phone that night. But she couldn't take long to talk to him since both Jean-Louis and Damien had stomach flu, and she had no nanny over the weekend to help her. Both their lives were suddenly more complicated by virtue of being separated and five thousand miles apart. And Jean-Philippe was sorry he wasn't there to help her. They said goodnight hastily, and he took a stack of files to bed and fell asleep while reading them. And he decided to call Chantal on Skype the next morning.

'So how is it?' she asked when she saw his image appear on the screen. He was wearing a sweater and blue jeans, and looked no different than he had when he was in Paris.

'Interesting,' he said, trying to be generous about it, and Chantal picked up how lonely he was from his tone of voice.

'Interesting good, or interesting you wish to hell you'd never done it?'

'A little of both.' He laughed at the question.

'Unfamiliar mostly. And very strange to be somewhere where I don't speak the language. No one speaks English or French here. I'd be lost if they hadn't hired me a translator. But mostly it's weird being here, and I miss Valerie and the children.'

'I'm sure she misses you too. This is going to be a year you'll both remember, and maybe not so fondly.'

'So how's your romance? Cheer me up and tell me what's going on in your life.'

'Not much. I'm finally finishing my script at the moment, and I just signed a contract to do a new one. I haven't started it yet. And I'm having a good time with Xavier. We went to an antique fair this weekend and the Musée d'Orsay. We're just having fun together.' She smiled as she said it, and looked happy.

'Are you still crazy about him?'

'More than ever. He's such a terrific person. And I love his brother and sister-in-law. We had dinner with them a few days ago. We really enjoy each other.' He was pleased it was going well for her. She deserved it after so many years alone. And she seemed more excited about life since she'd met Xavier.

They talked for a little while longer, and then Chantal said she had to get ready to meet the producer of the new project. They signed off on Skype, and Jean-Philippe found himself alone again. Although his days were full at the office, his nights were long and dreary. Once he got back to his apartment at night, he realized how much he missed Valerie. He had already decided that this was the worst idea he'd ever had. And now they just had to get through it, on sheer grit if he had to, but he had to live with his decision. He just hoped that he would make a ton of money to compensate for it. It was the only possible justification he could think of for the loneliness and misery he was enduring. His year in China had only just begun, and all he prayed for now was that the time would pass quickly, the money would be worth it, and it didn't kill his marriage.

11

Chantal and Xavier fell into a comfortable routine once they got back from L.A. He spent most nights at her apartment, but occasionally he went back to his place for a night if she was working. They went to museums, movies, and art openings, and dined with friends. She introduced him to a few people, and he was enjoying having her meet his circle of friends, which was wider. Once in a while she felt like the elder statesman in the group, but he had friends of all ages, social strata, and walks of life. And by October, her children no longer sounded shocked when she said she was with him, or that they had gone somewhere together. She went to Germany with him to see a client, and afterward they drove to Berlin to have dinner with Eric, who was delighted to see her and meet Xavier after hearing about him from his brother.

They were slowly merging into each other's worlds, and the ripples around them seemed small. It all felt very natural and normal. Xavier was very interested in contemporary art, and Eric had liked him. Chantal was surprised to discover how much he knew about conceptual art, which impressed her son.

She occasionally still worried about his meeting a younger woman, and kept telling herself that their relationship was too good to be true or to last, and tried to remind herself not to get too attached to him, but by mid-October they had been together for four months, and it felt as if they had been in each other's lives for years. He even talked to Jean-Philippe with her on Skype one Sunday, and he thought they made a nice couple. He was envious when he saw them together and had admitted to Chantal that he missed Valerie and the kids terribly. She said she hadn't spoken to her since he left, but kept meaning to invite her to lunch.

'She sounds very busy. She's going crazy at the office, and she has a new consulting client who's eating up her time, and she's got the kids on her own on the weekends.'

'That'll teach her to let you move to China without her,' Chantal said, only half joking. She still thought it was a huge mistake that they were going to live apart for a year and too hard on both of them. But she didn't say it to Jean-Philippe. He had enough on his plate without his friend being a doomsayer, but she was worried about them both, and he sounded desperately unhappy in Beijing. The opportunities were fabulous, but the living conditions and quality of life were abysmal. He had no friends there yet, and no social life in the foreign community, and he missed his friends in Paris too. Chantal felt like she was calling him in prison every time they Skyped.

'Poor guy, he looks unhappy,' Xavier commented one day after they Skyped. 'Why did he go without his family?'

'His wife wouldn't give up her job to go with him.' It was a modern-day dilemma that they both knew didn't always have a happy ending. 'She's worked hard to get where she is at *Vogue*, and she's in line for the position of editor-in-chief. And initially, he wanted her to commit to go to Beijing for three to five years. Now he's trying it out for a year, although I don't know if that's clear to his employers. I hope they make it.' He nodded, thinking about how lonely it must be, but more and more women had careers and weren't willing to sacrifice them for their men. And their men weren't always willing to impact their careers for them. Too often it became a standoff, and the relationship became the sacrificial lamb they both put on the altar for their careers.

'I wouldn't want to be in his shoes either way,' Xavier said with feeling, and Chantal agreed. There was always the possibility that their marriage wouldn't survive the choice they'd made.

They went to the food hall at Bon Marché later that day, and stocked up on things they both liked to eat. They were learning each other's ways, and they enjoyed cooking together, although he claimed to be the better cook, and she let him think so. They had a nice way of accommodating and adjusting, and giving each other enough space to breathe. She never felt crowded by him, and he never felt she was intruding. They were both respectful people.

They went for long walks in the Bois de Boulogne, and sometimes drove out into the countryside on the weekends to have lunch at some small country inn. They came back happy and relaxed, made dinner on Sunday night, and curled up in her bed to watch a movie, since she had the bigger TV. Everything about the arrangement seemed to suit them. She didn't see how it could last, given the difference in their age, but it worked and just seemed to get better and better.

★   ★   ★

In mid-October, after a business trip to Rome, Dharam went to Milan for the weekend to see Benedetta. She was still reveling in the success of her new line at Fashion Week, and she was happy to see him. The orders were pouring in, and everything she had done to streamline her business so she could manage it on her own had worked. She was the talk of the fashion press, and their sales figures were better than they ever had been when she and Gregorio ran the business together. She had taken a huge risk forcing him out of the business, but it was paying off big time, and his brothers were gnashing their teeth and blaming him for what could turn out to be the downfall of their family business. Benedetta had no regrets at all. Years of silent humiliation had suddenly turned to rage, but instead of waging war on him, she had put a positive spin on it and restructured the business. It was the ultimate revenge, and Gregorio had become the laughingstock of Milan.

Benedetta didn't waste time talking about it to Dharam. He had come to see her, and had waited three months to do so, since his trip to

Sardinia in July. He stayed at the Four Seasons, and took her to Ristorante Savini in the Galleria Vittorio Emanuele II for dinner. And they drove into the countryside on a gloriously sunny Saturday afternoon. At the end of the day, they came back to her chic apartment. She had made some changes to it since Gregorio left, and Dharam admired the classical paintings she had collected.

'So when are you coming to see me in India?' he asked her with a warm smile. 'It would be fabulous inspiration for you. You would love Jaipur, Jodhpur, Udaipur, and of course the Taj Mahal, but there are so many beautiful things to see and places to go in India. I would love to share them with you. I would be your personal tour guide.' She smiled and handed him a glass of wine. 'The light and the colors in India are exquisite. There is a hotel in Srinagar that is the most romantic place in the world, and the Shalimar Gardens on Lake Dal are unforgettable.' His dark brown eyes were warm and gentle as he said it. He was offering his world to her on a silver platter. 'Even the jewels might inspire you for your work. We could go to the Gem Palace in Jaipur.' She knew of them from the designers there who came through Europe to sell their magnificent jewelry.

'You make it sound very enticing.' She smiled at him, and sat back comfortably in an oversized chair in her living room with a sigh. She had enjoyed being with him in Sardinia in July, and had thought of him often ever since, but she'd been busy unraveling her marriage

184

and reorganizing her business, and she hadn't felt ready to see him, knowing that he had more than just a friendly interest in her.

'I would love to spend some time with you, Benedetta,' he said simply, 'if you'll let me.'

'Yes, I would like that now.' She wanted to be candid with him. Even though her husband had left her for another woman, and he had a daughter with her now, she needed time to get her head out of her twenty-year marriage. Gregorio's and her lives had been so entwined for so long that sometimes they felt like one person, and she had needed a meat cleaver to separate their two worlds. 'The divorce is filed, and it seems right to me. It takes a long time in Italy, but at least the intention to divorce is clear. I didn't want to be as sloppy as Gregorio has been.' She realized now how wrong she had been to turn a blind eye to his affairs, but he had always come back to her and assured her that the other woman meant nothing to him.

'Is he going to marry the girl?' Dharam asked cautiously, not wanting to upset her, but curious about her husband's plans and how they might impact her.

'I have no idea. It sounds ridiculous, but he didn't expect me to divorce him. He thought we should just stay married, keep the business intact, and he would live with her and their baby. Once he told me he was leaving me for her, I didn't see any point staying married. And we couldn't run a business together. Now he'll be free to do as he wishes.'

'I wouldn't want a young Russian supermodel

as a wife,' Dharam said ruefully, and Benedetta shrugged and then laughed.

'Maybe he won't either. That's up to him now. In any case, we're both free to do what we want.'

'Do you really feel that way, Benedetta?' Dharam asked her. 'It's not easy separating from someone you've been married to for that long.' He didn't want to ask her if she was still in love with him, and hoped she wasn't.

'No, it's not,' she agreed.

'I had a hard time when my wife and I divorced. At least you don't have children, which complicates matters even more.'

'No, but we had a business. And our families have worked together for generations.'

'It must have come as quite a shock to him when you wanted him out.'

'Yes, it did, and to his brothers.' She smiled at Dharam then. 'It's amazing how life changes sometimes in the blink of an eye. When we went to the White Dinner in June, I thought we'd be married forever. Now my whole life is completely different.'

'Sometimes that's a good thing. Sometimes change brings wonderful gifts,' he said, looking at her intently. 'I felt a strong connection to you that night, but I know these months have been hard,' he said and sounded as though he meant it about how drawn to her he felt.

'How would we spend time together, though? You live in Delhi, I live here. We both have businesses we can't ignore. I could never live away from Milan. All my work is here.' She wanted to be honest with him right from the

186

beginning. She wasn't going to drop everything and move to India if they fell in love.

'I know that. I've thought a lot about it. There's no reason why we can't go back and forth to see each other if we want to be together. People do that. I'm quite mobile and can work almost anywhere. I spend a lot of time in London, Paris, and Rome. And New York.' She knew that from his calls and emails in the past four months — he was always traveling somewhere, or writing to her from his plane or from a hotel room in the different cities he had mentioned. 'Would you be willing to give it a chance?' He was a good person, and very appealing, and what he was saying to her was very tempting.

'Yes, as long as you understand that I have to live here. This is my home base. My business is here, and even more so now that everything depends on me.' She could have sold the business and retired, or given it up to Gregorio and his family, or continued to run it with him. Instead she had chosen to run it all herself. She wasn't about to lose that now, or give it up for someone else. And he didn't seem to expect that of her.

'I think we're both modern people,' he said sensibly. 'You're not a housewife somewhere. I don't run a grocery store in Delhi. I think we both have options that people with less imagination don't,' he said, smiling at her. He put down his glass of wine, and came to sit in the oversized chair with her. 'I think we were destined to meet that night at the White Dinner.

Something sad and difficult was happening to you, and I think the fates, or the gods, or whatever you wish to call them, sent me to be with you.' She had thought of that once or twice too. The coincidence of their meeting that night had seemed impressive, and he had called her faithfully, though not intrusively, ever since. Had she told him that she was staying with Gregorio, she knew that Dharam would have accepted it with grace. And he had waited a respectable amount of time to come to see her. He had let her do what she had to do. 'I think we're forgetting something important,' he said, gazing at her seriously.

'Like what?' Benedetta looked surprised.

'How we feel about each other,' he said gently. 'You can't legislate everything and figure it all out. The heart can't be dictated to or managed. It does what it wants.' And as he said it, he leaned down and kissed her, gently at first and then passionately as he put his arms around her and she responded. It was a long time before they pulled away from each other, and he glanced at her again. 'I think we should just relax and see what happens. Perhaps you will hate India, or take a strong dislike to my children, and they're very important to me.' Now it was her turn to explore his life, how they got along, and the people in his world. He kissed her again then, and she forgot everything he had been saying.

They sat and talked for a long time, and then he took her out to dinner, and asked her again about coming to India.

'November is always busy for me, I work on our new designs. And in January and February I get ready for our show. What about the beginning of December? I could get away then,' she said, looking at him shyly. She was about to discover a whole new place, a whole new universe, and a new man. It frightened her a little, but it was exciting. And he had assured her she would be safe with him. She believed him. From everything she knew about him, she trusted him. He was a responsible, thoughtful person, and she also knew that he already cared about her. He had demonstrated that to her in his patience for the past four months. And now she was excited about going to India with him. And he couldn't wait to make plans for her trip.

By the time Dharam left Milan on Monday morning, Benedetta felt totally at ease with him. She went to have breakfast at his hotel, in his suite, before he left. And he held her in his arms and kissed her again. It had been a wonderful weekend, and worth waiting all these months for. If he had pursued her any sooner, other than with occasional phone calls, it would have felt wrong to both of them. Now they had nothing to feel guilty about. He hadn't swayed the balance of her decisions. He had stayed low-key while she worked it out for herself, and now they could move forward together, in measured steps, to see what life had in store.

He walked her to the lobby when she went to work. Her driver was waiting, and he kissed her lightly on the lips.

'I'll call you when I get to London. See you

189

soon,' he said, beaming at her. 'In Delhi.'

She waved as the car pulled away, and Dharam walked back into the hotel with a smile and a wave at her. He was a happy man.

★ ★ ★

When Anya returned to Milan after Fashion Week in Paris, she had worked a lot, had a great time, and her career was taking off again. She had bookings set up in London, New York, Berlin, Paris, and Tokyo in the coming weeks and months. And she was restless in Milan as soon as she got back. She was happy to see Gregorio and the baby, but in a matter of weeks Milan had become a place for her to visit, but not her home.

Gregorio could sense the moment he saw her that she had changed. She was back in her old life, and she didn't belong to him. He tried to talk to her about it, but she denied it whenever he brought it up. But even the baby reacted to her differently and cried whenever Anya held her. The center of Claudia's universe was her father, and Anya felt left out, and complained about how fussy the baby was.

'You need to spend more time with her,' he chided Anya gently. But once home, she was always out, at an exercise class, shopping, or on the phone with her agent and friends somewhere else. She seemed younger again suddenly, and not ready to settle down. She wanted to forget what had happened at the hospital, not grow into motherhood by his side.

All Anya thought about now was fun. She wanted to make up for lost time. She was acting like herself again, the woman he had had the affair with, not the one who had given birth to a daughter and grieved over their infant son who had died. She acted as though Claudia were someone else's baby, and it unnerved her to watch Gregorio with her, bathing or feeding her or taking pictures constantly. It made him seem like less of a man, and she didn't find it sexy. He had been so much more exciting the year before, when their affair started and she got pregnant. She shuddered to think of that now. They both had changed. He had gotten more serious, and she was more anxious to play. And Gregorio was sobered by all he had lost, and had grown deeper from the experiences they had shared.

He walked past his old house sometimes and wondered what Benedetta was doing. He wanted to ring the doorbell and see her, but he didn't have the courage. He knew that she wouldn't want to see him, and even if she did, he had no idea what to say. How did one apologize for dropping an atom bomb on their life? He realized now that he had gone insane when the twins were born, fatherhood had gone to his head, and facing tragedy together had made him delude himself that Anya was more than she was. The only blessing for him was the baby girl he loved holding in his arms. He had fought too hard to save her to lose her now. And Anya couldn't wait to leave Milan to go on her next assignments all over the world. Her personality and her work made it easy for her to escape the responsibilities Gregorio had assumed she would share with him, after he gave up everything for her. But she seemed to have lost interest in building a life and family with him. The depth and substance he had glimpsed fleetingly in her in the hospital in Paris had been a mirage.

The real Anya had come to the fore again, and a week after she returned to Milan, she left for her jobs in London, Paris, and Berlin. And she was only too happy to let Gregorio and the nanny care for their child. She looked relieved when she kissed him goodbye and left, promising to come home soon. But the falseness of the connection they had shared was glaring. Terror and tragedy had formed a powerful bond between them, but it wasn't strong enough to keep them together now.

By the end of October, he had picked up some of the threads of his old life. Two of his friends met him for lunch and felt sorry for him. But everyone else agreed, he had wrought destruction on himself. And he and Anya were invited nowhere as a couple when she was in town. Most of their friends and acquaintances felt compassion for Benedetta, not for him. He was paying a high price for his mistakes, and Anya was seldom there, so he was lonely a lot of the time and came home after work. The bright spot in his life, that always brought him joy, was his baby girl. She was worth it all.

12

Chantal's cellphone rang on the last day of October at four A.M. She heard it distantly in her sleep and thought of letting it go to voicemail, but with children scattered all over the world, she never dared. Her motherly instincts won out, and she picked it up off the charger, assuming it would probably be a wrong number at that hour, but she couldn't take the chance.

'Yes?' she said sleepily, as Xavier rolled over and opened one eye. And then Chantal sat up in bed and was wide awake. It was a hospital in Berlin, and they told her that her son Eric had had a motorcycle accident. He was alive and conscious, but had broken a leg and an arm and was going into surgery to have a pin put in his hip.

'Oh, my God,' she said, not realizing that she'd said it. 'I'll come immediately. May I speak to him?' The nurse said that he was already being prepped for surgery, but he would be out in a few hours. She looked devastated as Xavier sat up next to her, wide awake now too.

'What happened? What's wrong?' He was instantly concerned. He had no children of his own, but now he shared her worry about hers. He considered it part of their joint life.

'Eric had a motorcycle accident,' she said, looking at him with terror in her eyes. 'He's alive. They're about to put a pin in his hip. He broke a leg and an arm. Thank God he wasn't killed.' They hadn't mentioned a head injury, but she was sure they would have if he had one. And she knew he wore a sturdy helmet on his bike. 'I hate his goddamn motorcycle. He thinks it's bourgeois to own a car. He's got to get rid of it now.' She reached for her cellphone again then, and called Air France. She got a seat on an eight A.M. flight to Berlin.

'Do you want me to come with you?' Xavier offered immediately, but she was used to handling emergencies alone. She had been doing it for most of their lives.

'You don't need to do that.' She leaned over to kiss him to thank him. 'You have work today.' She knew he had important meetings all week. And Eric was her child, not his.

'Are you sure? I can cancel what I'm doing today. I'd like to be there with you,' he said, and she could see that he meant it, but she didn't want to disrupt his work. 'You shouldn't go alone.' They could both guess that Eric would be in the hospital for a while, and need help at home when he got out. And with a broken arm, he couldn't manage crutches for the broken leg.

'I wonder if Annaliese was on the bike with him. I never thought to ask.' She was worried about that too, as she went to pack a bag, and then showered and dressed. Xavier got up when she was in the shower, and made her coffee and a piece of toast, which was normally all she ate for breakfast. It was five-thirty in the morning by then, and she had half an hour before she had to leave. He sat at the breakfast table with

194

her and held her hand.

'Call me if you want me to come,' he said with a look of concern, both for her and her son. 'I hate to say it, but I agree with you, motorcycles are just too dangerous. Especially in Germany on the Autobahn, they go at crazy speeds. It's bad enough here. He'll probably hate me for saying it, but you should make him give it up.'

'Hopefully the bike was destroyed, but I won't let him get another one. I'll get him a car.' He couldn't afford one on his own.

'Nothing too bourgeois,' Xavier teased her, and she smiled. It was nice having his support, but she was in full mother mode now, and all she could think of was Eric in surgery. She wanted to get to Berlin, and wondered if she'd be there before he woke up. She was anxious to leave. She picked up the small bag she'd packed with sweaters and jeans, some toiletries, and her makeup, and she was wearing a warm duffle coat in case it was cold. Xavier walked her to the door and put his arms around her.

'I love you. I'll drop everything and come if you want me.'

'How did I get so lucky when I found you?' she asked, smiling at him. The cab Xavier had called was already outside, waiting for her.

'How do you know that wasn't my wish that night at the dinner? To find a beautiful, smart woman to love for the rest of my life?' It made a shiver run down her spine when he said things like that. How could he love her for the rest of his life when she was almost twenty years older? The math didn't add up well. But she didn't challenge him on it now. He kissed her again then, and she ran out the door. It was six in the morning, and he went back to bed, thinking about her and her son. He shuddered imagining how awful it would have been if Eric had died. It didn't bear thinking, and he didn't know if she'd survive it. People did, and she was a strong woman, but he hoped nothing like it would ever happen to her. He loved her and hated to see her in pain, worried about her injured son.

Chantal got to the airport in plenty of time for her flight and was one of the first to board. It took off on time, and she landed in Berlin at nine-thirty, ran through the gate, and got a cab to the hospital. The information desk told her that he was out of surgery and in the recovery room, and what floor the appropriate waiting room was on.

She went to the nurses' station when she got there, and they said that Eric was in stable condition, and he would be in his room at noon. And she thought to ask then if there had been anyone on the motorcycle with him, and they said he had been alone. She called his apartment then, and Annaliese answered. She was in tears and told Chantal that Eric hadn't come home the night before, which wasn't like him, and she was panicked. Chantal realized then that her own name and number were on his emergency papers, and Annaliese had no way of knowing what had happened. No one had notified her.

'He's all right,' Chantal said calmly, trying to reassure the girl. 'He had an accident on his motorcycle. He broke a leg and an arm, but he's okay. I'm at the hospital now.' Annaliese cried even harder when she heard the news and lapsed into German, and then reverted to her halting French.

'I thought maybe he was dead,' she said, sounding shaken.

'He's lucky he isn't,' Chantal said with feeling. 'He's still in the recovery room after surgery. He won't be in his room for a couple of hours. You can come over to see him later.'

'I have classes today,' she said, upset by the news, but relieved to hear that he was alive. 'I can come tonight.'

'He'll be happy to see you,' Chantal said kindly, and hung up. She was standing in the hall waiting for him when they rolled him out of the recovery room, toward a room with three other men. And he looked up at his mother gratefully. She was always there for him, and the others, and always had been. He had known that somehow she would come.

'I'm sorry,' he said to his mother, as she leaned down and kissed his face, still grimy from the accident. They hadn't taken the time to wash his face. They had bigger things to deal with. He had a cast on his arm, and a full cast on his leg. And the doctor she had spoken to while she was waiting said he would be in the hospital for a week. The arm was a clean break, and the cast would be off in a month. The leg would take longer, two or three months. And he had to go to a rehab hospital for therapy until he could get around on his own.

'You should be sorry,' she scolded him. 'That

motorcycle is history. You can join the rest of the bourgeoisie now and drive a car.' He smiled, and she left him then to go and do battle for a private room for him. And an hour later he was in his own room, and she and a nurse had cleaned him up. They treated him like a child, and he drifted off to sleep after the nurse gave him a shot, and his mother sat beside him, watching him, grateful that he was alive. And then she went down to the cafeteria to get something to eat. She thought about calling Xavier, but didn't want to bother him at the office, and it was a strange, lonely feeling as she went back to Eric's room. She had been doing hospital duty alone for them for more than twenty years. Stitches, sprained ankles, cuts when the boys fell out of trees when they were growing up. Charlotte's emergency appendectomy when she was nine, a kidney stone when Paul was fifteen. She had always been alone in hospital corridors and emergency rooms, worried about them, and faced with the decisions. She was used to it, but as she thought about it now, she realized just how long she'd been doing it and how lucky they'd been this time.

She turned the corner to go back to Eric's room, and as she glanced down the hall, she saw Xavier waiting for her. He looked serious and concerned as he started walking toward her. Tears of relief filled her eyes as she saw him.

'What are you doing here?' She was totally amazed. No one had ever been there for her the way he was.

'I didn't want you to be alone.' He had taken

the next flight after hers. 'This is more important than what I had to do today. How is he?'

'Pretty groggy. He was in a room with three other guys. I just got him moved to a private room.' Xavier smiled as he put an arm around her.

'Why am I not surprised? Mom to the rescue.'

'That's what mothers are for.' And in his opinion, she was a great one. She had just demonstrated it again when she flew out of bed in Paris and came straight to Berlin.

'Was the girl with him?' he asked her.

'No, she was at the apartment. No one had called her. She thought he'd been killed.'

'Thank God he wasn't,' Xavier said soberly, as Chantal kissed him lightly on the lips and slowly pushed open the door to Eric's room.

'I'll wait for you out here,' Xavier whispered. 'I don't want to intrude.'

'At least come in and say hello.' Xavier followed her in reluctantly, but Eric was still sleeping soundly. They went back outside then to sit in the chairs in the hall where they could talk. He had brought a stack of things to read in his briefcase, assuming she'd be busy with her son. She still couldn't believe that Xavier was there for her. She had had no one to share the burdens with for so many years, or the terror when something happened. It always seemed like too much to ask of anyone.

'Why don't I go and check in to the hotel,' he suggested after a while. 'I'll come back later.' He had already reserved a room at the Adlon Kempinski in the cab after he landed in Berlin.

He had thought of everything.

'How will I ever thank you?' she asked him before he left, and Xavier smiled at her in answer.

'I'll figure out something. We can talk about it tonight.'

She laughed and went back into Eric's room, and sat quietly next to his bed.

He slept for the next two hours, and then stirred and smiled when he saw her.

'Hi, Mom . . . I should call Annaliese. I never got a chance to call her last night.'

'I already did. She's coming tonight after her classes. I'm glad she wasn't on the bike with you.'

'So am I,' he said, trying to move in the bed, which wasn't easy with both casts. Chantal called a nurse, and they changed his position, and his mother left the room when the nurse got him a bedpan. 'How soon can I get out of here?' he asked when Chantal got back.

'Not for a while. You've got to go to a rehab hospital after this, until you can manage by yourself. I think that'll be for about a month, and a week here.'

'Shit,' he said, looking glum. 'I was working on a show.' But he'd had a hell of a lesson, a valuable one if it kept him off a motorcycle in the future and kept him alive.

'At your age, you'll probably heal pretty quickly. Do you want to come home to Paris while you recuperate?' she asked quickly, and was disappointed when he shook his head.

'I'd rather be here.' By now, this was home. He

200

wanted to be near his friends, his studio, his girlfriend, and his work. 'I'll be fine,' he assured her, although he was looking tired and uncomfortable by the time Xavier came back at dinnertime. He came in for a few minutes with Eric's permission, and Eric thanked him for being there for his mother, and then Xavier went down to the cafeteria to get Chantal a sandwich and a piece of fruit. 'He's a nice guy,' Eric commented about him. 'Did he come with you?' He was curious about him, but he liked what he'd seen so far, and his mother looked happy and comfortable with him.

'No, he came after. It was thoughtful of him.' Eric nodded and smiled at her.

'It's nice to see you with someone, Mom.'

'I'm glad you feel that way.' He was the kindest and most compassionate of her children, and always had been.

'Why should you be alone? We're not.' They each had a significant other, but it had never occurred to them before that she might want one too. And she had never made an issue of it since she hadn't met anyone important to her in years, until Xavier.

He sat in Eric's room with them, while Chantal ate her sandwich and an apple. She and Xavier left when Annaliese came, so the two young people could be alone. Annaliese cried and threw her arms around him, and Eric looked happy to see her, while she berated him for driving like a maniac. Chantal promised to come back in the morning, and they went back to their hotel.

Xavier had reserved a beautiful room for them, and Chantal lay on the bed, exhausted. She had been up, and tense, worried about her son, since four A.M.

'Oh, my God,' she groaned. 'I didn't know how tired I was till I lay down. I'm dead.' He ran a bath for her, and they took a bath together, and then lay in the bed, talking. It made him realize how hard it was for her to have her children live so far away. They were still her children, even though they were grown. And this was the kind of event she dreaded, or worse. And she could no longer be there for their daily joys and sorrows. She had become an outsider in their lives, except for an emergency like this, when she flew to their rescue, but as soon as Eric was back on his feet again, he would be on his own and she would be irrelevant again.

'It's not easy having kids,' Xavier said thoughtfully.

'No, it's not,' she admitted. 'You're always doing too much or too little for them, not there when they want you to be, or too present and driving them insane. You have to let them try their own wings, and pick up the pieces when they fall. And whatever you do, no matter how hard you try, there's always something you did wrong that they never forgive you for. It's a thankless job. But the best one in the world.' She smiled at him. 'It's hard to get it right, and they always blame you for something. If you're lucky, one of them thinks you're cool, for about five minutes, and the others think you're a disaster, or they all do. Charlotte has always been tough on me. Eric always forgives me my mistakes. Even in the same family, they're very different people. And it's a miracle if you get it right even some of the time, no matter how hard you try.'

'That's why I've never wanted kids. You have to be Einstein to figure it out.'

'No, you don't. You just do the best you can and love them a lot, no matter what.' And let them go when it was time, which was the hardest of all.

'Children never seem to forgive their parents. It seems very harsh to me.'

'Do you really not want children?' she asked him thoughtfully. Sometimes she felt like she was keeping him from a woman his own age who could give him kids.

'Not really. I never thought I'd be good at it. I'd rather deal with yours or my brother's. It's easier when they're grown up, and they're blaming someone else for whatever is wrong in their lives. Little kids are too scary. And I'd probably screw that up. And women who are desperate to have babies always make me nervous. I'm much happier with you,' he said, leaning over to kiss her. He knew what she was thinking and wanted to put her mind at rest. He had no regrets about being with her, and hadn't since they'd met. 'You're not depriving me of anything. If I wanted kids, I'd have figured it out by now.'

'Lucky for me,' she said, and kissed him back.

When they woke up in the morning, Xavier ordered breakfast from room service, and Chantal went back to the hospital, relaxed after the night she'd spent with Xavier. It was a whole different story than it would have been if she were alone. He told her he'd come to meet her at noon, and bring them lunch. And when she got there, Eric was complaining about his casts, and the food, and he wanted to go back to his apartment. She calmed him down, and one of the nurses gave him a bath. And by the time they were finished, Xavier arrived with two big bags of food from a beer garden down the street.

'I have schnitzel, sausages, more schnitzel, and more sausages, and schnitzel,' he said, and Eric laughed.

'I like them both.' They set the food out on paper plates, and Eric ate a hearty meal, and afterward the nurse gave him another shot and he went back to sleep, while Xavier and Chantal took a walk around the neighborhood, and then decided to try and get to a museum for an hour. They went to the Neue Nationalgalerie to see the spectacular glass structure. They only had time to see a small portion of the museum, but it was a nice break for both of them from the tedium of the hospital, and Chantal told Eric about it when he woke up. Xavier had gone back to the hotel to do some work and return calls to clients, and said he'd be back with dinner.

And miraculously, when he showed up, he had found a Chinese restaurant near the hotel, and brought Chinese food for all of them, and Annaliese joined them. It was more of a waiting game now, until Eric was well enough to be transferred to the rehab hospital, which was scheduled for the end of the week. And the following day Xavier went back to Paris, since the worst was over, and Eric had to face his long convalescence. Chantal was planning to go back to Paris once Eric was settled at the rehab, and she was eternally grateful that Xavier had come with her for the initial crisis. She would never forget it.

'Who's going to bring me schnitzel and sausages?' Eric asked him, when Xavier came to say goodbye, and they both laughed.

'Be good to your mother,' Xavier admonished him. 'No more motorcycles.' Eric reluctantly nodded agreement.

'Come back and visit when I can walk again,' he said to Xavier, and thanked him for the meals.

After Xavier left, Chantal sat with Eric every day till the end of the week, and then helped settle him at the rehab, which was big, sun-filled, and modern, and there were several other young people there, who had had similar accidents or worse. She stayed for the weekend, and then left him. He was going to be busy every day with physical therapy, although he couldn't do much yet. His friends had started to visit him, and Annaliese was with him every night. He didn't need his mother there anymore. She promised to come back and see him in two weeks, and again when he went home in a month. She had begun feeling redundant sitting there as his friends dropped by day and night. And he was busy with therapy in the daytime, to get his arm and leg strong again. She kissed him when she left, and flew back to Paris that night. She always hated leaving her children. It was such an empty feeling. She was happy to find Xavier at the apartment, waiting for her.

He suggested they go out to dinner, and they went to their favorite bistro and had a good meal. The weather was chilly and it was hard to believe it was already November. The year was flying past and almost over. And so much had happened in her life since June. They walked back to the apartment after dinner, arm in arm, and he looked down at her. Neither of them had expected to end the year together when they met at the White Dinner. Who could have guessed it, or that Jean-Philippe would be living in Beijing, or that Benedetta would divorce Gregorio? Life was so unpredictable. And she was excited to think that Jean-Philippe would be home in a few weeks to visit Valerie and his children. She had so much to tell him, and on her side, all of it good news.

13

It had been a juggling act for Valerie as soon as she took the consulting job with Beaumont-Sevigny, while carrying her full workload at *Vogue*, at the same time that Jean-Philippe left for Beijing. And without him, she had to manage the children on her own all weekend. Some days she ran from morning till night, and had to bring home work from the office, and do it the moment the kids went to bed. She fell asleep late every night, trying to keep up, and often woke up exhausted.

The consulting job was time-consuming but not complicated. She gave them a constant assessment of their products and if they were heading in the right direction. They tapped into her knowledge after years of working at *Vogue*, and her own taste and style. Their target market wasn't as sophisticated as the high-priced lines she usually worked with on the pages of *Vogue*. But it was fun advising them, and she had made three presentations already to suggest ways to improve their lines. They were interested in an international market, and were currently focusing on Asia, for the same reason Jean-Philippe had gone there to work. There was so much money to be spent there, and fortunes to be made. Valerie put a lot of work and thought into her presentations to them, and they were receptive and anxious for her advice.

She worked closely with their director, Charles de Beaumont, who was one of the owners of the company and had developed the concept of their business. His father had owned a major fashion brand, which he had sold to the Chinese two years before, and now the son was targeting the same market. He was more of a money man, but clever about fashion, and he collaborated with Valerie on her presentations. He was a thirty-six-year-old Frenchman who looked more like a model than a businessman, and he flirted relentlessly with every female in the office. Charles de Beaumont was possibly the best-looking man Valerie had ever seen, although she was put off by the fact that he was an obvious womanizer, and she stuck to business whenever she was with him, despite his best efforts to charm her. And she had to admit, his taste was flawless. He understood what she was trying to achieve with the direction of her summaries and presentations, and often contributed new features that improved them. And much as she hated to admit it, even to herself, they were a great team. His partner was less involved in the fashion aspect of the business, and only dealt with financial issues, so Valerie had less contact with him. All of her direct dealings were with Charles.

He always managed to schedule their meetings at the end of her workday at *Vogue*, supposedly as a convenience for her, but invariably she found herself alone with him in his office after everyone had gone home. He usually invited her to dinner, and she thanked him and told him she had to go home to her children.

'Can't your husband watch them?' he asked one night, looking exasperated. 'There's so much more I want to discuss with you about the next presentation.' He was artful about prolonging their meetings.

'My husband is in China,' she said one night, as she put her coat on. It was nine-thirty, her nanny would be furious, and her children asleep. She hated not seeing them at the end of the day, but her meetings with Charles always went late.

'Is he on a trip there?' Charles asked with interest.

'He works in Beijing,' she said, looking distracted, thinking about her nanny, who complained about leaving late since she had to be back early the next morning in time for Valerie to leave for the office and drop Jean-Louis off at school.

'Are you separated?' he asked her, curious, which shocked her.

'Not at all. He had a great opportunity there, and I stayed here, for *Vogue*.'

He nodded. 'How does he like it? I worked there myself for two years,' Charles said easily.

'Not much. He's only been there since September.'

'That must be difficult for you with your kids,' he said, with a sympathetic expression.

'It is.' She smiled at him. 'That's why I don't want to make the nanny angry. I need her.'

'You should get a live-in. It would give you more freedom. You can't run out of meetings to rush home to your children,' he said with a slightly disapproving tone.

'I'm not exactly running out of the meeting. It's nearly ten o'clock,' she corrected him politely. She'd been putting in extra days and long hours for consultations.

'Why don't we finish this tomorrow? And let's plan on dinner,' he said practically. 'That way we don't have to hurry through it.' He made it sound like it was purely business, but she felt odd having dinner with him. Inevitably, it would run late. And he was a handsome bachelor, and she was married. She didn't flatter herself that he was after her, but she didn't like the way it looked. And she had a feeling Jean-Philippe wouldn't either. She wouldn't have liked him taking late meetings with women in China, followed by dinner. And from what she could tell, he was working at home every night, and had no social life whatsoever. Neither had she since he'd been gone. She was already spreading herself as thin as she could, and had no time for anything but work and kids. She hadn't had any fun, or even been to a movie in the six weeks since Jean-Philippe had left.

'I'm serious,' Charles reiterated as they went down in the elevator in the deserted building. 'Let's get together tomorrow at the office to finish this, and continue it through dinner at my place. I'll pick up sushi, if you like.'

'I'd rather not,' she said honestly. 'I'm a married woman. I'd feel awkward working with you at your apartment.'

He laughed at her. 'Oh, for heaven's sake, I'm not going to rape you, Valerie. Relax. I have a

210

girlfriend.' And then she felt stupid for what she'd said and agreed to meet him at his office the next day. 'Do you need a lift?' he asked her innocently, as he saw her reach for her phone to call a taxi, and she looked embarrassed.

'I'm fine. I didn't bring my car today. Sometimes I use G7. They'll come in a minute.'

'Don't be silly. Where do you live?' She told him. His car was parked at the curb in front of the building. She was impressed to see that he drove an Aston Martin. 'I live just around the corner from you. You'll be home before the cab can get here.' She hesitated and slid into the sleek sports car when he unlocked it, and he talked business with her until they reached her building. He was totally circumspect, and she felt foolish for her earlier concerns. He must have thought she was crazy, and more than anything she felt stupid.

'Thank you for the ride home.' She glanced at him apologetically for her suspicions.

'See you tomorrow.' He smiled at her and roared off, as she put the door code in and hurried upstairs. And predictably, her nanny looked annoyed.

'I'm so sorry, Mathilde. I was stuck in a meeting. And I've got one tomorrow night too. Can you stay late? I'll be out till after dinner.' The woman nodded, it was money for her, and she was used to their going out when Jean-Philippe was home. But she had a husband she wanted to get home to, which was more than Valerie felt she had at the moment. Everything was so complicated without Jean-Philippe. She

211

had no partner present, no backup, only hired help, which was limited at best, but better than nothing.

Once the nanny left, Valerie took out her presentation, made some more notes on it, and wondered what he wanted to discuss the next day. It looked finished to her. She put it back in her briefcase, answered some emails, checked her messages, and peeked in at her sleeping children. She felt as though she never caught up anymore. She was always behind, and she had the same impression at her office at *Vogue* the next day. They had several crises, and she arrived at the meeting with Charles half an hour late.

'I'm sorry. I had a crazy day at the magazine.' She looked flustered and had rushed there.

'Don't worry about it,' he said easily. 'In fact, why don't we go straight to my place? I had my houseman pick up the sushi. That way we can eat and work without interruption. There's no point starting here.' She felt awkward disagreeing with him, and she followed him meekly out of the office. He drove her to his apartment in the Aston Martin, and although he only lived a few blocks from where she did, he had a beautiful penthouse in an old building overlooking the Seine on the Quai Voltaire. She walked out onto the balcony to admire the view as the barges and bateaux mouches slid by, and Charles handed her a glass of champagne.

'Thank you.' She hadn't expected it, and took a sip as she looked at the Right Bank of the city lit up across the river, and the glass dome of the

Grand Palais. It was one of the prettiest views in Paris.

'It will help us work,' he assured her with a smile, and she followed him back inside. His houseman had set the table in his handsome black granite kitchen, and she took the presentation out of her briefcase and spread it out on the kitchen counter.

'Let's do that after dinner,' Charles said easily, and took the platter of sushi out of the refrigerator. It was obvious that it had come from a very fancy Japanese restaurant that catered and not the kind of neighborhood place where she bought hers. And as soon as they sat down, he opened a bottle of very fine white wine. She drank sparingly so she would still be able to work, and the sushi was delicious. And as soon as they were finished, he presented her with his latest ideas for their project, all of which were excellent, and inspired her to be more creative too. They fed off each other in adding to the original plan, and improved it immeasurably. He was a genius at what he did, and his suggestions sparked more of her own. And two hours later, they agreed that they had a highly polished product they were both proud of. She was pleased they'd spent the extra time together to get it right. And it was fun creating the final version with him.

'I love working with you, Valerie,' he said, sitting back in his chair and smiling at her, echoing how she felt about him. 'We should do more of this. Brainstorming sessions always evolve better for me at home than in the office.

213

There are no distractions here.' She had to agree it had certainly been true that night. Some of his concepts had been brilliant, and what she had added to them made them even better.

'And I enjoyed working with you.' She smiled at him. He was very quick, smart, and efficient.

'Would you ever consider going to the theater with me?' he asked her randomly as they relaxed after their evening of concentration and productivity. 'Even as a married woman,' he teased her. 'If your husband is living in Beijing and you're here, you need to get out and have some fun. How often does he get home?'

'He's planning on trying to get home every two months. He'll be home in a few weeks.'

'Precisely. I'd love to go to the theater with you. Or dinner sometime. The more we know about each other, the better we'll collaborate.' He looked serious as he said it, and she wondered if it was true. 'Or do you like the ballet?' he asked innocently. 'There is a wonderful production of *Swan Lake*.'

'I like both, theater and ballet.' She smiled at him. 'That's very nice of you.' It seemed a little awkward to her, but it was generous of him, and she didn't want to appear ungrateful. He had been a perfect gentleman and focused on business.

'You need a night off from work and kids.' She knew that what he said was true, but so far she hadn't managed it, and was beginning to feel like a total drudge. She had nothing to tell Jean-Philippe anymore because all she did was slave away at the office and run home to see their

214

children before they went to sleep. She hadn't seen a single one of their friends since he left.

'It would be fun,' she said easily, and a little while later she got up from the table, and he insisted on taking her back to her apartment. And she had to admit, it felt very glamorous being driven home in an Aston Martin. He was fully committed to the firm's success and a perfectionist about the product. And on the way, he told Valerie how impressed he was with her dedication to her projects. He kissed her lightly on both cheeks before she got out of the car and thanked him for dinner.

She was surprised to hear from him two days later. She didn't have another presentation due for three weeks, and the one they had done together over dinner was complete.

'All set,' he said victoriously. 'I had to promise my first-born to get them, but I got tickets for us to the ballet tomorrow night. It's the production of *Swan Lake* I mentioned. I hope you like it. It's very traditional, but the young prima who's dancing is fabulous. I saw her last season.' She hadn't expected him to come up with tickets so rapidly, or at all. She thought he was just being friendly when he said it, and since he'd had so much trouble getting the tickets, she was embarrassed not to go.

'That's very kind of you, Charles,' Valerie said, feeling awkward again. 'I didn't realize you were going to get them so quickly.'

'I'd like us to get to know each other, Valerie. You're a very impressive woman, and I think we're a good team. We could do a lot more

215

projects together.' He made it sound like he had something specific in mind for her, which made her even less willing to turn him down.

'Thank you. I have to see if my nanny is willing to stay late again.'

'Tell your nanny she has no choice,' he said cheerfully, 'or we can drop the children off at my mother's,' he teased her. 'How many kids do you have?'

'Three,' she said easily. 'They're five, three, and two. Your mother may not be so thrilled.' He laughed at the thought.

'You've been busy, three kids in four years. Wow!'

'They're very cute. And they're good kids.'

'So is their mother. I'd like to meet them sometime. Actually, I'll pick you up tomorrow night before the ballet. You can introduce us. And I booked a table at Alain Ducasse at the Plaza Athénée for after the ballet.' He was going all out for her, and the evening he had planned for them was expensive. The only thing she didn't like about it was that it felt a little, even a lot, like a date. But since technically she worked for him, or with him, she thought it would be rude to refuse, particularly with *Swan Lake* tickets as part of the deal.

'Thank you very much,' she said politely. And the following night, she was waiting for him in a simple black cocktail dress and a black coat when he came to pick her up. Mathilde had agreed to stay, without complaint. Charles looked very handsome in a dark suit, and as promised, she brought her children out to meet him in their pajamas. Jean-Louis shook hands with him, and Isabelle did an awkward curtsy as they had taught her to, in old French style, and Damien just stared at him.

'Where are you taking my *maman*?' Isabelle asked him with a worried look.

'To the ballet,' Valerie answered her, 'where beautiful ballerinas wear tutus just like yours, and pink toe shoes.'

'Can we come?' Isabelle asked, her eyes lighting up, and her mother bent down and kissed her and said that they would go to the ballet one day.

'That's just for girls,' Jean-Louis said with a look of disgust, and then Mathilde shepherded them back to their rooms for a story before they went to bed.

'They're very sweet,' Charles complimented her, touched. 'Good work.' She smiled, and they left the apartment, and chatted on the way to the Opera House.

Their seats were fabulous, in a box. And they went to the bar at intermission and had champagne, and afterward the meal at Alain Ducasse was superb. They had delicate white truffles, which were in season and had come from Italy. They shaved them over their dinner, and they were so insanely expensive that they were sold by weight. And Charles selected the finest wines for her. It was an exquisite meal.

'I feel terribly spoiled,' Valerie said to him over chocolate soufflé for dessert. 'I don't normally go to dinners like this.' The white truffles had been unforgettable, she'd only had them a few times before. They were very rare, and came from one specific region in Italy and nowhere else.

'You deserve to be spoiled, Valerie,' he said quietly. 'You work too hard.'

'So do you,' she said easily, but he disagreed.

'I only have one job. You have two now, and you're doing wonderful work at both. Don't think I don't notice all that you do, above and beyond the call. And I don't go home to three children at night. And it looks like you do a great job of that too. You're a kind of Wonder Woman.' And then he looked more serious for a minute. 'I'm surprised your husband took a position in Beijing and left you to manage three very young children by yourself. That's a lot to ask.'

'We didn't have much choice. An irresistible opportunity came up that was too good to pass up. And I didn't feel I could leave. I don't want to lose my place at *Vogue*. And then your firm made me the offer right before he left. I feel like I belong here for now. And he felt he had to be there. We're trying to make it work.' She said it sincerely with a serious expression as he listened.

'And how is it for you?' He seemed sympathetic and concerned.

'It's too soon to tell. It's been kind of a relay race for me since he left, but so far so good.'

'It's challenging keeping up a marriage from five thousand miles away. And China is a whole different world. I think you were right not to go. I don't think you'd be happy there. Shanghai maybe, or Hong Kong, but not Beijing. It's still too rough, although all the big French designers are opening stores there. But you have an

218

important role here, especially now with us.'

'I'm very excited about it,' she said, smiling at him. 'It's a wonderful opportunity for me. I've always wanted to consult, it gives depth to my job at *Vogue*, to work in the real world, not just the lofty world of editorial.'

'You're helping us a lot. I hope we have a lot of opportunities to work together,' he said quietly, and then put his hand over hers. 'You're an extraordinary woman. I hope to see more of you.' Valerie blushed and took away her hand as quickly as she dared. He was very charming and she had the feeling that he was courting her, although that seemed impossible, and she decided she was imagining it. He couldn't be. Even though he was flirtatious, she didn't think he'd pursue a married woman with three children.

Charles drove her home after dinner, and she didn't invite him up for a drink — that seemed too personal. And then he turned to her before she got out of the car. Her long shapely legs were crossed over each other in the chic little black dress.

'When can I see you again? Would tomorrow be too soon?' She was shocked by the question. He knew that she was married and had young children, but he also knew that her husband was gone for a year. She wondered if he thought their marriage was in trouble and that was why Jean-Philippe left.

'I — I don't know if we should,' Valerie said as directly as she could without offending him. She worked for him, after all. 'I had a wonderful

219

time, but I don't want to give anyone the impression we're dating. That would be wrong.' He liked how proper she was, he respected women like that, although he wasn't always equally proper himself.

'Is your husband as faithful to you?' he asked her bluntly.

'I hope so,' Valerie said in a soft voice.

'Are you sure?' he inquired, sowing a seed of doubt that she refused.

'Yes, I am,' she said more firmly, trying to remember how much Jean-Philippe loved her, and she loved him. She had never been in a situation like this before, with a man who wanted to go out with her even though she was married.

'No one has to know we're dating,' Charles said carefully. 'That's between you and me. All anyone needs to know is that we work together and we're friends.'

'I can't date anyone,' she said clearly. 'I'm married.'

'We'll be friends, then. Until you see things in a different light. Perhaps when we get to know each other better.' He was refusing to take no for an answer and hear what she was saying. It was unnerving to realize how determined he was. He kissed her lightly on the cheek then, and she got out of the car, and he watched as she went to the door, entered her code, and let herself in. She waved, and then it closed behind her. Her heart was pounding as she ran up the stairs.

And the next morning she received the largest bouquet of red roses she'd ever seen, with a note from him. 'I am haunted by you, and in awe of you, Charles.' She had no idea what to do about him. She didn't want to lose the consulting job, and she couldn't date him. He called her again two days later, and invited her to lunch, which seemed harmless and less risqué than dinner, so she went, to try and explain her situation to him again, and at the same time, his pursuing her so elegantly was embarrassingly appealing in some ways. She would never cheat on her husband, but Charles's attention was flattering. She told herself that lunch was hardly an infidelity, and she didn't need to feel guilty about it.

Charles looked thrilled to see her when she arrived at Le Voltaire, which was just below his apartment, and one of the chicest bistros in Paris for many years. She had been there often before, and felt more at ease there than she had at Ducasse. He brushed aside her qualms, and they talked about myriad subjects. And she was shocked when she realized they had been at the table talking for three hours, and she was late getting back to the office. He dropped her off again, after darting the Aston Martin expertly through traffic, and she was smiling when they got to *Vogue*. She'd had a wonderful time, and felt more at ease with him every time she saw him, which worried her a little.

'Thank you, Charles. I had a great time at lunch.'

'So did I. I always have fun with you. I'll call you tomorrow.' Had she been single, she would have been excited about him. But as things were, she was panicked. What if Jean-Philippe was doing the same thing in Beijing? Sending women

221

roses, and having elegant dinners with them, and meeting them for lunches at chic bistros? Without meaning to, she felt herself sliding into deep waters and was afraid to get in over her head. Charles was very smooth, and clearly very smitten with her. Or was he just looking for another conquest? Or playing with her? He could have any woman he wanted.

She tried to slow him down when he called again, and she told him she couldn't see him, she was taking her children to the park and needed to spend time with them. And he arrived at the Luxembourg Gardens where she said she was going, with a gift for each of them, and they were excited. And worse, she realized that she was happy to see him too. He bought them all ice cream and stayed with them for quite a while, and then he left and the children waved goodbye to him as though he were an old friend.

'I like Charles,' Jean-Louis announced. He had given him a little red model car that Jean-Louis loved, Izzie a small doll, and Damien a teddy bear he was clutching.

She didn't hear from Charles after that all weekend, and he called Monday and invited her to dinner. He said there was a new Indian restaurant he wanted to try, and Valerie started to tell him she couldn't, and then gave in. He was a very persuasive man, and incredibly seductive. At dinner he behaved respectfully toward her and didn't try to kiss her, and much to her horror she realized that she wished he would. She was suddenly totally confused. She didn't understand his motives or her own. She was in love with her husband, but was she falling for Charles? How real was it? This had never happened to her before, but she had never felt so alone as she did now with Jean-Philippe in Beijing. Jean-Philippe called her that night after she got home from dinner, and she was nervous when she talked to him on Skype, and he could see that she was troubled.

'Is something wrong?' She didn't want to tell him that she'd just been out for dinner with Charles. She didn't want to lie to him, nor tell him.

'Just tension at the office. The usual stuff,' she said vaguely, feeling guilty. Then she changed the subject: 'How's Beijing?'

'I had an interesting weekend. I did some exploring. The shopping malls here are incredible. You would love them. And then for balance, I went to the Great Wall.' He had been meaning to do it for weeks and hadn't had time. 'There are so many things I like about this city, and unfortunately just as many I don't.' And then he sounded wistful. 'I can't wait to come home,' he said in a tender voice. 'Another ten days. I'm counting the hours until I see you and the children.' It made her feel even guiltier, and reminded her that she was Cinderella at the ball, and she was about to turn into a pumpkin. When Jean-Philippe came home, she couldn't go out with Charles, and she didn't know how he'd react to that, but he knew she was married, and she had been honest with him.

The one she wasn't being honest with was Jean-Philippe. He had no idea what was going on and she felt terrible about it. But there was no way she could tell him, and there was really nothing to tell. The only thing that had happened was that she had had some lovely evenings and was now confused. She hadn't been unfaithful to him. Yet. But in her heart of hearts she knew that it had crossed her mind, about what would happen if she had an affair with Charles. She would never have thought it possible that she would think that way, but he had been subtly seductive and incredibly appealing since they'd started going out together. And he was even sweet to her children, which she realized they might tell their father. What had she been thinking to be so open with him? But with Jean-Philippe no longer part of their daily life — sometimes it felt as if he didn't exist. And she wondered if it was the same for him.

'I can't wait to see you too,' she said weakly, and then she said she had to go to bed, she had an early meeting the next day, which wasn't true. But she had run out of things she could tell him. He looked disappointed to end the conversation so quickly, but at least he'd see her in ten days. He told her he was longing to see her and she assured him she felt the same. She closed her computer after that with a groan. What had Charles done to her? He had spun her totally around. Or had she done it to herself? She was no longer sure.

Charles could hear the guilt in her voice when he called her the next day, and asked the same question her husband had. 'What's wrong?' She was transparent to both of them. There was no artifice to her. She was an honest person, or always had been until now. Now she wasn't so sure.

'I don't know what I'm doing,' she said, sounding anguished. 'I talked to my husband last night, and I lied to him. I can't tell him we're having dinner all the time. I'm acting like a single woman, but Charles, I'm not.'

'I know you aren't. You haven't lied to me. I know the rules. And I haven't pressed you about anything. I know this must be confusing for you. He's not here, and I am. And I'm not asking you to make any decisions now. I don't want to pressure you. I want you to be with me, Valerie, not with him. And that takes time. You can take as long as you want.' What he had just said to her almost made her gasp for air. He wanted to steal her from her husband, and he was being completely open about it, and she had been playing along with him.

'That's not right, Charles. I've never cheated on him before.'

'And you haven't now. And I assume he never moved to Beijing before. What did he expect? You don't leave a woman like you alone to fend for herself, and park you like a car in a garage. You deserve a man who adores you at your side, not one who goes off to seek his fortune and leaves you alone with three children. I'm sorry, but he deserves whatever he gets. You're the only woman I know who would put up with that, and feel guilty about being with another man.' They were harsh words, and she was shocked.

'He's doing it for us, for our future,' she insisted.

'He's doing it to feed his ego, because it's exciting for him to be on the new frontier and make a name for himself. I know, I've been there. I've done it too. But I didn't leave a wife and three children in Paris.' She couldn't help wondering if what he said about Jean-Philippe's motives was true. Maybe men recognized those things better than women did. 'And you're the one who feels guilty, when you've done nothing wrong. He should be lying awake at night, consumed with guilt, not you.' It was the most candid he had been with her, but she had been honest with him too.

'I refused to go with him. Don't forget that.'

'You had a right to do that, with three little kids to consider and a career of your own. He should have dropped it then and stayed here. Let me tell you, married to a woman as fabulous as you, I wouldn't let you out of my sight.'

'Thank you for the compliment,' she said sadly, 'but I can't justify my questionable actions with his.'

'What have you done wrong? Have you lied to me? Slept with me? Cheated on him? No, you haven't.'

'I've cheated on him in my heart. He doesn't know what I'm doing. And I'm lying to him now. Sins of omission, remember those.'

'Oh, my God.' He laughed at her. 'Sins of omission, impure thoughts, and lusting in your heart. I'm happy to hear it,' he said, sounding pleased. 'At least I'm not the only one with

226

impure thoughts. I'd be disappointed if I were.' She laughed at what he said, and he teased her for a few minutes and she relaxed. 'Let's go to a movie this week and a pizza dinner and stop worrying about it. Destiny will decide. If we belong together, Valerie, we'll know it. And if not, he'll be the lucky winner, although I hope he's not.' Charles had never been in a situation like this either. He had taken her out to be collegial at first, and get to know her better for work. But little by little, as he discovered her, he had found a woman he admired, with honest values, and realized what he'd been missing all his life with the superficial women he went out with. He wasn't a man who accepted defeat easily. And now he wanted to win her away from Jean-Philippe. By being so honorable, she only made herself more appealing to him, and made him try harder to convince her to be with him. And the power of his arguments was heady stuff to Valerie. No man had ever courted her with such determination before. She didn't know if she was dazzled by him, infatuated, or falling for him. And he was harder and harder to resist.

Although she didn't plan it that way, Valerie had dinner with Charles the night before Jean-Philippe came home, and he kissed her passionately in the car when he dropped her off. He had restrained himself till then, and she was stunned, and hadn't resisted his advance, much to her own despair.

'I wanted to give you something to remember me by,' he whispered. 'How long will he be here?' The way he said it made her feel like a woman being torn between two men.

'Two weeks,' she whispered back, and he kissed her again. And she responded just as fiercely.

'I'll be waiting for you. And call me when you can. I'll be worried about you.'

'You don't need to,' she said quietly. 'I'll be fine, and I'll call you.' She tried to sound calm about it but looked longingly at him, and then let herself into the house. And with horror, she realized that she didn't want Jean-Philippe to come home. Not now. She didn't want to lose Charles, and she knew she would miss him, and she felt desperately guilty about it, and utterly confused about her feelings for him. He was the forbidden fruit she was desperately trying to resist. And for a moment, she was angry at Jean-Philippe for leaving her in this situation, unprotected and vulnerable to the advances of other men when he went to Beijing. But more than him, she blamed herself for being so drawn to Charles and allowing it to go this far. She knew she should never have gone out with him, and had slipped into it so innocently.

And all Charles wanted now was to win her.

14

When Jean-Philippe came home, his children squealed with delight and threw themselves into his arms, and Valerie smiled at him from across the room, and then came quietly to put her arms around him. Seeing him there suddenly made him seem real again. He wasn't just an image on Skype, and as he looked at her, she remembered all the things she loved about him. For the past few weeks, Charles had pushed everything about him out of her head. He was so powerful, attractive, and convincing. And she felt confused all over again when she kissed Jean-Philippe. She knew she loved her husband, but if so, how could she be so attracted to another man? Her head was reeling when she and Jean-Philippe went to bed that night and he made love to her with all the longing of two months without her. And there were tears on her cheeks afterward that she couldn't explain, and didn't try to.

Jean-Philippe watched her closely for the next few days whenever they were together. He kept sensing something different about her, and oddly subdued. He couldn't put his finger on what it was, and he wondered if the strain of juggling everything herself, two jobs and three kids, was too much for her. But she didn't complain about it. She was unusually quiet, and yet she was very loving. He tried to explain it to Chantal when he had lunch with her, and she had told him all about Xavier, and how well they got along. She was still obsessed with the idea of his running off with a younger woman one day, but she seemed divinely happy, and said she was. She was thriving, and he had never seen her look so well.

'For heaven's sake,' Chantal said in response to what he told her about Valerie, 'the poor woman is probably exhausted. You run off to China, leave her with three kids. She works like a slave at *Vogue*, which is a stress factory for any normal person, and now she has a huge consulting job on top of it. What do you expect? I'd be subdued dealing with all that, and you're not here to help her. She's totally on her own. I keep meaning to call her. But I've been busy, working on two projects, and spending time with Xavier. Eric had the accident, and I've been back and forth to Berlin to see him. I promise I'll call her this time when you leave.' Chantal wasn't worried about Valerie. She and Jean-Philippe adored each other. That couldn't have changed in two months.

'I know this sounds ridiculous, but do you suppose she's having an affair?' Jean-Philippe insisted. Something was gnawing at him. Valerie was not the same.

'Don't be ridiculous. When would she have time? You said yourself, she doesn't even have a nanny on weekends. Who's she going to have an affair with? Your pediatrician?' But they both knew that odd things happened, and the people you never expected to leave their spouses often did. But she just couldn't see Valerie doing that to Jean-Philippe. They were crazy about each other, and had been since the day they met, although Chantal knew they'd had a rough patch about the decision to move to Beijing. But she couldn't imagine Valerie having an affair, she was totally devoted to Jean-Philippe.

'She meets a lot of interesting people at *Vogue*. Writers, photographers, designers.'

'Most of the designers are gay, so you can rule them out.' Chantal was trying to jolly him out of it, but not succeeding. He was on a witch hunt.

'Her new consulting job is a big deal,' he said. 'The guys who own that company are hot stuff in the financial world, and now they're investing in fashion because there's real money in it. They're money guys, and they're not gay.'

'Who are they?' Chantal asked with interest.

'Serge Sevigny and Charles de Beaumont. I know Sevigny, and he's kind of a jerk, and very full of himself. I've never met Beaumont, but I've heard a lot about him. He made some big money deals in China, invested in all the right things, and made a killing.'

'I know who he is,' Chantal acknowledged. 'I think he went out with the daughter of a friend of mine. He's a good-looking guy, if he's the one I'm thinking of, but he's given to pretty young things from fancy families, debutantes, not married women with three children. I think he's kind of a playboy.'

'My wife is pretty and young, and maybe he's grown up,' Jean-Philippe said, looking panicked.

'Valerie is too much trouble for guys like that. She's married to you, and you're stiff competition for any guy. She has kids, she's married, she

231

has a demanding job. She's not exactly free to romp and play. And now she's a single parent to your kids with no help on the weekends. She's hardly a candidate for a hot romance, unless the guy wants to babysit your kids on the weekend. And I don't know a guy alive who would do that if he wanted to have an affair. They want a woman who is accessible and has free time. Valerie must be drowning without you now.' She made him feel guilty when she said it, and he knew it was true. He had left her with a tremendous burden when he took the job in Beijing. Maybe too much so. 'Maybe she's tired, or depressed. She can't be having a great time these days without you. Maybe you need to do some fun things with her while you're here, and not just spend time with your kids. Put some of the romance back in your life. It sounds like she needs that.'

'You're probably right. Maybe it was selfish of me to take the job there.'

'Is it working out?' she asked, concerned. He looked tired and thinner, but his eyes were alive.

'The deals we're doing are fascinating. And the money's there, for all of us. But I hate the place. It's not a city where I'd want to spend the rest of my life.'

'You're only planning to spend a year, right?'

'Or two or three. I haven't told Valerie yet, but now I can see why they wanted me to commit for three years. You almost have to, to get anything major done.'

'Maybe you need to be careful of that,' Chantal said cautiously. 'Don't push her too far.

Her life can't be easy right now, and she may get tired of being a part-time wife.'

And that night, following Chantal's advice, he took Valerie to dinner at the Voltaire. She hesitated when he suggested it, and then she agreed. He knew it was one of her favorites, and went there with editors all the time, so he was surprised she wasn't more enthusiastic about it.

They were halfway through dinner, when a man walked in with a young woman, and Jean-Philippe saw Valerie stiffen, as she and the man glanced at each other and their eyes met and then he walked by to the corner booth. Something strange had passed between them that Jean-Philippe had sensed, and he asked her in an undertone who the man was.

'He's the style director and one of the partners at Beaumont-Sevigny where I consult. Charles de Beaumont,' she said almost too nonchalantly. And Jean-Philippe had a sinking feeling in his stomach as he took another look at the man in the corner booth. He was with a very attractive young woman, but he was watching Valerie, and his eyes were hard when he looked at Jean-Philippe. Jean-Philippe could sense a predator on the loose and a major threat.

'Why didn't he say hello to you?' Jean-Philippe asked her. She was picking at the food on her plate.

'I don't know. I don't know him socially, and he looks like he's on a date.' She made a point of not looking at his table, and didn't order dessert, and Jean-Philippe wasn't sure if he'd imagined it, but she seemed anxious to leave.

He paid the check and they drove home after dinner, and she was quiet in the car. He heard her get a text message, but she didn't look at it until they were home, which was odd for her. He saw that she didn't answer it, she just turned off her phone. The text was from Charles. 'I wanted to kidnap you when I saw you.' She responded and just told him she missed him, and erased the message. Jean-Philippe would have felt like a fool asking her who the text was from, she got so many of them. So he didn't, but he sensed something odd about her behavior. As they were getting ready for bed, he couldn't help wondering if there was something going on between her and Charles de Beaumont. Jean-Philippe was unnerved by how handsome he was, but Valerie didn't seem impressed. Maybe he was crazy, or paranoid because he had left her alone. But he realized now more than ever that this was not going to be easy if he stayed in Beijing for a year, and worse if he signed on for a second year, which he was beginning to realize he would have to do.

It took them about a week to get used to each other again, and feel at ease. He could feel Valerie start to relax with him by the second week, and by then he was leaving. Even two weeks were not enough to restore the damage from his absence. They had celebrated Thanksgiving with their children, which was a tradition she wanted to share with them, although they were French, but it still meant something to her.

Jean-Philippe noticed that she seemed profoundly sad before he left. He reported it to

Chantal at lunch the day before he was going back to Beijing.

'I think she's depressed. And I saw Beaumont by the way, at Le Voltaire. He's a very attractive guy, but Valerie didn't seem to react. But I think my being away is taking a hell of a toll on us. It took her nearly two weeks to warm up and seem at ease with me, and now I'm leaving tomorrow. I don't know if this is going to work.' He looked heartbroken as he said it. Maybe he had asked too much of her. He no longer thought she was cheating on him, but he was beginning to wonder if they would grow so far apart that they'd get divorced. He had never thought that could happen to them. Now he wasn't so sure.

'That was always the risk,' Chantal reminded him. 'You knew it when you left. And you did it anyway. Men are stupid sometimes. When are you coming back?'

'Not quite four weeks. I land on Christmas Eve.'

'That's cutting it a little close,' she said sternly.

'I'll be here for two weeks. And then I'll be back again at the end of February, beginning of March.'

'Just pray that your kids keep her busy, and no handsome guy like Charles de Beaumont crosses her path.' He still looked worried at the end of lunch when he kissed Chantal on the cheek, and they left the restaurant.

He and Valerie spent a quiet last night together, talking in bed. She seemed like her old self again, although he found her quiet and sad at the prospect of his leaving. But this time he'd be home in less than a month, and they'd have

235

Christmas with the children. She'd have to put up the tree and have done all the decorating alone before he got home, since he was coming home so late.

'Valerie, is this too much for us?' he asked her honestly before they turned out the light. 'Are we going to survive this?' He was beginning to have doubts. Maybe Chantal was right, and he had been a fool to take the risk. She was a beautiful woman, and any man would want her. And he knew that it would kill him if she gave up on him and their marriage.

'I don't know,' she said, looking him in the eye. 'I hope so. I guess we just have to wait and see.' It was the most honest she had been with him. She was making him no promises for the future, which was a terrifying prospect, especially the night before he was leaving.

'I don't want to lose you,' he said miserably.

'I don't want to lose you either, or myself. This is harder than I thought it would be.' He nodded, hearing what she was saying, and wondering what he should do about it.

'I thought you were having an affair when I came home. You were so distant and removed from me at first. But now I realize you're not.'

'No, I'm not,' she confirmed to him, and he was relieved.

'I hope you never will,' he said fervently, looking up at her, and there was something sad in her eyes.

'So do I,' she said softly. It wasn't a promise. It was a hope. It was the best she could do for now, and he had to content himself with that.

Before he left early the next morning, he kissed the children in their beds, and went to kiss his wife. She clung to him for a long moment as he held her tight against him, wishing he wasn't leaving again.

'I'll be home in a few weeks,' he reminded her, and she nodded and kissed him again, and then he hurried down the stairs with his bag, to the cab waiting to take him to the airport to go back to Beijing.

She sent a text to Charles as soon as he left, and asked him to meet her for lunch. She was seeing him at the office the following week for their next presentation, but she didn't want to wait till then. Other than the night they had run into him at Le Voltaire, she hadn't seen him in two weeks, and she had missed him even more than she'd thought she would, and more than she wanted to.

They met at a quiet bistro near his office, and she was wearing a red coat and black boots when she walked in, and she looked incredibly chic. His face lit up as soon as he saw her. He was wearing an exquisitely cut tweed suit and brown suede shoes and was as fashionable as she was. And he kissed her fervently the moment she walked in. She didn't resist.

'Oh, my God, those were the longest two weeks of my life,' Charles said, looking her over and drinking her in as she smiled at him. 'How was it?' She had only called him once, and texted him a few times about work. It was too awkward trying to contact him while Jean-Philippe was there, and she wanted to give him the respect she felt she owed him as her husband. Calling Charles while he was in town didn't seem fair.

'It was fine,' she said quietly in answer to his question. 'It wasn't easy. It was strange having him back again, like I'm not used to him anymore, I'm used to being by myself now. And by the time we adjusted to it, he had to leave. He told me last night that at first he thought I was having an affair. And he wanted to know all about you when we saw you at Le Voltaire. I think he had a sixth sense about us, which he decided to ignore.' She was relieved he had.

'I had an overwhelming urge to grab you away from him that night and run out the door.' She smiled at what he said and would have liked it too. Charles was a much more exciting person, but Jean-Philippe was her husband, and she remembered that now. His two weeks in Paris had driven that point home, and reminded her of what their marriage meant to her. She didn't want to lose that, even if it was a hard time now.

'I wanted to see you for lunch today to tell you that I can't do this. I want to, I would love to. And I wish I'd met you eight years ago, before I met Jean-Philippe. But I'm married to him now. I have to try and do this. It may not work, but I have to do it right. Or I'll never forgive myself later. I can't do us behind his back, and look him in the eye when he comes home. If I want out, I have to tell him. But I don't know if I want out yet. I have to give it a chance.'

Charles was quiet for a long moment as he

listened to her, and something told him he couldn't change her mind, and he was right. He was bitterly disappointed and pained by what she'd said. But he respected her loyalty and honesty. It was part of why he wanted her so much. In his eyes, she was the perfect wife and had just proven it to him. She played it straight, and was an honorable person.

'If I do this with you, you'll never trust me, and I'll never trust myself again, and everybody will get hurt. Do you want me to resign from consulting with your firm?' He thought about it for a minute and shook his head.

'No, I don't,' he said, looking her in the eye. 'We need you too much. And so do I. I wish you'd give us a chance, Valerie. You know as well as I do, it's not going to work. You're going to suffer your way through it for a year or two, and then come to the same conclusion I believe now. He's a selfish man to have gone to Beijing without you. I would never do that to you. Why not give us a chance instead? We could be so happy together.' He was entirely sincere when he said it. More than he had ever been in his life. He was not playing with her, and she could tell.

'I'd love to try,' Valerie said sadly. 'And if I were single, I would. I was sorely tempted to. But I married him for better or worse seven years ago, and I meant it. This is 'worse' for now, but that's what I signed on for. We had seven years of 'better.' Now I'll stick it out through 'worse.' For as long as I can. I owe him that, and our kids. And it's not fair to ask you to wait. I may not know how this turns out for years.'

239

'I envy him,' Charles said, looking desperately unhappy. He kissed her when they left the restaurant, the way he had wanted to for two weeks. And after he left her, he walked along the street with his hands in his pockets and his head down, thinking about her, and the kind of woman she was, and he thought what a lucky man Jean-Philippe Dumas was. And Charles hated to be the loser in the piece. He never had been before. As he walked back to his office, his ego was as bruised as his heart.

★　★　★

Two days after Valerie had lunch with Charles de Beaumont, her editor-in-chief called her into the office, and she thought she was in trouble for a minute. But instead the editor had a project for her.

They were 'doing' the April issue in China, and they wanted her to go to Shanghai and Beijing, to do a scouting mission and decide what to focus on, and which models and photographers to assign to it. They wanted it to be spectacular. The bad news, as far as *Vogue* was concerned, was that they wanted her to go the following week.

'I know it's short notice, but you'll be back in time for Christmas with your kids,' the editor-in-chief said apologetically. Valerie just sat there, smiling at her, thinking what it could mean. She had just let go of a man she cared about and thought she wanted to be with, and now she had a chance to spend time with the husband who had become a stranger to her in the past two months. It was almost like a sign. 'Your husband lives in Beijing, doesn't he?'

'Yes, he does. He's only been there for two months, but he can give me some tips.' She was intrigued about going and seeing where he lived. It sounded like a very exciting trip to her, and consolation for just having done the right thing with Charles. She missed him.

She sent Charles an email when she left the editor's office, and told him she wouldn't be able to meet with him the following week to deliver her presentation. She was being sent to China by the magazine, but she would have the full presentation delivered to him before she left, and he could contact her to make any changes he needed while she was away. She wasn't going to let him down. He sent her a short response, thanking her for advising him, and being so diligent about her work. She was professional to the core, which he appreciated.

And then she texted Jean-Philippe and told him about the trip. He had been sitting in his apartment, depressed to be back, and thinking of her, wondering what he was doing there, when he had a wife and family he loved in Paris. He was ecstatic she was coming, and responded that he'd go to Shanghai with her.

Her trip to China was exactly what they both needed to try and reestablish the bond between them and save their marriage.

'When are you coming?' he asked, smiling, when he called her on Skype.

'Next week.' She was beaming at him, and so grateful she hadn't done anything foolish with

Charles. He had been so appealing, but just as she had said to Charles, Jean-Philippe was her husband, for better or worse. And all she could hope now was that there would be better times ahead. Charles de Beaumont had almost swayed her, as dazzling as he was, but Jean-Philippe was the man she loved.

15

When Benedetta boarded the flight from Rome to Delhi, she had no idea what to expect. She had taken the short hop from Milan to Rome early that morning and boarded the second plane shortly before noon. She had heard about the extreme poverty in India, the beggars and maimed children in the streets, conditions that would shock her, but she had always heard tales of the country's extraordinary beauty too, the light, the colors, the temples, the people, the fabrics, the jewels, the atmosphere and the magic of India. She had been reading a little about it, but she wanted Dharam to unveil its wonders to her. She was excited to have him show her as much as he could. The flight seemed endless as she thought about the places he had described and she wanted to see. They were going to use his plane to get to the various locations, which seemed ideal to her. It was such an easy, comfortable, luxurious way to travel.

They landed in Delhi after the eight-hour trip, at nearly midnight, and he was waiting for her as she came through customs, with two local policemen and an agent from the airlines escorting her. He had arranged for all of it to facilitate her arrival. She smiled broadly as soon as she saw him, and he kissed her immediately.

'I can't believe you're here.' He looked as excited as she was, and he couldn't wait to start the trip. He had set two weeks aside for her. It barely seemed like enough, the country was so huge.

The first thing she noticed were the women all around her in saris in a rainbow of colors, many of them wearing jeweled sandals and bangles on their arms. Some of them had red bindis on their foreheads. The men were in traditional dress of long tunics and loose pants. The effect was instantly exotic. In any European city, you couldn't be sure if you were in Paris or Cincinnati at the airport; in Delhi you were cast into another culture and universe immediately. There were foreigners in Western dress too. It all combined into a canvas of vibrant colors that fascinated Benedetta as they walked through the airport, and an employee of Dharam's appeared to take her bags. He had booked a suite for her at the Leela Palace Hotel in the city, and they drove there in his deep blue Bentley with his driver at the wheel. Dharam introduced the driver to Benedetta as Manjit, and they rolled through the Chanakyapuri diplomatic section on the way to the hotel.

Doormen, runners, porters came to relieve them of her bags when they got there, to send to her room as soon as she checked in. And Dharam accompanied her upstairs to make sure that she was satisfied with her suite as two managers and a concierge stood by. Dharam was a hero here, and a very important man, so they wanted to make sure his guest was pleased.

The suite was spectacular, with an enormous living room with a view of the gardens, and a bedroom that Benedetta said was the largest she'd ever seen in any hotel. There were champagne, strawberries, a basket of fruit, and a box of candy on the table, as well as little cakes, and the moment they had walked into the suite, a liveried butler offered to serve them champagne or tea. It was difficult to imagine going back to a Western hotel after this. There were armies of personnel scurrying everywhere to meet her every need.

They were planning to spend two days in Delhi, and Dharam stayed to talk to her for two hours, as the maids unpacked for her, and he left her reluctantly at three in the morning to get some rest.

When she woke up in the morning, the weather was perfect, and she put on gray slacks with a red cashmere sweater, and she had a short jacket with her in case it got chilly. She could hardly wait to start.

She was ready when Dharam appeared in her suite after she had breakfast, and he had gone to his office for an hour.

'All set?' he asked her, so pleased that she had come.

'I can't wait,' she said excitedly as they set out. It felt like a huge adventure to her, and Dharam looked happy. His driver and the Bentley were waiting for them downstairs.

The first things he took her to were the traditional monuments, Lal Qila and Purana and Humayun's Tomb. They got out and looked around. They strolled across the lawns and through the Lodi Gardens, and she could sense

245

the peaceful atmosphere. From there they went to see Qutub Minar, the tallest brick minaret in the world. She was constantly aware of the contrasts in the city, the old and the new, the opulence, the poverty, the beggars clamoring as she'd been warned, the beautiful women in saris bustling along every street.

He took her to the Olive Bar and Kitchen for lunch, and afterward to the Crescent Mall to see some of the Indian clothes, which Benedetta found fascinating. And then they returned to the hotel, and had tea overlooking the gardens before she went back to her room to rest for a while before dinner.

'How is it so far?' he asked her. He was so proud of his country and his city, and it was obvious that she was loving it, and falling in love with his city too.

He left her at nearly seven to go home and change, and promised to be back at eight-thirty for dinner at the Smokehouse Room, which he had told her about when they were in Sardinia, and now he wanted to share it with her. It had a panoramic view of the Qutub Minar minaret, which they had seen that morning.

The restaurant was very impressive, and the dinner was exquisite. He ordered several dishes for her, and explained to her what they were, as a fleet of waiters served them the delicious food. She was amazed by how many waiters there were, and the service was excellent. She was already overwhelmed by India's magic and beauty and she had only been there for a day. It had lived up to every expectation she'd had so far, and this was only the beginning. She could already tell it would be an extraordinary trip. Dharam had seen to that and orchestrated everything perfectly for her.

After dinner, he kissed her again and left her in the living room of her suite. He still couldn't believe she was there. He kept thanking her for coming, while she thanked him for everything he'd arranged. He promised he'd be back in the morning, and urged her to get some sleep. He wanted her to have the energy to do everything he'd planned. There were so many sights to show her.

When he appeared the next morning, she was already dressed and ready, and had been up for hours. They left a short time after and explored the old part of Delhi. They had even more locations on their schedule for that day. They went to the Lotus Temple, Dilli Haat, and the National Museum, and at the end of the day, she went back to the hotel for a massage and a swim in the pool.

They had dinner at Le Cirque in her hotel that night. They wanted an early night, as they were starting at dawn the next day to begin their trip. She wanted to meet Dharam's children too, but his son was away playing polo and wouldn't be back before she left, and his daughter lived in Jaipur, which was one of the stops planned on their trip.

Their odyssey began in Khajuraho, where they visited dozens of temples through the day. There were gods, goddesses, warriors, and musicians depicted in the carvings, and Benedetta took

247

dozens of photographs with the camera she'd brought. They had dinner at their hotel that night, and he walked her back to her suite before going to his own.

In the morning they flew to Agra to see the Taj Mahal, and nothing had prepared her for its staggering beauty. It was truly the most magnificent structure she'd ever seen, infinitely more so than the photographs she'd seen of it for years. They walked around and took pictures of the reflections and then checked into the Oberoi Amarvilas Hotel, which was an extraordinary Moorish- and Mogul-inspired palace right next to the Taj Mahal. There were beautiful terraces, fountains, pools, gardens, and lush flowers. And the rooms were spectacular with inlaid wood, marble floors, and heavy silk drapes, with the Taj Mahal visible from every room. Dharam had ordered her bath filled with rose petals when she returned to her room to relax after dinner. He had thought of everything.

And after a night in Agra, they went to Ranthambore National Park to stay at the Hotel Vanyavilas, in the luxury camp, and in each place, Dharam had a room or a suite next to hers. He wanted to be close to her to protect her if necessary, but mostly to enjoy her company. They hadn't stopped talking for days, since she'd arrived. He had so much to tell her about each location.

They went to Jaipur, where they visited the Jantar Mantar astronomical observation site, the Hawa Mahal, an eighteenth-century palace, the City Palace, and the Chandra Mahal Palace.

Even more exciting for Benedetta, they had dinner with his daughter, Rama, at her palatial home. She introduced Benedetta to her three young children, who were adorable and impeccably behaved. Her husband was away playing polo with her brother, but she provided a feast for them that night, and then sat for hours afterward, chatting with Benedetta and her father. The two women hit it off perfectly, and Dharam looked proud and pleased.

They were staying at the fabulous Rajvilas Hotel, and had a drink there on the terrace after dinner. The hotel had thirty-two acres of spectacular gardens, and the scent of jasmine was everywhere.

'I'm sorry you didn't meet my son-in-law,' Dharam said with regret. 'He's a charming young man. His family is one of the most important in India.' But so was Dharam, although he was a modest person. With all the wonders he was showing her, what impressed Benedetta the most was his constant kindness to her, his gentleness and grace.

Benedetta was sad to realize that the trip was already halfway over. It was moving past her with lightning speed, and she wanted it to last forever.

'I wish I could stop time so I could see more of everything, and engrave every detail on my mind.'

'You will anyway.' He smiled at her, and she agreed. How could she ever forget any of this? Each experience, each vision, each temple, each building was unforgettable and unique, and yet so typical of India. And each moment was special and tender as he shared the beauty of his country with her.

After they regretfully left Rama, they flew to Udaipur in his plane, and visited the City Palace, and the marketplace so she could see the fabrics there. She wound up taking samples of everything so she could reproduce some of the simpler styles and vibrant colors of their textiles that would have been impossible to describe at home.

Dharam had a terrible time getting her to leave the marketplace. She was so excited by everything she saw there. Benedetta wanted to explore it all and take as much as she could with her. She had stacks of fabrics when they left and an armload of bangles to bring home to friends as souvenirs of her trip.

The next day they explored the Eklingji and Nagda temple complexes, which were among the most beautiful they'd seen, and then went back to relax at the hotel. They had planned to spend the last few days of the trip taking it easy in Udaipur before going back to Delhi. Dharam wanted some quiet time with her, and they explored some little back streets and shops where she found more treasures. She was insatiable, she wanted to take every sound, every smell, every sight and memory home.

'So, Benedetta, are you pleased that you came to India?' he asked her on their last night there.

The trip was almost over, she was going home in two days, and they had crammed in a remarkable number of sights, cities, experiences, and historical visits, and the culture of his country enveloped them like a magic spell. She was totally enamored and enchanted by the trip he had planned for her, and grateful for the time they had spent together. She had not only gotten an extraordinary look at his country, but a better understanding of the man himself. When they had met in Italy and Paris, she hadn't fully captured his full depth and scope as a human being. He was steeped in the traditions of his culture, its gentleness and beauty, and seeing him with his daughter, how much he loved her and how proud he was of her, had shown Benedetta an additional side of him as well. And although it was impossible to compare them, it made her realize even more how much she had tolerated from Gregorio, how shallow he had been, how narcissistic and uncaring he was toward her. Dharam had a depth of soul and compassion that exceeded anything she had known in any man. She loved his traditions, the myths and stories and history he shared with her. His only goal for the past two weeks had been to make her happy and show her his country, life, and culture. And as they sat chatting that night about what they'd done and seen, he slipped a bracelet on her arm that she had admired when they visited the Gem Palace in Jaipur. It was a wide diamond bangle, set with the rough diamonds of India that had captivated her. Her eyes flew open wide when she saw it, she was stunned by the remarkable gift.

'Dharam, no!' It was far more than she felt she should accept from him, but she loved it and was thrilled to have it. She knew he would be deeply hurt if she refused it, and she leaned over to kiss him on the cheek to thank him. He looked enormously pleased that she loved it so much.

'I want you to have something to remember our trip by. I hope it will be the first of many visits here. This country still has many riches for us to explore. Next time we will travel more slowly, but I wanted you to see as many aspects of our life as possible on your first visit. A kind of overview. We will explore it in greater detail when you return.' And he wanted there to be a 'next time,' many of them. He had made that much clear. Her eyes clouded for an instant, as she touched the beautiful bracelet and looked at him. She was still worried about the one thing that had concerned her since the beginning. Their lives were worlds apart.

'How would we do this?' she asked softly. 'You live here. I live in Milan. And it's hard for either of us to get away.' It had taken careful planning, and a great deal of thought on his part. And he had kept his professional obligations at bay now for two weeks and would have to work harder than ever once she left, and so would she when she got back to Milan, to pay the piper for the time she'd been away. They both knew that was true, they had demanding careers, many employees who depended on them, and major jobs and responsibilities. She didn't see how it could work out, except as a romantic interlude from time to time, although she knew that he came to Europe often, and had considerable mobility with his own plane. But his life was here, and hers was 3,800 miles away in Italy. It

252

saddened her to think about it.

'We can do anything we want,' he said gently. 'If we want it to work, it will. It depends on us, Benedetta, and how much effort we want to make, how much time we put aside. I don't expect you to give up your life in Italy. I have obligations and family here. I believe we can have both. Perhaps we cannot be together every moment, but I would rather have a part of you than nothing at all. I have never met a woman like you, who works as hard, is as creative, and has such a vision about life. You are a genius at what you do.' And he knew she was a warm, loving, wise woman besides.

'So are you.' She smiled at him, touched by the compliment. She was as modest as he was in her own way. She had given Gregorio all the credit, but she had been the talent and creative force behind the throne, and the world was now giving her her due, and Dharam was pleased for her. He was well aware of how talented she was.

'Geniuses have unusual lives. Perhaps we will not have breakfast together every morning, but we can combine our two worlds, adding to each other's happiness, blending two remarkable people, worlds, and careers. And you have no children, mine are grown. I enjoy spending time with them, but they don't need me on a daily basis anymore. Fifteen years ago, this might not have worked. Now it could if you are willing to enter one of life's great adventures with me.' And as he said it, he held his hand out to her, and she took it silently and looked at him. 'I love you, Benedetta. I fell in love with you the night we met. When I saw you and I spoke to you, I could not believe my misfortune that you were married to another man. And then, without warning, he left, and I saw the look of pain in your eyes. I wanted to wrap my arms around you and take you home with me, but there was nothing I could do then. Now life has been kind to us, or to me. And you're here with me. I want to take care of you, and love you. I won't let anyone hurt you, Benedetta. I offer you my heart and my life.' She was bowled over by what he said, and the look in his eyes. They weren't even lovers yet and had only kissed. She had been cautious with her heart after the pain of what she had gone through with Gregorio. But Dharam was a totally different kind of man, giving and loving, protective and generous. She knew that now. She was safe.

'I love you too,' she said softly, and meant it. They were brave words for her.

'Will you walk with me on the path we have been given?' And as he said it, the image of the Taj Mahal came into her mind, of immeasurable love that defied reason or explanation, but that lasted for centuries through time. She nodded, and he kissed her and held her for a long moment, and she felt an extraordinary sense of peace wash over her. She had never experienced anything like it before and recognized it for what it was. The love of a good man.

They went upstairs together afterward, and he stopped at the door to her suite, as he had every night. She opened the door to him, and her heart. And their dreams came true that night.

They didn't know what would happen, or how it would evolve, but as she fell asleep in his arms after they made love, Benedetta knew they would be together. Her destiny was with this wonderful man. It was a priceless gift life had given her. One that could not be denied.

16

When Valerie landed at the airport in Beijing on her trip for *Vogue* at the beginning of December, she was overwhelmed by all the sights and sounds that assaulted her. The sheer number of people, the noise, the chaos in the airport, the traffic, the pollution. She had never experienced anything like it as they drove into the city, and Jean-Philippe pointed out sights and buildings to her and explained what she was seeing. There were fascinating colorful remnants of China's history in Beijing, along with some new, intriguing aspects of the city, for her to report to *Vogue*, but her first view of it was how he lived as a foreigner who worked there, and she was shocked at the ugliness and discomforts of his life. She was horrified at the tiny apartment and how unpleasant it was. Had he gone there with his family, he would have made more effort to find a decent place to live. As it was, he made do with a company apartment, and didn't care. His heart was in Paris, not here. He was here only to work.

After she saw his Spartan bare-bones apartment, they went to her hotel. *Vogue* had booked her into the Opposite House, which was sleek and modern and had a great pool. She was stunned again by how few people spoke English, despite the Western-style hotel filled with foreigners. Nothing felt familiar here. In a way, she liked that, as something completely different, but she could see now how hard living there would have been. *Vogue* had hired a translator for her, who was to meet Valerie later that morning for a tour of the city. She had much to do and see while she was there, on her scouting mission for the magazine. And she intended to see all she could in the daytime when Jean-Philippe was at work. He had tried to slim down his schedule for the duration of her stay, but he was in the middle of several new big deals, and it had been a victory freeing himself up to accompany her to Shanghai. Valerie was excited at the prospect of going there with him. She had heard great things about the city, but Beijing interested her more because he lived there now, and she could see firsthand what she had missed by not going with him.

She showered and changed at the hotel, while he ordered breakfast from a room service waiter who barely spoke English, but got most of their order right in spite of it. And after they shared eggs and croissants, which arrived with a bowl of rice with bits of fish in it, Jean-Philippe had to leave her to go to the office for a meeting, and Valerie went to meet her interpreter in the lobby, who was a pretty young girl. She spoke accurate though halting English, and had never been out of China. Hers was a government position, she was assigned to foreign businessmen, and was pleased to see that Valerie was a woman. Valerie had a copy of French *Vogue* with her, and explained what she was doing there. Since they were going to use Chinese models for the photo

257

shoot as well as the famous models they brought from Paris, she had to contact a modeling agency about the shoot while she was there. The models were state trained as well.

But that day she planned to scout locations with her interpreter and a driver she had hired at the hotel. They covered a lot of ground, as Valerie took photographs at the Silk Market, and the more rustic Dirt Market, which would provide great backdrops for their photographs. It was a flea market with a vast variety of wares. The interpreter took her to several enormous shopping malls, which Valerie found less interesting. The girl said that there were over a hundred of them in Beijing, but Valerie wasn't excited by those she saw. She wanted more unusual locations to show *Vogue* than shopping malls.

They wandered through 'hutongs,' narrow ancient lanes and alleys that were scattered throughout the city and could provide an exotic backdrop for photography. Valerie was excited about the 798 Art Zone, an exhibition space for modern art that was originally an electronics factory built in the 1950s turned into gallery spaces, where she thought the models would look fabulous, and it would be an easy shoot. And in addition there were the obvious locations, the Forbidden City, the Great Wall, and the Peking Opera, for more traditional options. Valerie didn't stop taking photographs all day, and she and her interpreter were both exhausted when they went back to the hotel, where Valerie lay down, while waiting for

Jean-Philippe to come back from work. He would be staying at the hotel with her, and he found her sound asleep when he got there. She had let her translator go home, and he didn't have the heart to wake her. He lay on the bed next to her, smiling and looking at her. He was happy and at peace in Beijing with her, for the first time since he'd arrived. It made all the difference in the world having her there.

Valerie woke up at nearly midnight, and smiled when she saw him next to her. Jean-Philippe was reading quietly and had ordered something to eat without disturbing her. She was starving when she woke up, and they ordered room service, and she ate a midnight supper while she told him what she'd seen that day.

'You covered a lot of ground,' he said admiringly. 'I haven't seen all that in two months.' But he'd been working all the time.

'I tried to. I don't have much time, and I have to figure out how to work the shoot.' One big problem they were going to have when they shot it in January would be the weather. The girls would be freezing in subzero temperatures.

Jean-Philippe loved how enterprising she was, how creative and competent. It was one of the many things that had attracted Charles de Beaumont to her as well. His name never passed her lips while she was there, afraid she would give something away, or her husband would see her near-betrayal in her eyes. She never wanted him to find out that she had almost cheated on him, knowing that if he did, he would never trust her again. He seemed more in love with her than ever, as they shared the excitement of her trip to China. And there was something about being in a hotel, and only there with him for a short time, that made it more romantic.

On their last night in Beijing, Jean-Philippe took her to an important dinner that he had to attend, invited by a client. It was a sumptuous affair with endless courses of delicacies, which Valerie found fascinating, and she enjoyed going with him. And he was visibly proud of her. He loved having his wife with him.

And by the time they left for Shanghai, four days after she'd arrived, Valerie felt as though they were falling in love all over again. The trip had saved them. Everything felt new and fresh, as they rediscovered each other. And they both loved Shanghai, much more than Beijing. Valerie found it a far more appealing city, and they explored it together, almost like a honeymoon, except that she was doing it for work. He was on vacation and free to join her everywhere.

She flew back to Beijing with him the night before she had to leave for Paris. And they spent their last night in the hotel like honeymooners. She hated to leave him the next day, and he dreaded going back to his lonely apartment after she left.

'At least I'll be home for Christmas in two weeks,' he said sadly, thinking about her leaving. His life was so much happier while she was there. But he had the holidays at home to look forward to. His life without her in Beijing was intolerably dreary. With Valerie at his side, everything was better, and he could face anything. But he no longer tried to convince her to move to Beijing with him. He could see now how unpleasant it would be for her, and how much better off she and the children were in Paris. This was a sacrifice he was making for them, not one he expected of her any longer, and he was sorry he had ever asked it of her and strained their marriage before he left. He felt lucky that by some miracle their marriage had survived it. He could hardly tear himself away from her when he left her at the airport. It had been a wonderful trip for both of them, and a great piece of good fortune that *Vogue* had sent her, for which she was very grateful.

'See you in two weeks,' she said happily after they kissed for the last time. They had made love at every opportunity, as though to make up for the agonizing months when things had started to go so wrong between them over this decision. Somehow, miraculously, in China they had found each other again.

She waved at him and then disappeared into the security area. All he could think of now was flying back to Paris in two weeks. He had never before been as in love with her as he was now.

* * *

When Valerie got back to Paris, she reported to her editor-in-chief everything she had seen in China. They spread all her photographs out on an enormous screen, and examined them carefully, and they loved the locations. The shoot in China was going to be fantastic. And she had photographs as well of all the models she had seen in Beijing. They all agreed, the April issue was going to be a knockout.

And the following day she had a meeting with her consultation client. She was grateful that Charles was in New York and didn't attend. She didn't feel ready to see him yet, although she knew that eventually she'd have to, and she didn't want to lose the client. But she felt more sure of her relationship with Jean-Philippe again, and she knew she had done the right thing with Charles. If she had cheated on her husband and he'd found out, particularly if it became serious with her and Charles and it might have, it would have broken Jean-Philippe's heart. And although she had doubted it for several months, she was sure again that he loved her. And she knew she loved him as well. His decision to move to China had put their marriage on the line, and somehow their feelings for each other had survived, and even gotten stronger.

She had a presentation due to her consulting client the following week, and agreed to send it to Serge Sevigny, Charles's partner. And she was interested to hear that they were considering introducing some of their lines into stores in the shopping malls in Beijing, and when she discussed it with them, she could do so knowledgeably, having just been there. Serge Sevigny was impressed. Clearly, she was as good at what she did and as on top of the current markets as Charles said she was. Serge said they would talk more about China after the new year, when Charles was back. He said Charles was traveling for most of December, working in New York, and then planning to spend the holidays at his house in St. Barth's. She tried not to react when she remembered that he had invited her there with her children, and she had told him that she had to spend the holidays in Paris with her husband. There was an unreality now to what had happened between them. And she hoped that it would only seem more that way when she saw him again after the new year. She trusted him to be professional, he didn't want to lose her as a consultant either. She was too good at what she did.

Valerie reported to Jean-Philippe on her meetings at *Vogue* when she got back to Paris. She could hear in his voice and see on Skype how excited he was to be coming home soon. After everything they had shared in China recently, and the renewal of their relationship, they both could hardly wait. It had been a terrible six months, but hopefully now the worst was behind them. What they had to do now was live with his decision. And she wondered if maybe, living on separate continents, their marriage could be more exciting and their romance fresher. All she could do was hope so.

★   ★   ★

While Valerie was visiting China with Jean-Philippe, Chantal and Xavier had gone to an early Christmas party in Paris. She had just visited Eric in Berlin. He was out of the casts, had graduated from rehab, and was back at his apartment with Annaliese. Chantal had bought him a car to replace his motorcycle. He had insisted on a second-hand one, said he didn't want anything too new or recent, and had fallen in love with an old postal delivery truck he could carry his installations in. She had tried to talk him into a used Volkswagen or Audi, but the battered postal truck was all he wanted, and she finally gave in. At least he couldn't kill himself going at high speeds in it. It barely made it to fifty miles an hour, and she laughed at the vision of him driving away in it, and told Xavier when she reported it to him that he looked like the mailman, and he had even found himself a mailman's cap to wear when he drove it.

'I don't know where I got such crazy children.' Charlotte had recently bought a brand-new Range Rover in Hong Kong, befitting her status, and her fiancé drove a Jaguar. Paul had invested his savings in a 1965 Mustang that was his prize possession, and Rachel's parents were planning to buy her a Mercedes station wagon before she had the baby. They were putting pressure on her and Paul to get married before she gave birth. Paul had mentioned it to his mother, and she was staying well out of it. She wasn't going to influence whether he married Rachel or not, although with a baby on the way, she advised him to get a full-time job so he'd have a reliable income, which he didn't have making indie movies. She didn't think either of them was ready to marry, but if they were going to have a baby, it was time to grow up and take responsibility. For now, Rachel was dependent on her parents, and Chantal gave Paul help when he needed it.

The big day was coming closer. And Charlotte's marriage was only five months away. And Eric was back on both feet after his accident, and driving a mail truck.

Xavier reminded her that they were going to a party the night she got back from Berlin, given by one of his law partners. They were a little bit stuffy and very traditional, in their late sixties with grown children, and they lived in a very fancy area of the sixteenth arrondissement, but Chantal liked them. She wasn't sure what to wear, as their friends were conservative, and his partner's wife was exceptionally so.

Chantal decided to wear a sober black wool dress that was longer than she liked and very serious, with long sleeves and a high neck, and she added a string of pearls to it that made it even more so. But she didn't dare wear anything wilder, and she wore her hair in a bun, which she rarely did, because she thought it made her look older, and Xavier preferred her hair down. She wasn't sure about the dress and stared at herself in the mirror before they went out.

'Do I look like a secretary or a Greek widow in this?' she asked Xavier, feeling unsure of herself. He was wearing a new black suit, and a black Prada shirt she'd bought him, and looked very hip. She was worried that she looked like his mother.

'You look very grown-up,' he said diplomatically.

'Do you mean old?' She looked unsure of herself.

'Personally, I like your hair down, and skirts to your crotch, but I have to admit, in this crowd, you'll look appropriate.' It was not a high compliment, but it was true. She took her hair out of the bun, kept the dress on, put on her coat, and they left. It was a big festive holiday gathering at his partner's home, with everyone from the law firm and their friends, and a long buffet in the dining room, catered by an excellent catering firm that had provided delicious food. And their hostess was wearing a dress almost identical to Chantal's, so she knew she had worn the right thing.

Chantal found herself talking to a female lawyer she had met before, and got locked into a group of very interesting, very liberal women who were discussing the dire situation of women in the Middle East, and how that could be changed. She talked to them for almost an hour, before she stopped to get something to eat at the buffet, and went to look for Xavier, and was mildly surprised to see him talking to a sexy-looking redhead in a skin-tight white dress that barely reached her crotch. From the smooth outline of her hips, it was clear that she was not wearing underwear, and she was standing in mile-high black suede stiletto heels.

'Wow,' Chantal said in an undervoice, and wondered if she should leave him to it, and not look like an overbearing jealous girlfriend, so she engaged some other people in conversation and waited for Xavier to move on. He didn't.

Instead, he and the girl sat down on the couch, and he was laughing heartily at everything she said, as she inched closer and closer to him, while Chantal watched but did not approach.

She waited an hour for him to break up the conversation with the redhead. Finally the girl stood up, took a card out of her handbag, and gave it to him, and Chantal saw him thank her and slip it into his coat pocket, as she walked away. Chantal waited a few minutes and then went over to him with a stern expression, and said she was tired and wanted to go home. They had been there for nearly two hours, and it seemed long enough to her, except that they usually stayed late at gatherings, and he looked like he was having a good time.

'Are you okay?' he asked with a look of concern as he put an arm around her. She was stiff as stone and walked out of his embrace.

'I'm fine,' she said icily. She got her coat, and a few minutes later they left. It was obvious to him that she was furious about something, although he had no idea what. He wondered if someone had been rude to her or if she'd just had a lousy time. He thought it had been a nice party, and there had been about eighty people there. It was a good group and had a festive feeling. The hosts had made a lot of effort.

'Is something wrong?' he asked her as they drove from the Right Bank to the Left.

'Wrong? No. Predictable, yes. Who was that woman you were talking to?' She hated the way she sounded but couldn't seem to stop herself.

'What woman?' He looked blank as he drove

and then glanced at Chantal.

'The redhead with no underwear. You looked like you were having a great time together.'

'She's pretty funny. She's our new intern. She's a nice girl. And how do you know she wasn't wearing underwear?' He looked puzzled.

'I have eyes in my head.' She had no pantyline, but she wasn't going to stop to explain that to him. 'How old is she?'

'I don't know — twenty-five, twenty-six — she's a law student. She wants to be a divorce lawyer,' he said easily.

'I'm sure she'll cause plenty of them,' Chantal said with a grim look as they got to her apartment and he parked.

'What are you so upset about?'

'Oh, I don't know — you spend an hour talking to a gorgeous twenty-five-year-old who crawls all over you while you laugh like a schoolboy. She hands you her card, and you slip it into your pocket. I'm nearly twenty years older than you are. What would be your first guess about why I'm upset? I didn't like the smoked salmon?'

'It was very good, by the way. The caterer was great,' he said, trying to change the subject, which only made Chantal madder. 'And it wasn't her card. It was her brother's. He's an architect, and we need to do some remodeling at the office. She was recommending him for the job.'

'She could have given it to you at work. And frankly, I don't believe you. She may be a law student, but she looks like a Hollywood starlet, and she dresses like a hooker. I don't love that combination when she's crawling all over the man I live with and I'm old enough to be his mother and by some stroke of shit luck dressed like his grandmother tonight. Your partner's wife is twenty years older than I am, and we were wearing the same dress. Remind me to burn it.' He smiled at what she said. Even when she was angry, she knew how to make him laugh.

'Chantal, baby, please, I love you. I was just talking to her. It was harmless. I don't give a damn about her. And you could wear our bedspread, you're sexier than any woman alive.'

'I told you a long time ago,' she said, as they got out of the car and rode up in the tiny elevator in her building, 'I don't want to be made a fool of or get my heart broken. One day you'll run off with a girl like her, and her age, and I'm not going to be left in the dust crying my heart out. If you're starting to look at younger women, Xavier, I'm done. I'd rather get out sooner than later if that's where we're headed.' He was shocked by what she'd said, although he had heard it before, and he realized now that she meant it. She was terrified of his falling for a younger woman and dumping her.

'I promise you, I'm not looking at younger women. I love you. I probably should have stopped talking to her, but I was having a good time, and I didn't want to be rude.'

'That's my point. The 'good time' part. You have a right to do whatever you want, but I have a right to save my ass before you break my heart.'

'I won't do it again,' he said quietly as they walked into the apartment.

'I'm sure you will,' she said, walked into her bedroom, and slammed the door. And he heard her lock it a moment later. He spoke through it half an hour later, hoping she had cooled off.

'Do you want me to stay at my place tonight?' he asked politely, hoping she'd say no.

'Yes,' she responded through the door. And he decided not to press her about it. He left quietly a few minutes later, with a sinking heart. He felt badly that she was so upset and realized now how it must have felt to see him talking to the young woman. He wouldn't have dated her even if he'd been single. She wasn't his type. He always liked smart, intellectual women, not sex bombs. And the exchange had been entirely harmless, whatever Chantal believed now. She was in a jealous rage, but it was unfounded. He sent Chantal a text before he went to bed that night, and told her he loved her. She didn't answer, and he called her on her cell the next morning. She didn't pick up, and it went straight to voicemail. And when he got to the office, he nearly had a heart attack when Amandine, the cute redhead, told him she had called him at home. His home number in their roster now was Chantal's.

'I gave you the wrong card for my brother last night. I told him that you might call him, and he gave me hell. I gave you his old one — here's his new one,' she said, handing it to him and walking away. Xavier could just imagine the effect on Chantal when she had called. And he didn't want to send her a lengthy explanation by text or email. He would save it till he saw her that night. But he had a knot in his stomach all day. He never heard from Chantal, and he was worried that she was truly on the warpath now after the girl's call, which wouldn't have looked innocent to Chantal, no matter what he said.

He walked into the apartment that night, with a bouquet of roses in his hand, and felt like an actor in a sitcom. It was so trite as to be pathetic, but he didn't know what else to do. He was truly sorry he had upset her and made her jealous.

The only lights on in the apartment were in her study, where she wrote. The rest of the apartment was dark, which he didn't consider a good sign. And he tripped over a large suitcase in the hallway outside her office. She looked up with a stony expression when he opened the door and walked in holding the bouquet of red roses, which she ignored.

'Are you going somewhere?' he asked, trying to sound nonchalant, referring to the suitcase.

'No, you are,' she said coldly, but her eyes were two pools of pain. 'I packed your things. It's over. I can't do this. I'm not going to wait for the other shoe to drop. I'm too old for you. I've been through enough in my life. You need to be with a younger woman, the redhead or someone else. I need to be by myself. I'm a hundred fucking years old, and you're thirty-eight. You need to find someone your age to play with.'

'Chantal . . . please . . . don't be ridiculous . . . I love you. You're the smartest, sexiest, most beautiful woman I've ever known. I wouldn't care if you were two hundred years old. Don't blow this out of proportion.' He was standing

271

next to her by then, and had dropped the roses into a chair. He tried to put his arms around her, and she wouldn't let him. There were tears rolling down her cheeks.

'I love you too, and I want you to leave . . . now. That scene last night is exactly what I don't want to live through one day, for real. Me crying and brokenhearted when you fall in love with some girl half my age. You have to go, Xavier. I can't do this anymore.' He looked horrified. 'It's over,' she said for good measure, in case he hadn't understood the suitcase and the speech.

'This is crazy.' He was near tears too.

'No, I was. Now I want to be sane again, and alone. I thought this could work. It can't. Last night reminded me of that. Please go, Xavier, this is too painful.' She was crying harder, and with a last desperate look at her, he left. And not knowing what else to do, in case she really meant it, he took the suitcase in the hall and left the apartment with it, feeling as if someone had died. He couldn't understand how such a small thing could turn into a big one. Everything had been perfect between them for six months, and now it was over, because he 'might' fall in love with a younger woman one day. She could fall in love with someone else too, older or younger. Either of them could die. Anything could happen, or they could be together for the rest of their lives. And who knew who would outlive who? He could die young, she could live to be a hundred. No one could predict how it would turn out. It was insane to end what they had.

Her idea of preventive medicine was very extreme, kill the patient immediately, in case he might die later.

He bumped down the stairs with the suitcase full of his clothes and books, and when he opened it at home, he found photographs of her in it, and set them on the table next to his bed, and on his desk, and put his clothes away with a heavy heart. He felt terrible about what had happened and what she'd done. He sent her a text that night, telling her how much he loved her, and there was no response. And when he woke up the next morning, he felt as though he had died. And Chantal was sure she had, but she was certain she had done the right thing. And she was not going to turn back. Xavier was history.

17

Chantal's children came home for Christmas again, as they did every year. It was the only time that they were all together as a family. All three of her children were at home in Paris.

Eric arrived first, and spent a quiet evening with his mother the day before the others arrived. He was almost recovered from the accident, although the pin would have to be removed from his hip in a year when the bones were stronger and fully meshed. But he had been surprisingly lucky, and said the leg only ached now occasionally. It had been nearly two months since the accident, and he told his mother he was very happy with his mail truck and used it to transport his work. She was pleased.

And he was very disappointed, when he asked where Xavier was, to hear that Xavier wouldn't be with them, and he and Chantal had broken up.

'He's not here anymore,' she said, looking tense, and her son could see that her eyes were sad.

'You broke up?' She nodded. 'That's too bad. I like him. Did he do something really bad?' He was worried and she shook her head, not meeting Eric's eyes.

'No,' she said honestly, 'but he would have eventually.'

'Does that make sense?' He was puzzled by

what she said. 'Why not wait till he does?'

'I'd rather not. When you know how something is going to turn out, it's smarter to act accordingly.'

'What if you're wrong?' Eric was the voice of reason, despite his youth.

'Trust me, I'm not. And I don't want to talk about it,' she said firmly. Eric said nothing, but he could see how unhappy she was about it. He had liked that Xavier wanted to be with her in Berlin and was a support to her. He worried about his mother alone in Paris. Xavier had seemed like a good guy to him, and they got along well. He was sorry it had ended, for her sake. She had been alone for so long before she met him.

Paul's flight from the States arrived the next morning, and he and Rachel were at the apartment by eleven, while his mother and brother were sitting at the kitchen table, having breakfast. And there was a flurry of activity when the American contingent walked in, and Chantal was shocked by how big Rachel's belly was. She was six months pregnant, but looked as if she were having twins. She was huge, and Eric was impressed too as the two brothers embraced and Paul asked his baby brother where his girlfriend was.

'She's with her family for Christmas. Germans are very big on Christmas. I'm going back for New Year's,' Eric explained, and Paul said they were too. They were only staying for a week, and meeting Rachel's parents in Mexico for a week over New Year's on the way back to L.A. Her parents invited them every year, it was a tradition, at a fabulous hotel in Cabo called the Palmilla. Chantal couldn't compete with that, and was grateful to have them for a week.

Unlike his brother, Paul didn't ask where Xavier was. He didn't even think about it until Eric told him quietly that they'd broken up recently, and he was sorry about it.

'Is that a big deal to Mom?' Paul asked, surprised.

'I think so,' Eric said.

'I thought they were just kind of hanging out. It was bound to end, with him so much younger. Mom must have known that. He was never going to stay with a woman her age.' Paul dismissed the whole notion summarily, and hadn't really expected to see him again. He assumed it was either a brief summer romance or some kind of weird friendship so she didn't have to travel alone. He couldn't imagine it was a big deal to her, and she was used to being alone. He never noticed, as Eric had, that she looked upset, was quieter than usual, and seemed sad.

And shortly after they arrived, Rachel wanted to go shopping on the Avenue Montaigne. Her credit cards were paid by her father, and she loved shopping in Paris. She had slept on the plane so she was ready to go after they changed, and Paul went with her. And Eric wanted to see some of his friends and check out some galleries at the Bastille that showed his kind of work.

Chantal was alone at the apartment when Charlotte and Rupert arrived from Hong Kong. He was extremely polite, very British, treated

276

Chantal like the queen mother, and said he hadn't been to Paris in years. Charlotte reminded her mother as soon as she arrived that she wanted to check out wedding dresses with her, and they didn't have much time since they were going skiing two days after Christmas, a passion of Rupert's, and they were flying back to Hong Kong from Zurich, so she was staying less time than her brothers. Chantal knew the drill, in less than a week they'd all be gone, but at least for now they were here, however brief the visit, and they knew Christmas was important to her. It wasn't the way it used to be when they were younger and stayed home for whole school vacations, but it still meant the world to her.

Charlotte and Rupert went out that afternoon. Chantal had made no plans while they were there, she never did, she wanted to be totally available to them. And she waited in the apartment for the others to return.

Paul and Rachel came back at six, laden with packages. She said she had found several 'cute little outfits' that she could get into, a bag at Hermès, and some baby clothes at Baby Dior, since they knew it was a boy. Paul could hardly get all the bags into the elevator, and Rachel went to his boyhood room to take a nap before dinner. She was exhausted from shopping all afternoon. It gave Chantal an opportunity to talk to Paul, while Rachel was lying down. She found him in the kitchen, having something to eat. She talked to him again about getting a job before the baby came.

'You can't be supported by her parents,' she

said firmly and he nodded.

'I'm going to pay for the baby. They're going to support her.'

'That doesn't bother you?'

'I can't afford her, Mom. Her father buys her whatever she wants.' Rachel was very spoiled. 'I've been taking production jobs, and I've got some money put aside to support the baby. That's the best I can do for now.' It seemed to satisfy him, knowing he would take care of his son. And Rachel was well beyond his means, and had no desire to cut down what she spent for him. It seemed like an unhappy arrangement to Chantal, but Paul had made his peace with it, and living with a girl he could never support. As long as he could pay for himself and his son, he was happy.

Half an hour later Rupert and Charlotte returned. They hadn't bought anything, and Charlotte was anxious to shop with her mother the following morning. Eric didn't show up till eight, after gallery-cruising at the Bastille. Chantal made a big dinner for them at home that night, since she assumed those coming from far away would be tired and jet-lagged. She made a leg of lamb with garlic, one of their favorite dishes, with string beans and mashed potatoes. It reminded them all of their childhood as they ate dinner. It was delicious, and she had made a big salad and put cheese on a platter. There was an ice cream cake for dessert, which they had loved as kids. It was their favorite dinner.

She was putting the finishing touches on the meal when Charlotte glanced at Paul and asked in a low voice, 'Is the boyfriend coming?' She seemed nervous at the prospect, and her brother filled her in in a low tone.

'Eric says it's over.' He sounded neutral about it, not sympathetic, since he hadn't taken it seriously himself.

'Well, that's a relief,' Charlotte said, visibly satisfied. 'I wasn't looking forward to that. And he would have been ridiculous at the wedding if he's that much younger. I have no idea why she'd get into something like that in the first place.' Paul agreed with her. He had met him and liked him, but felt no great attachment to him. 'She's fine on her own.'

'What makes you so sure of that?' Eric challenged her, annoyed. He had been listening to their exchange. 'None of us are alone, why should she be?'

'She's had her life and kids. She doesn't need a man in her life,' Charlotte said, firmly convinced of it.

'She's fifty-five years old, not ninety. Don't you think it gets lonely without us? You guys only see her once or twice a year for a few days, and I don't see her a lot more. She's alone all the time. What if she gets sick one day? And why shouldn't she have someone to have fun with now?'

His brother and sister stared at him as though he were speaking Chinese. Not a single one of the concerns he expressed for their mother had ever occurred to either of them.

'If she gets sick, we'll hire her a nurse,' Charlotte said tersely. 'She has enough money to pay for it. We'll put her in some kind of care facility when she gets older. She doesn't need a boyfriend.'

'You guys are all heart,' Eric said, angry at them. 'She's not a dog that you can ship off to the vet, board, and have put down when she gets old. She's a human being. She took great care of us, and still does when we need her. Why can't she have someone in her life to take care of her? Most people are married at her age, or even have boyfriends. She should too.'

'Oh, for God's sake.' His sister rolled her eyes, and Paul looked uncomfortable. He hated discussing serious issues. He liked everything to work out easily, and her not having a man in her life was certainly easier for all of them. And they didn't have to deal with some guy when they came home. Eric thought Xavier was a good one, and he had never seen his mother as happy in his whole life, except when they were small. She had always been happy then, when they were home. In recent years, he found her sad at times and worried that she was lonely, and he felt guilty about it, although he wasn't about to move back to Paris to solve the problem. None of them were, which was the issue. Without them, if she had no man in her life, she had no one. And Eric worried about it.

'Well, I think it's much simpler that he's not here and we're not stuck with some stranger at Christmas,' Charlotte said petulantly.

'Rupert is a stranger. We don't know him,' Eric said, loudly enough for his future brother-in-law to hear him, and Charlotte looked as if she wanted to kill her outspoken baby brother.

'He's not a stranger,' she corrected him. 'We're engaged.'

'Great. I'm happy for you. So why shouldn't Mom have a boyfriend?'

'What's the point here? She broke up with him, so obviously she didn't want him either. So what are we arguing about?' Paul asked them, and the other two backed down.

'It's a matter of principle,' Eric said firmly. 'I don't think you two ever wonder if she's happy or okay or alone.'

'She's used to it,' Paul answered, 'and she has friends.'

'Friends aren't the same thing. I was lonely as hell before I met Annaliese. Friends go home to bed with each other, not with you.'

'Oh, for heaven's sake, Eric, it's not about sex at her age.' Charlotte looked disgusted.

'How do we know? Maybe it is. Some women have babies at her age nowadays.'

'Shit,' Paul said in horror. 'Imagine if she had a baby with some guy. That's all we need.'

'You are,' Eric, the devil's advocate, said, 'and we all think it's okay.'

'I'm thirty-one years old. That's a big difference.'

'And you're not married. And if Annaliese and I ever have a baby, we won't get married either. We don't believe in it. So maybe we're a lot more 'shocking' than she is, and whatever we do, she puts up with it and acts like it's okay. If we get married, if we don't, if we have babies, whoever we want to live with. She never gives us a hard

281

time about it. So why are you two so determined to give her crap about what she does, and why do we all assume that she's supposed to be alone?' Eric was dogged in her defense.

'She must want to be alone,' Charlotte pointed out. 'You said she dumped him.'

'That doesn't mean she's happy about it. She looks sad to me.'

'She looks fine to me,' Charlotte said staunchly. 'We're going to look for wedding dresses tomorrow. That'll make her happy.'

'That will make *you* happy. What do we do for her?' The other two looked at each other and didn't answer. They didn't think about her that way. She did for them, but it never occurred to them to do for her, and Chantal never asked them to, nor expected it. She was a wholly undemanding person. And while they were thinking about it, she called them to the table, put red wine in a decanter, and served dinner. They all sat down, and a moment later they all dug into the delicious meal. And they agreed by the end of it, her cooking was better than ever. Dinner was superb.

'I'm going to gain ten pounds,' Rachel said nervously, 'and I don't have a spinning class here.'

'It's good for you, and the baby,' Paul assured her. 'You need to eat more.' And he thought she did too much exercise. Pilates, spinning, yoga, and she worked out every day. She had a great body, and worked hard at it, but now she was pregnant.

'Are you going to get pregnant right away?'

Rachel asked Charlotte over dinner. Chantal listened to their exchanges with interest, but spoke very little.

'No, we want to wait a few years. We want to buy a bigger apartment, and maybe a small flat in London before we deal with babies, and I'm in line for a promotion. I don't want to lose that.' It sounded typical of Charlotte, and no one was surprised. She liked having everything planned and organized far into the future, and Rupert agreed. Paul was more haphazard, which was why Rachel was pregnant. It had been an accident, but now they were happy about it. And her parents had hired a baby nurse for her, who was going to stay for a year, so the baby wouldn't impact their life too much. They were relieved. Unlike Chantal, who had been married to a struggling writer, and had three children in five years and took care of them herself, with no help, and was under even more pressure when their father died a few years later, and she had to go to work at various jobs. None of them would have wanted to be in her position. They forgot the struggles she'd been through. She made it all seem effortless, and always had.

Rachel and Charlotte helped her clean up the kitchen after dinner, while the men went to play video games in the living room, and afterward they played charades. Everyone laughed and was highly competitive, even more so now that Rupert and Rachel were part of the group. And at midnight, they all went to their rooms, and Chantal was happy when she went to bed. She loved having her kids at home. She missed

Xavier terribly and tried not to think about it. And she thought it interesting that neither Paul nor Charlotte had asked about him, only Eric. She knew nothing about their conversation in the living room before dinner — she'd been busy in the kitchen. And had she known, she would have been even more upset than she was. They thought the idea of her having male companionship, and a man to love her, was completely superfluous, and both Charlotte and Paul were delighted that she and Xavier had broken up and hoped there would be no replacement. It would have made her heart ache even more than it was if she'd heard it.

★ ★ ★

Jean-Philippe had flown back from Beijing the morning of Christmas Eve, but Chantal had no time to see him that week, and they promised to have lunch when her kids left. She never saw anyone when they were there and didn't want to lose a moment with them. They made a date for lunch on New Year's Eve, since she knew her whole brood would be gone by then, and Jean-Philippe would be in town for another week.

Valerie had the tree up and decorated when he walked in. She had done it with the children, and they even made decorations for the tree in cardboard and papier-mâché with glitter on them, and a crèche they had read how to make in a magazine. And they all went shopping for the little animals and Baby Jesus. The apartment looked like a Christmas card when he got home, and all the presents were neatly wrapped under the tree. He hadn't had time to buy much in Beijing, except a little Chinese dress for Isabelle, a fire truck for Jean-Louis, and a stuffed tiger for Damien. And he had bought a gold bracelet at Cartier for Valerie when he was home in November.

They put the children to bed together on Christmas Eve, and after they opened their gifts and the ones from Santa Claus the next morning, they went to church as a family. They had a big Christmas meal at lunchtime. The smells in the apartment were delicious, and the children were thrilled to have him home, and so was she. They were still coasting on the fun they'd shared during her trip to China two weeks before. It seemed aeons ago now, but she was going back in January to oversee the shoot for *Vogue*. So even when he left after the holidays, they'd have time together in Beijing, and he would be home again in February. Their situation was a challenge, but one they felt they could win now, with careful planning and effort on both their parts. And the children seemed to be fine. As always, Valerie was doing a good job, and she saw to it that they talked to their father on Skype often, so he was part of their daily life, as much as possible.

She loved the bracelet he gave her, and he loved the watch she had given him, and the children had a ball with their gifts. They all agreed when they fell into bed that night after a long day that it had been one of their best

Christmases ever. And Jean-Philippe was sure of it when Valerie fell asleep in his arms with a smile on her face on Christmas night.

$$\star \quad \star \quad \star$$

Xavier told his brother that Chantal had broken up with him, and Mathieu was sorry to hear it. When Annick heard about it, she was equally sad. They liked Chantal, had enjoyed her time with them in Corsica, and thought they made a good couple. Her reason for ending it didn't make sense to them, but there was no accounting for what brought people together, or pulled them apart, and Xavier assured them it was definitely over. They invited him to spend Christmas with them, they had an army of people coming over, the kids' friends and their own, but he declined and said he just wasn't in the mood. The breakup was all too recent, and he said he wanted to be alone. He had nothing to celebrate this year.

On Christmas he read and watched movies on TV, went for a long walk along the Seine, and for a crazy moment thought about going into one of the pet shops on the quais and buying a dog. But he had heard that most of them arrived sick from Eastern Europe, so he didn't, went home instead, and mourned the woman he had fallen in love with who no longer wanted him because one day he might fall in love with someone younger than she was. It didn't seem fair. He hadn't cheated on her. He truly loved her. He hadn't even flirted with the girl she objected to, he had just talked to her. He knew her fears about being older than he, which had sent her into a panic, beyond reason. Chantal hadn't returned a single one of his calls, nor answered them, nor any other form of message he had sent her for the past three weeks and clearly didn't intend to. He believed her. It was over. Now he just had to go on with his life, but he didn't want to. He needed to mourn her for a while, out of respect for all he felt for her. It hadn't been a casual affair to him. It was the real deal. For him. But apparently not for her. He had easily imagined them staying together forever since they had the same values, enjoyed the same things, and got along so well.

His office was closed till after New Year, and he spent every day taking long walks along the Seine or in the Bois de Boulogne, thinking about her, and wishing that there were some way to convince her that their ages didn't matter to him. He could no longer imagine his life without her, nor did he want to.

18

Charlotte and Rupert were the first to leave, two days after Christmas. They had stayed with Chantal only for four days, but they had saved their vacation to go to Val d'Isère to go skiing. Charlotte still had friends who went there, and she had promised Rupert the best skiing of his life.

She and her mother had found the perfect wedding dress at Christian Dior, and Charlotte was ecstatic. It fit her perfectly, and needed no alterations. Her mother was bringing it to Hong Kong with her in May for the wedding. And they had found a navy blue dress Charlotte thought was suitable for her mother across the street at Nina Ricci. It was a little more severe than Chantal would have liked, with a grandmotherly bolero over it, but she wanted to make Charlotte happy, and wear what her daughter felt was right for her wedding. It wasn't an exciting dress for Chantal, but she didn't care. She wouldn't know most of the guests anyway — they were the bridal couple's friends. And Rupert said his mother was wearing pale gray, which Chantal thought sounded even more depressing. And given all the rules and restrictions and traditions Charlotte was adhering to, it wasn't going to be a lighthearted event, but a very formal one. And neither of her sons was thrilled that they had to wear morning coats, but their sister was adamant about it. Rachel was worried that she'd still be fat after the baby in May, two months after he was born. But the bride's dress was going to be spectacular. She was having eight brides-maids, but their dresses were being made in Hong Kong by a terrific seamstress she knew. The wedding was taking shape. And Rupert and Charlotte left for Val d'Isère in high spirits and thanked Chantal for the wonderful Christmas. Rupert had told her that they would be spending it in London with his family next year, but they would share holidays with her on alternate years. And Paul's response was that he and Rachel might stay in L.A., since it would be hard to travel with a baby during the holidays, and Rachel's parents wanted them to stay there. But he told Chantal she would be welcome in L.A. And trying not to complain about it, or cry, she realized that she had possibly just had her last real Christmas with all three of her children present. Eric had heard them too and saw the look in her eyes. But as always she was gracious and didn't argue with them about their plans, or even comment. She tried to respect them as adults, and they had other families to satisfy now, not just her.

Although he hated to do it, Eric left for Berlin to meet up with Annaliese the day after Charlotte left, and Paul and Rachel flew to Mexico to meet Rachel's parents the day before New Year's Eve. Chantal was sad to see them all go, and the apartment was agonizingly empty that night. It always was when they left and felt like someone was ripping a bandage off her heart. She wanted to scream in pain at first, but she got used to the dull ache after a while. It especially hurt when they all thanked her for a lovely Christmas, while casually letting her know that they wouldn't be back next year, except for Eric, who never knew his plans until the day before.

She tried not to look depressed when she met Jean-Philippe for lunch the next day. But he saw the pain in her eyes immediately. She told him about the kids' comments, their partners and babies. It was a trend she couldn't fight, and she knew it wouldn't be right to try. They had a right to their own lives. The problem for her was that she didn't have enough of her own, and hadn't for years, except for a brief interlude with Xavier. Jean-Philippe hated to see her so sad about her kids, but he saw the dilemma from both sides. He felt sorry for her. And he didn't think they made enough effort to be with her, especially since she was alone, and always so willing to be there for them, which they didn't seem to notice.

'How were they with Xavier?' he asked as they ordered lunch, wondering if they had given him a hard time. He knew that Charlotte was certainly capable of it, and always hard on her mother.

'They didn't have to be anything,' she said, avoiding his gaze.

'Why not?'

'He wasn't there. We broke up a few weeks ago.' She looked devastated when she said it, and Jean-Philippe was horrified.

'Shit. Why didn't you tell me?'

'I needed some time to get used to the idea, before I could talk about it.'

'What happened? It was going so well every time we talked.'

'I decided to cut my losses before that changed.'

'Excuse me?' He was puzzled.

'Preventive surgery. We went to a party, and he spent the whole evening talking to a beautiful young girl. And I realized that that's what I had to look forward to. That's who he belongs with, not me. I looked like her grandmother, and his. He's a handsome young guy. He doesn't belong with someone my age, and sooner or later he'll figure that out. I decided not to wait.' He knew she had worried about that since the beginning of their relationship.

'What did he say?' Jean-Philippe was crushed for her. He was so sorry to hear it.

'That he loves me, and he doesn't want anyone younger . . . until he does one day. It would kill me. Well, no, not quite,' she corrected. 'But it's an agony I don't want to go through, so I decided to bite the bullet and end it now. There's never a good time. So I did it.'

'And how do you feel now?' He was worried about her.

'Miserable. But it's still the right thing to do. I didn't expect to be happy about it. But it's right.'

'Has he called you?'

'A lot. I'm not calling him back. There's nothing to talk about. I'm done, and I mean it. I don't want to see him or talk to him. He has to move on.'

'And you?' Jean-Philippe saw the profound sadness in her eyes and hated it for her.

'I don't have to do anything. I just sit here. I'll write, see my kids when I can. There's nothing to expect now, except seeing them less and less as they establish their own families and lives. That's the way life works with kids these ages who don't live in the same town.' She accepted it. She had no choice, and as her friend, Jean-Philippe detested what it did to her life. It was no one's fault, but he knew it was heartbreaking for her, and if she had no man in her life and no life of her own other than work, it would only get worse over time, and she knew it too.

'You can't just end it that way with him. If he says he loves you, and you love him, why can't you give it a chance?'

'Because it will hurt too much one day when I lose him. And I will.'

'He could lose you first. You might fall in love with someone else before he does.' But that wasn't her style, and they both knew it. She was a faithful, loyal, loving woman. But Jean-Philippe had a feeling Xavier was the same way. He hated to see her give that up, out of fear of something that might never happen.

'Trust me. I know I'm right.'

'I don't think so.' He disagreed with her, which was rare, but when he did, he said so. But she refused to follow his advice about Xavier. She was convinced she knew better.

'What are you doing tonight?' she asked him, to change the subject. It was New Year's Eve.

'Staying home with the kids. I'm going back to

Beijing next week. I want to spend every minute I can with Valerie and the children. And you? Any plans tonight?' But he could guess the answer to his question before he asked, given the rest.

'Bed at nine P.M.' She smiled at her friend. 'Or earlier. I hate New Year's Eve.'

'So do I,' he agreed, but he wished she had something happier planned than going to bed alone. These had not been easy holidays for her, and she had put a good face on it for her children so they wouldn't know how sad she was about Xavier. Only Eric had guessed and was sorry for her.

When they parted outside the restaurant, Jean-Philippe promised to call and try to see her again before he went back to Beijing. And he was desperately upset for her about Xavier.

★   ★   ★

Benedetta went to London with Dharam for New Year's Eve. He flew in from Delhi the day before on his plane, and stopped to pick her up in Milan. He had taken his usual suite at Claridge's, he made a reservation for them at Harry's Bar for dinner, which was their favorite restaurant, and they'd been invited to a party by friends in Knightsbridge, but they didn't stay long. They were anxious to be alone, and at the stroke of midnight, he put his arms around her and kissed her, and then they went back to the hotel and went to bed.

On New Year's Day, they had brunch, and

took a brisk walk in Hyde Park. She was wearing the beautiful bracelet he'd given her, which hadn't been off her arm since she received it. And that afternoon, they lay in bed at the hotel and watched movies, and made love several times. It was not by any means the way she had expected to spend New Year's six or seven months before. She had been sure she would be married to Gregorio, no matter how badly he behaved. And Dharam had fallen out of the sky like a miracle, or one of Xavier's magical Chinese lanterns in reverse.

'Happy?' he asked her as she looked up at him with a broad grin.

'Totally,' she answered as she reached up to kiss him.

'Excellent,' he said, beaming. It was the perfect way to start the New Year.

★ ★ ★

Gregorio and Anya were spending the New Year holiday in Courchevel. He preferred Cortina, in the Italian Alps, but Courchevel was perfect for her. It had been taken over by Russians, and even some of the street signs were in Russian now. Menus in restaurants, salesgirls in shops were Russian, and all of Anya's fellow Russian models were there, and a flock of Russian men. Some with their families, and others with their mistresses stashed away in other hotels so the two groups never met. Several of the men were rough and disreputable-looking, although they had a lot of money to spend. The fancier Russian men were in houses they had rented. And Gregorio knew she'd enjoy being with her countrymen.

They brought the baby and the nanny with them, and Gregorio went for long walks every day, with Claudia in a baby pack strapped to his chest where he could see her and talk to her and make her giggle. He let the nanny go skiing because he preferred taking care of the baby himself, except at night, when he and Anya went to the local restaurants. He liked showing her off, and he was thrilled to have a vacation with her. She'd been traveling a lot, and her career was booming again. She had hardly been in Milan since September. And he didn't complain, she was still getting over the trauma of the twins' birth, and he thought she'd settle down eventually. And she seemed happy to be in Courchevel with him. She went skiing every day with her Russian friends while he stayed with the baby.

He bought her a red mink coat at Dior on New Year's Eve, and she wore it proudly after she came back from the slopes, and that night she put it on over a black miniskirt with a see-through top, and tall suede high-heeled boots that reached her thighs when they went to dinner. She was a spectacular-looking girl, and the twins had done nothing to damage her figure, possibly because they had been born so prematurely and were so small. She was more beautiful than ever, and Gregorio was proud to be with her.

She had been on the cover of several

magazines that month, and had just been booked for a shoot in Japan. It made him feel sexy and young to be with her, although his family still refused to see her. His sisters-in-law disapproved of her, and he was sure his brothers were jealous of him, whether they admitted it or not. But being with her fed Gregorio's ego.

Their relationship was not as close or as warm as it had been right after their babies' birth, for those harrowing three months, but he was still happy to see her when she came home to Milan, and she seemed pleased to see him. They got along better when he took her out, although his social life in Milan was greatly diminished and the invitations he got never included her. They'd had none for New Year's Eve, which was why he had brought her to Courchevel, so she could hang out with the people she knew there to her heart's content.

On New Year's Eve he suggested they spend a cozy night in their suite having a romantic dinner, since all the restaurants would be crowded. Anya was disappointed, and said they had been invited to several parties, all by people he didn't know.

'Your friends only speak Russian,' he pointed out to her. And then he suggested she go out after midnight. That way they could have a nice evening together, and see the New Year in. He had given the nanny the night off, so he would stay home with the baby. Anya seemed mollified by the idea, and she was wearing a fabulous red evening gown that clung to her when she sat down to dinner with him in the suite. He had ordered caviar and champagne and lobster. They had a feast, while Claudia slept peacefully in her bassinette next to them. Anya glanced at her occasionally, as though she were mystified by how she'd gotten there. The whole experience of motherhood still seemed unreal to her, and now that she was traveling so much, she had had no time to bond with her child at all.

Gregorio noticed Anya staring at the baby, and smiled. 'She's like a little doll, isn't she?' She was tiny, but she was lively when she was awake and lavished smiles on her father. At six months, she still seemed hardly bigger than a newborn.

They kissed at midnight, and Gregorio wanted to make love to her, but by then Anya was anxious to meet up with her friends, and promised to come home early. And twenty minutes later, he found himself alone in the suite with their sleeping baby. It wasn't the New Year's Eve he had dreamed of, but the one he got with a twenty-four-year-old girlfriend, and he still believed it was worth it.

He watched a movie on TV and then went to bed after rolling the bassinette into their bedroom, and fell asleep instantly. He felt Anya climb into bed next to him at three A.M., and he curled up next to her, wanting to make love to her, but she was already sound asleep before he could arouse her. And he suspected she'd had a lot to drink with her friends.

Anya was already up and dressed when the baby woke him the next day. He took her to the nanny to change and feed and was startled to see Anya looking serious and drinking coffee.

'You're up early,' he said, as he bent to kiss her. 'Happy New Year, by the way. How was last night?' He sat down at the breakfast table with her in his robe and poured himself a cup of coffee, as he noticed that she was wearing slacks and high-heeled boots and not ski clothes. 'Are you going somewhere?' He was confused.

'I'm leaving,' she said in a low voice and didn't look at him when she said it.

'To go home?' They'd been planning to stay for a few more days. And then she raised her eyes to his.

'I'm going to London with Mischa Gorgovich.' He knew the name. He had made a fortune in finance in London.

'Why are you going with him?' Gregorio didn't understand what she was saying.

'I'm going on his plane,' she said quietly, without answering his question. 'He invited me.'

'Does he know about me and the baby?' Gregorio looked worried. Anya's eyes filled with tears then. She wasn't heartless. Her heart just didn't belong to him or the baby, or anyone for now.

'I can't do this . . . you . . . the baby. It was different in the hospital. It all seemed so real then. Now it doesn't. I don't know what to do with her, or how to take care of her. She screams every time I touch her, and all you want to do is be with her. We had fun in the beginning, before the twins. Now you don't want to go anywhere or do anything except take care of the baby. I'm not ready to be a mother yet. I thought I was, but I'm not. I feel like I can't breathe when I'm

298

with her, or with you. And I want to go to London with Mischa.' It was all about her now, not about him or the baby.

'You're leaving me?' He was shocked as he stared at her, unable to believe what she had said. 'Are you coming back?' He still didn't understand what she was saying and didn't want to. He had given up so much for her that what she was saying was inconceivable to him. She shook her head in answer to his question.

'I hate Milan, and I can't work there because of your ex-wife.'

'What about us, and Claudia?'

'I think you should keep her. I can't.' She was being truthful with him, but she had the grace to appear embarrassed as she said it, and then stood and went into the bedroom to pack her suitcase. He followed her with an expression of disbelief as she put things in her valise.

'That's it? You just walk out on us and go off with someone else?' She didn't answer and just kept packing until she finished, put her bags on the floor, and turned to look at him as she put on the red mink coat he had given her the day before.

'I'm sorry,' she said. 'I loved you in the hospital, but it was like being in prison, or on a desert island.' She didn't love him once she was back in the world that seduced her so easily. And staring at her, and seeing her, he knew he didn't love her either. He loved what she could have been, but not who she really was. And he knew now that the only woman he had ever loved was Benedetta.

'Do you want to see the baby before you go?' he asked in a gruff voice, and she shook her head, and then called the front desk for a bellman for her bags.

It was strange and brief and bloodless when she left. She gazed at Gregorio from the doorway and told him again that she was sorry, and he didn't try to stop her. He knew he couldn't. He couldn't compete with Mischa Gorgovich and didn't want to.

'Claudia is better with you,' she said, and he nodded, grateful that she didn't want to take their daughter with her. It would have killed him if she had. And then without another word, she closed the door behind her, as Gregorio stood staring at it, and sat down heavily in a chair. The insanity was over.

He flew back to Milan that afternoon with Claudia and the nanny, and walked around the apartment he had shared with Anya for a few months. There were closets full of her clothes, and a safe full of the jewelry he had bought her. She hadn't taken it to Courchevel, and he wondered if she would contact him to have it sent to London, and assumed she would.

He waited two days before he contacted Benedetta. He sent her an email, several text messages, and a number of voicemails, and she answered none of them. He finally called her assistant and asked for an appointment. Her assistant said she would get back to him after she spoke to Mrs. Mariani, and he was sure now that he wouldn't hear from her, but her assistant called him the next day. He thought it was a hopeful sign.

'Mrs. Mariani will see you at nine o'clock tomorrow morning,' she said in a dry voice. 'She has a meeting at nine-forty-five, so she can't stay longer than that,' she announced precisely.

'That's fine. I won't take up too much of her time. Please thank her for according me the meeting,' he said politely.

'I will,' the secretary said, and hung up.

He arrived promptly at her office the next day, which gave him a strange feeling since his own had been just down the hall, in another lifetime. He tried not to think of it as he walked into her office in an impeccably tailored dark gray suit, with a white shirt and navy tie.

Benedetta noticed that he was as handsome as ever as he walked in and looked at her with his smoldering eyes that used to melt her. They no longer did. There was a time when she would have dissolved at his feet. But she was relieved to feel that he did nothing to her now. Those days were gone. She sat down behind her desk and motioned to a chair across from her.

'Thank you for seeing me,' he said soberly. They had not laid eyes on each other since July when he had come to tell her that he was leaving her for Anya, and she responded by wanting a divorce. It had been almost six months, and everything had changed. But he told himself that they were the same people, and had loved each other for a long time. This wasn't an affair like Anya, which had been fireworks for five minutes and burned itself out. The only thing that had prolonged it and made

301

it more serious was the twins.

'It seems ridiculous for us to avoid each other now that you've moved back here,' Benedetta said coolly. 'This town is very small. We don't need to hide. I understand you're working with your brothers now.' She had the good taste not to mention Anya or the child.

'It's a big change,' he said quietly. 'They run an antiquated business, as you know.'

'But it works.' She smiled at him. He had the feeling he was looking at a stranger, not the woman who had been his wife. He noticed too that she was thinner and had done something different to her hair, and she was wearing an enormous Indian diamond bangle that had a lot of style. He liked it and wondered if it was real and where she got it. She didn't usually buy pieces like that, and was given more to traditional jewelry. She and Miuccia Prada were known to have the most beautiful jewelry in Milan.

'You look well, Benedetta,' he began cautiously.

'Thank you, so do you,' she said politely.

'I don't know where to begin. I came here today to ask you something, and tell you something too. I want to tell you how sorry I am for what happened. I was a fool, and I put you in a terrible situation. A bad situation that got completely out of hand.' She nodded agreement and wondered if he had really come just to apologize and beg her forgiveness. If so, he was a better man than she thought, not that it mattered now. 'I really didn't know what to do once the babies were born.' She nodded again and looked pained. It was not a happy memory for her.

'We don't have to go through all that, Gregorio. We both know what happened and why.' He agreed with a remorseful look, and knew he was getting in deep waters.

'I just want you to know how bad I feel about it, and that I know how wrong I was. I can assure you nothing like it will ever happen again.'

'I hope not,' she said sternly, 'for the sake of whatever woman you're with. No one deserves to go through that.' It had been hell for her, and for him too, but he had signed on for it, she hadn't. 'Thank you for apologizing.' She glanced at her watch then. She only had twenty minutes left, and he hesitated for an instant.

'I want to ask you humbly, and with my deepest apology, if you would come back to me, Benedetta, if we could try again. We threw away twenty years.' He had tears in his eyes when he said it, and Benedetta's eyes were hard as she gazed at him in disbelief at what she'd heard.

'I didn't throw them away. You did. When you had the affair with her. And all the others. And you told me you were leaving me for her. I only asked for the divorce then. I wouldn't have otherwise,' she reminded him.

'She's gone. She's not coming back. And I don't want her to. It was momentary madness on my part.' Like so many others, she thought, but she didn't say it. 'I will have full custody of the child, she doesn't want her, and I do. She's a wonderful baby.' He smiled when he talked about her, and for an instant Benedetta was touched, but not by the rest. Clearly he cared about his daughter, but he had made a mockery of their marriage for twenty years, and she had put up with it. She no longer wanted to. And she was in love with Dharam now, genuinely and fully. Not Gregorio. He had missed the boat. At last.

'I can't,' Benedetta said sincerely, as she looked across the desk at him, and she wasn't even angry suddenly. She felt nothing for him except pity. He had run off with someone else, had babies with her, and when she dumped him, he wanted to come back. Benedetta had read the tabloid stories too, as had the entire world. Anya was making a spectacle of herself in London with Gorgovich and said it was over with Gregorio.

'Why not?' he asked Benedetta. He didn't even ask if there was someone else. It never even occurred to him, but she wouldn't have told him if he had. It was none of his business. 'We have loved each other for more than twenty years.'

'I don't love you anymore, not like that. I'm sorry about what happened, for both of us. A lot of people got hurt, not just us — our families, people who believed in us, people who lost their jobs when I had to restructure the business. And most of all the two of us, maybe even your child. But I can't do it again. I believed in you for all those years. I trusted you to do the right thing in the end. I don't anymore. I could never trust you again. And there can't be love without trust.'

'I learned my lesson. It was a harsh lesson for me too.'

'I hope you did. And so did I.' She stood up then, she had heard enough. 'Thank you for the offer, it means a lot to me,' she said sadly, 'but I can't do it again.' He looked shocked, as though he had been sure he could convince her to try again, but he couldn't. Even if Dharam didn't exist, she would never have gone back to him.

Gregorio sat staring at her for a long moment and then stood up.

'Will you think about it?' She shook her head in answer.

'I would be lying to you if I said I thought I could do it. I can't. And I never lied to you, Gregorio. Never.' She couldn't say the same for him, and he knew it too. He had woken up too late. Way too late.

He stood up, put his head down for a moment and then walked to the door, and then he turned to glance at her with his smoldering brown eyes. 'I will always love you, Benedetta,' he said dramatically, and she didn't believe him. She wasn't sure he ever had, or was capable of it. And now he was saying it to get what he wanted. He was desperate to come in out of the storm and bring his baby with him. And she was sure he wanted to come back to their business. He was trying to turn the clock back and break her heart again. He started to walk out of her office and then stopped to gaze at her. 'Call me if you change your mind,' he said, and she shook her head and smiled at him.

'I won't,' she said firmly, and with that, he closed the door behind him, and walked down the hall of what had once been his business, as he wondered what to do next. Plan A had failed.

And in her office, Benedetta was thinking about him, and didn't feel anything at all.

19

The night before Jean-Philippe went back to Beijing, he and Valerie had a quiet dinner with the children in the kitchen. He gave them their bath afterward, read them stories, cuddled with them on their beds, and tucked them in. He missed that so much when he was in Beijing. And Skype just wasn't the same as holding and loving them. He was sad when he got back to their bedroom, and talked to Valerie for a long time. She was coming to Beijing herself in a few weeks, to run the shoot for *Vogue* for the April issue. She had everything organized and the photographers and models booked. Her assistant had helped her pull the clothes, and she was taking it all with her, and two assistants. And they were hiring ten of the models she had seen in Beijing. It was going to be fabulous, and he was going to stay at the hotel with her again. She'd be busy most of the time, but at least he'd see her late at night. And then he'd be back to Paris for a week in February. She looked strangely calm about his leaving this time, which worried him. He hadn't completely forgotten his concerns about her getting involved with another man while he was away.

'I have something to tell you,' she said as they lay on their bed. His bags were already packed. 'I talked to my editor. They're interested in China now. They would accept my being a contributing

307

editor there for a year. Not forever, but for a year. The editor-in-chief isn't going to make any moves about her own job till then. They're going to let me go to Beijing, starting in June. And if I still want the job as editor-in-chief, I'd have to come back. But if I do it, that would give us a year together there. By then, you'll have been there almost two years, and you could come back. But I can spend a year there with you with the children, starting in June. I might even be able to continue my consulting job. They're more and more interested in the Asian market, and they want me to scout locations for a store. I could be their point man there while I'm in Beijing. What do you think?' He was stunned into silence for a minute and then held her tight.

'I think you are amazing. I never expected you to do something like that. And I saw how wrong I was to pressure you once I got there. Are you sure you want to do it? It's not a great place to live.' She hadn't met a single person who had told her they loved it, and many who didn't, but she could do it for a limited amount of time, and it was an interesting opportunity for her too.

'I can do it under these circumstances,' she said, and he could see she meant it. She was a brave woman, and a strong one, especially to make the move with three very young kids.

'Oh, my God, Valerie. How do I ever thank you for something like this?'

'Come back to Paris when your two years are up. Don't reenlist,' she said seriously.

'I won't. I promise.' But he was already on the trail of some very major deals that would be profitable for him, and she could understand that better now that she had been there, and she still had a lot to learn about it. But she thought it would be fascinating to work there for a year. 'I have to get a bigger apartment,' he said immediately. And a better one, in one of the nicer areas where foreigners lived.

He could hardly sleep that night, what she had told him was so exciting. They had found a compromise that worked for both of them. She had done it. And he knew that what she had negotiated would save their marriage. It was the greatest gift she could ever give him, and he bounded out of bed the next morning, ready to conquer the world, excited to go back to China, and more in love than ever with his wife. She was smiling at him as he dressed after his shower.

'I love you, you're a fantastic woman,' he said, and kissed her, and she laughed.

'As they say where I come from,' she said in English, 'you're not so bad yourself.'

★ ★ ★

Before Jean-Philippe left, he called Chantal from the airport to tell her the good news about Valerie and the children coming to Beijing. She was stunned, impressed by his wife, and happy for him that it was working out. She sounded terrible when she congratulated him. She said she had the flu, and he told her to take care of herself and then got off.

Chantal had caught a rotten cold and stayed in bed for a week. It turned into bronchitis and a

309

sinus infection, and she was miserable. She finished her script about the concentration camp, finally, but she felt too lousy to go out for nearly two weeks, and she was living on whatever she found in her kitchen cupboards. She didn't care, she wasn't hungry, and she'd been depressed for a month. She still missed Xavier terribly, but was more certain than ever that she had done the right thing.

It had been raining for days and it turned into snow and sleet the day she finally went to the grocery store and the pharmacy, for the antibiotics her doctor had called in. She bundled up in an old duffle coat and a wool beanie, and she was soaking wet by the time she got to the market, and then the pharmacy, and she trudged home with a bag of groceries, her head down in the wind, wondering if her flu would turn into pneumonia. She felt like Mimi in *La Bohème* as she had a coughing spell and walked into someone at the crosswalk, not looking where she was going. It was a man with a woman next to him. She collided with him, glanced up, and gasped when she saw it was Xavier, and she knew just how bad she looked. Her nose was red, her lips were chapped, her eyes were watery. She was deathly pale and had a coughing spell as soon as she saw him, and nearly strangled when she saw the girl he was with. She was a waiflike blonde who couldn't have been over nineteen years old. He had gone from one extreme to the other, predictably, she thought.

'Are you all right?' he asked, catching her by the elbow before she fell. And the irony of it was hideous. The girl was wearing almost the same outfit as Chantal, only she looked adorable and Chantal felt like Methuselah's grandmother, and she couldn't stop coughing.

'I'm fine,' she managed to choke out, 'I have a cold. Don't get near me, you'll catch it.' She smiled at the girl, who was uninterested and waited for Xavier to move on. The weather was so awful, with sleet coming down in sheets, that none of them could stand there long, but he was worried about Chantal. He could see how sick she was.

'You should go home,' he urged her, while she assumed he just wanted to get her away from his fourteen-year-old girlfriend. It was a Saturday, and they were obviously spending the weekend together since it was still early. 'How've you been?' he asked before they all ran off to escape the weather.

'Great,' she said, which was unconvincing given how sick she was. 'Happy New Year,' which the French always wished each other until the end of January, ad nauseam, and then she waved to both of them and scampered across the street with her grocery bag and package from the pharmacy. It had been a shock to see him, and she was still feeling shaken when she got home and took off her wet coat and her boots. Her feet were wet too, and she put on another sweater, made herself a cup of tea, and took the antibiotic before doing anything else. Then she sat down, replaying the scene in her mind of running into Xavier and his beautiful new girlfriend. She hated the fact that she herself looked so bad.

Couldn't the fates have been a little kinder when they slated them to meet that morning? She was sure it was a sign to prove her right and show her she had done the correct thing by breaking up with him.

She wrapped herself in a cashmere blanket and went back to bed still in her jeans and sweater, and put on warmer socks, while wondering if the flu was going to kill her, or maybe she'd just die of a broken heart. People in the eighteenth century had done that, and she wondered how. She just felt like shit and looked worse, but she didn't seem to be dying. She just felt like it. And when the downstairs bell rang half an hour later, she ignored it. She didn't get mail on Saturdays, and if it was a registered letter from some credit card company, she didn't want it. She had all the credit cards she needed, and whoever it was was sitting on the bell and wouldn't let up. Grumbling, she got out of bed and went to the intercom in the hall and asked who it was.

'It's me, Xavier!' he shouted into the intercom against the wind, and she groaned. 'I'm soaking wet. Can I come up?'

'No . . . why?'

'I need to talk to you.' She wondered if his girlfriend was with him, but she didn't want to ask.

'What about?' She negotiated through the intercom, and she could hear the wind howling outside.

'I'm pregnant. You can't abandon me like this.' He sounded desperate, and she burst out laughing. She shook her head and pressed the buzzer to let him in. She heard him shout thank you, he knew the door code to the second door, and a minute later she heard the elevator and her doorbell, and she let him in. Water was running down his face in rivers, and his wool cap was soaking wet. There were pools of water in the hall where he was standing, as he looked at her. 'Thanks for letting me in.' They walked into the kitchen, and she handed him a towel and put the kettle on for tea. She still had the kind he liked, and she made him a cup without asking, as they both sat down at the kitchen table.

'Your girlfriend is very pretty,' she said as they both sipped the tea, and he set his down.

'She's not my girlfriend. She's my nephew's new girlfriend, and I promised to help her with her law school exams. I knew you'd think that when I saw you.'

'What am I supposed to think on a Saturday morning? Not that it's any of my business.' She tried to sound nonchalant about it, but she wasn't. And she gave a hideous hacking cough as he watched her intently.

'Look, Chantal, I love you. I have just spent the most miserable month of my life since you dumped me. You ruined my holidays. I can't live without you. I don't want a younger woman, or any other woman. I want you. Can you possibly try to understand that? What the hell are we doing? You look like shit, and you sound like you're dying. I can't think straight. I've never been as happy with any other woman as I am with you. Can't we please give this another

313

chance before you die of consumption in your garret, and I throw myself into the Seine?' She was smiling at him in spite of herself. They had a good time together. She had tried to forget that, but it was still true.

'You're very dramatic,' she commented.

'I'm very dramatic? I talked to a redhead for half an hour, and you dumped me. How dramatic is that?'

'It seemed appropriate at the time,' she said primly, as she gave them each a refill of tea and noticed that it was snowing harder outside.

'It was not appropriate. It was insane. But I swear, I will never talk to another redhead at a party, no woman under ninety, and you can blindfold me anytime we go out. Come on, Chantal, give us a chance.' He looked at her pleadingly, and she smiled at him. There was no escaping him. She loved him, and he was too good to be true.

'You screwed up my wish,' she said reproachfully, thinking of the lantern at the White Dinner.

'I screwed up *your* wish? You threw me out! May I remind you that you packed up all my stuff in a suitcase and dumped me? How friendly is that?'

'I was upset.'

'Yeah, me too. The bag is still packed, by the way. I cried every time I started to unpack it, so I didn't. And Merry Christmas to you too. Your timing sucked.'

'I'm sorry.' She looked remorseful and gazed at him tenderly. 'I'd kiss you, but you'd probably die from whatever I've got.'

314

'I don't care,' he said, and kissed her so hard he took her breath away. 'There. Now we can die together.'

'I just took an antibiotic. I might survive.' She was smiling at him, and he smiled as if he had just won the lottery. He kissed her several times and then followed her into her bedroom, and she patted the bed next to her, and he climbed in. They pulled up the covers like two kids with their clothes on, and snuggled beneath the comforter, as the snow fell and covered the rooftops, and they talked all day, made dinner together, and fell asleep in each other's arms that night. And when they woke up in the morning, with the city covered in snow, he glanced around the room as though he were lost.

'Did I die and go to heaven?' he said, looking at her, and she grinned.

'No, I did,' she confirmed.

'You couldn't have,' he said, smiling at her. 'You took an antibiotic yesterday, so you can't be dead. Want to go out and play in the snow?' She nodded, and a little while later they went out and made snowballs and threw them at each other. They came back drenched from the snowballs, their hair wet and matted to their heads, with snow on their eyelashes, and they laughed till they almost fell down.

They peeled their coats off when they got back to her apartment, and she frowned at him.

'We need to take a hot bath or we'll both get sick, and I'll get sicker. Trust me, I'm a mother, I know these things.'

'If you say so,' he said, as she ran a bath, and

315

they both took their clothes off and climbed in. They lay in the tub smiling and talking to each other, and then he kissed her, and it all began again.

20

Dharam came to Milan to see Benedetta's show during Fashion Week in February. It was only her second one since she had streamlined the business, and she had invited him to be there, since Dharam had never been to Fashion Week before. She had warned him that it was always wild and frenetic, with a thousand things going on, and she would be busy, but it was an important part of her life, and she wanted him to come. She had reserved one of the best seats in the house for him, and he stayed in the background for the entire week, not wanting to distract her, but wanting to be there for her.

He was staying at her apartment, and working from his computer every day while she was at her office, and she let him come to some of the fittings and for a brief glimpse backstage before the show, and then he took his seat, with all the important people in fashion seated all around him. Magazine editors, stylists, buyers from all over the world, hundreds of press were confined at one end of the room. The lights went down, the music came on, and the show started, with the models rolling out onto the runway like gumballs out of a machine. Backstage Benedetta gave each one the signal to go, checking them for a last time before they did.

The show was a major hit, and afterward they went to parties, met other designers, talked to

317

buyers, and charmed all the editors. The photographers got lots of shots of Benedetta with Dharam. They were the hot news in Milan by the end of Fashion Week, and the show got great reviews.

'Did you have fun?' she asked him when the evening was over, hoping he did.

'I loved it, and I love you.' And that night he gave her the second diamond bangle he had bought her when he got the first one, so she had a pair. They were spectacular, and it was easy to guess who had given them to her, since they were so obviously Indian. And she had used numerous details, colors, and fabrics that she had brought back from India, and other inspirations she had seen while she was there. She had integrated the Indian touches perfectly into the show, in a very subtle way. There was nothing subtle about her bracelets, however, which had caught the attention of the press immediately. Everyone was envious when they saw the two huge diamond bangles on her wrists, and she never took them off.

She told him about Gregorio's visit, and his offer to get back together, and he looked relieved when she said there was no question of it, and it was over for her. At one of the parties, she heard that Gregorio had been out with several models during Fashion Week. Gregorio wasn't wasting any time. He never did.

Benedetta went away with Dharam for a few days to rest and relax before she went back to work. They stayed at Il Pelicano in Argentario, which was a romantic spot on the sea. He was amazed by how hard she had to work every season, and he had huge admiration for how talented she was. Dharam wanted her to go back with him, but she had to start her next collection. She was hoping to visit him again in a few months, and in the meantime they would continue to meet in London or Milan every month. It sounded like an excellent plan to both of them.

He went back to India after their brief holiday, but promised to be back in a few weeks. Their schedules were in perfect harmony now, and all her worrying about it had been in vain.

'Happy?' he asked her as they snuggled in bed the night before he left.

'Always, with you.' She smiled sleepily, and he kissed her, as she looked up at him, thinking how lucky she was. He was the nicest man in the world, and it seemed like a miracle that they had found each other.

★   ★   ★

It was two months after they'd gotten back together, and Chantal and Xavier were sound asleep at three-forty A.M. when the phone rang. He heard it first and prodded her. He knew the drill now. She answered all calls at all hours, just in case something had happened to one of her kids. He handed her the phone off the charger, and she looked instantly worried, fearing another accident to one of them.

'Yes?' She listened for a long time. He watched her, wondering what had happened. He was beginning to think like her, and he couldn't tell what was going on from the questions she asked. 'At what time? . . . How does she feel? How far apart now? . . . Call me later and tell me how it's going.' And then she smiled at him when she hung up. 'It was Paul. Rachel is in labor.' They went back to sleep, and the phone rang again three hours later. Paul said she was almost ready to push, and the midwife didn't like the sound of the baby's heartbeat. They were going to the hospital by ambulance, and Rachel might need a cesarean. Paul was beside himself with fear for her and the baby. Chantal tried to calm him down, and then hung up.

'Why do I feel like we run an emergency hotline?' Xavier asked her as they both gave up the idea of going back to sleep. She hoped that Rachel and the baby would be all right. She had told them from the beginning that she thought they were crazy to do it at home.

Twenty minutes later they called from Cedars Sinai, and the contractions had picked up, and the baby's heartbeat was regular again.

'Sensible kid, he wanted to be born in a hospital,' she said to Xavier, and he laughed.

'I don't need children. I can live it all vicariously through yours.' The week before, Eric had called them when Annaliese's brother had been arrested on a DUI, and Eric wanted his mother's advice about what he should do about it, bail him out, or leave him there to teach him a lesson. He was eighteen and a student. Her advice had been to leave him in jail to sober up and pick him up in the morning, which was what they'd done. And now Paul was waiting for Rachel to deliver their little prince. Rachel's mother had arrived at the hospital by then and was driving Paul and the doctors crazy. She wanted to be in the delivery room, and Rachel didn't want her there. Listening to her son, she was very happy she was in Paris, and not another annoyance for them in L.A.

After the last report, they didn't hear for another three hours, and Chantal guessed that Rachel was pushing, and hoped that it was going well and nothing traumatic had happened. She didn't want to call and ask what was going on, and they probably wouldn't have answered anyway.

It was nine-thirty in the morning when they got a text from Paul. 'No go. C-section in ten minutes. Poor Rache.' Chantal felt sorry for her, and finally, an hour and a half later, at eleven, which was two A.M. in California, Paul called her sounding euphoric. They had a nine-pound, four-ounce baby boy and were naming him Dashiell. Dash for short. He told her everything had gone fine at the C-section, although Rachel was exhausted, the baby had been too big. Chantal didn't point out what a disaster it would have been if they'd had him at home. The water birth idea had fallen by the wayside with the first real pains. They were sewing Rachel up when Paul called.

'When are you coming to see him, Mom?' he asked her, but she'd already considered that. She didn't want to be an intrusive mother, they already had one of those. She was going to see

Dash at Charlotte's wedding, when he was two months old, not when Rachel was exhausted, trying to figure out how to nurse, and they were all frantically adjusting to a new baby. For once, she was not going to drop everything and run. The baby was healthy, and she didn't feel she needed to go. She had her own life to lead. She was happy for Paul about their baby, if that was what he and Rachel wanted, and it seemed to be. And she was sure he'd be a good father. He was a kind, responsible person, and he loved Rachel.

After she hung up, Chantal turned to Xavier, and told him all the details, how big the baby was, how Rachel was feeling, everything Paul had said, and how happy he sounded.

'You realize what this means now, though, don't you?' she asked him with a shell-shocked expression.

'What? They're going to call you every night for breast-feeding advice?' he asked, looking worried.

'No, she'll call her mother, who is an authority on everything.' Chantal wasn't crazy about her. 'It means you are now sleeping with a grandmother.' She seemed embarrassed and grinned at him, and he laughed.

'Does that make me a grandfather by proxy?'

'If you want to be.' She smiled at him, as they lay in bed together.

'I think I like that idea,' he said, vastly amused. And she was trying to adjust to the idea that she had a grandson now. It was shocking.

★ ★ ★

In April, Xavier moved out of his apartment. They both agreed, it no longer made sense for him to be paying rent on an apartment he never used.

'Unless you throw me out again,' he said cautiously when they discussed it. 'I haven't talked to a redhead since Christmas,' he reminded her, and she laughed.

'I think you're safe.'

He got rid of most of his furniture, which he didn't like anyway. She cleared a closet for him, and he moved his belongings in, and she let all three of her children know. She could almost hear an audible gulp when she told them, but only Eric, who was delighted, made any comment.

They went to the Cannes Film Festival in May, where they were showing one of her films, and it was very exciting. They had dinner with her producer and two major movie stars, and Xavier was duly impressed, and thrilled to be there with her. She won an award, which she didn't expect. And they stayed at the Hôtel du Cap in Cap d'Antibes, in incredible luxury, and had rooms in the lower portion on the water, called the Eden Roc. Xavier had heard about it for years, but never been there till he went with her. She stayed there every year when she went to the festival. And he was incredibly proud to be with her, and totally indifferent to the masses of starlets who fought to attend on some man's arm. And there were many famous actors, actresses, producers, and directors. It was a fascinating event, and they had fun at the hotel, and stayed for two days after. One of his clients had presented at the festival as well.

He had taken time off from work to attend, and two weeks later took another week to fly to Hong Kong with her for Charlotte's wedding. Chantal had been organizing it from a distance for months, but they also had a wedding planner, and Charlotte had handled many of the details herself.

Everything was in order when they got there. They stayed at the Peninsula Hotel, and Chantal finally got to meet her grandson, whom she had seen on Skype almost daily for the past two months, so much so that he recognized her voice and smiled as soon as he saw her. She was surprised by how moved she was when she held him. Xavier took a million photographs of her when she did.

'Is this so you can tease me later about being a grandmother?' she asked him, as he took more pictures from another angle.

'This is my first time being a grandfather, let me enjoy it!' he said, and she laughed at him.

'You're too young to be a grandfather,' she reminded him, and he looked insulted.

'No, I'm not. Do the math.' He had just turned thirty-nine, and could have had a twenty-year-old child himself.

'In that case, I'd be a great-grandmother. Let's not go down that path.' He laughed at that. And that night when she tried on her dress for the wedding, Xavier frowned at her.

'When did you get that?'

'In Paris when Charlotte was there for

Christmas. She likes it.'

'You must have been depressed. That was after you dumped me. Let's go shopping.'

'Now? Before the wedding?' It was two days away. 'I can't find anything here, at this late date.' She looked panicked. 'Is it that awful?' She stared at herself in the mirror in the navy blue dress with the old-lady bolero and hated it too.

They left the hotel early the next morning like two conspirators, and went to the malls on Victoria Harbour in the hotel's Rolls-Royce, and Xavier was relentless. He was normally not a shopper, but he had decided that this was an emergency, and he treated it like a legal crisis. She explained to him that she couldn't wear white to her daughter's wedding, or any wedding — the bride would kill her, justifiably. He had found a gorgeous white satin dress that fit her perfectly, but it was out of the question. And black was considered rude and seemed too severe. Pink was too girlish, although it was pretty. 'You can wear that to our wedding,' he teased her, 'although I liked the white one.' But she knew he was only joking. They had no need to get married, they were happy living together. She tried on a sad-looking gray dress, but she knew the groom's mother was wearing gray. And there was a spectacular red one, which was too showy for her daughter's wedding. It would seem like she was trying to upstage the bride, and she would have. She looked incredibly sexy in the red satin. And finally at Dior, she tried on a pale blue satin dress the same color as her eyes. It was sexy and yet demure, it was young-looking but not ridiculous, and the color was elegant and subtle, and by some miracle they had pale blue satin shoes to match, and she had brought a silver handbag for the rehearsal dinner.

'Bingo!' he said, beaming at her. It was even the perfect length and needed no alteration, and it fit her like a glove and showed off her youthful figure. And he told her to wear her hair down because he loved it that way. The dress was everything she would have hoped for if she had been in better spirits when she shopped with Charlotte in December. And she had brought a short emerald-green satin Balenciaga dress for the rehearsal dinner that was young and sexy and showed off her legs, with silver high-heeled sandals. The groom's family was giving the rehearsal dinner at the Hong Kong Club, the same place as the wedding, but they liked it and Charlotte had approved. She said the rehearsal was going to be very dressy and traditional, and so was the wedding the next day, in a different suite of rooms.

'Thank you for helping me find a dress,' Chantal said gratefully to Xavier as they rode back to the hotel with the package. It had taken them four hours, but it was well worth it. She loved the dress she was going to wear now. It was elegant but youthful, and it was great on her.

They had fun at the rehearsal dinner that night, in spite of how stuffy it was, and how conservative most of Charlotte and Rupert's friends were. They went dancing with her children at Play afterward, and Chantal danced up a storm with Xavier. Eric was thrilled to have him there, he felt a little lost with the traditional crowd, and Paul was all wrapped up in his baby and Rachel, so Xavier was good company for Eric.

And the next day Chantal helped her daughter dress for the wedding, which was a very special moment, and she had tears in her eyes when the wedding planner handed her her bouquet. Charlotte looked exquisite, like a princess, in the dress Chantal had hand-carried from Paris. Charlotte was surprised when she saw her mother in the pale blue satin dress, wearing her hair the way Xavier had suggested. Charlotte hadn't said a word of objection to him since they had arrived in Hong Kong, and Paul had actually been happy to see him, and was touched by all the photographs he was taking of the baby.

'What happened to the navy-blue dress we got at Nina Ricci?' Charlotte asked as they waited for Paul to come and get her so they could drive to the church. He was giving her away.

'I changed my mind and decided it was a little too serious. It seemed right in Paris last December, but it's a little wintry for May.' She didn't want to tell her that she felt a hundred years old in it and she and Xavier had hated it two days before.

'I like this one,' Charlotte said, smiling at her, as Chantal kissed her and had to fight back tears.

'You're the most beautiful bride I've ever seen,' she told her in a choked voice. Paul showed up then, and the wedding planner and Chantal helped Charlotte manage her train. The bridesmaids were ready in the palest of pink dresses, carrying pale pink roses. And they all got into the limousines the hotel had arranged for them, with Paul and Charlotte in a Rolls, and Chantal and Xavier in a Bentley right behind them, with Eric in the front seat looking handsome in a morning coat. Xavier was wearing a dark suit. Since he wasn't family or officially part of the bridal party, he didn't have to wear a morning coat. And he was very elegant.

Everything went smoothly at the church, and the reception was beautiful, and Chantal felt perfect in her dress.

'Thank you for encouraging me to get rid of the other dress.' She smiled at Xavier as she danced with him. They had a wonderful time at the wedding, and Chantal cried when the bridal couple drove away. She had refrained from trying to catch the bouquet and didn't think it was appropriate. She and Xavier had smiled at each other from across the room as the single women scrambled to catch it. They understood each other perfectly. What they had was enough.

And the next day Paul, Rachel, and Dash flew back to L.A.; Eric got a flight to Frankfurt, where he'd have to transfer for a flight to Berlin; and Chantal and Xavier flew back to Paris. The bride and groom were honeymooning in Bali. They were spread out all over the map again. But with Xavier at her side now, she was no longer alone. Her wish at the White Dinner had come true. She had a man she loved to love her and had a real life with him as a couple. It was exactly what she had wished, and now he was here. And it had happened very quickly, since their romance had begun right after the White Dinner, eleven months before.

21

Jean-Philippe came home to help Valerie pack what they were taking to Beijing. He had rented a furnished apartment, but there were lots of things Valerie wanted to send from home, for them and for the children. She had been packing for a week when he got back to Paris. They had timed it perfectly. The White Dinner was the following week, and they were flying to Beijing after that, with a stop in Hong Kong first so she could shop.

Valerie was taking a lot of research books with her for work. She would be *Vogue*'s contributing editor in Beijing, with occasional trips to Shanghai for them too, for a year. They wanted her back in Paris after that. And she had negotiated a satisfactory arrangement with Beaumont-Sevigny to consult for them in China.

'What are we doing with this?' Jean-Philippe asked her, holding up an enormous teddy bear that Jean-Louis insisted he wanted to take with him.

'Pack it, I guess.' There were mountains of toys, clothes, and books everywhere, and she was glad he had come home to help. She had been exhausted for the past two weeks. He had come back to Paris twice since Christmas, this was his third trip. And Valerie had been in Beijing in January for her shoot for *Vogue*. So they had seen each other regularly since the beginning of the year, but it was going to be wonderful to wake up in bed together every morning again. She had missed that so much in the past nine months.

They took a break from packing to have lunch, and afterward she disappeared for a few minutes. He assumed she was checking her emails or on the phone, and when she reappeared, she looked disoriented for a minute and then sat down on a box of books he had just packed, and she stared at him.

'Is something wrong?'

'I don't know. You tell me. It depends on how you look at it.' He stopped what he was doing and stared at her. Suddenly, he had a sense that a serious problem had come up. She held a test stick up to him. He had seen those before, but not in three years, and he looked shocked. 'I'm pregnant,' she said in a whisper. He had last been home at the beginning of May, and it had occurred to her to check, since she had suddenly realized a few days before that she was more than a week late, and had bought the test. But with the move and so much going on, she hadn't given it any more thought, and as she was packing the contents of her bathroom to ship, she found the test and decided to check. She hadn't thought it would be positive, and had done it as more of a lark. She wasn't prepared for this, not as they were moving to Beijing.

'Are you sure?' he asked, visibly stunned. She held out the test stick to him, and he checked. It was positive. There was no doubt. And he could see their plans for China going up in smoke. There was no way she would be willing to go to China if she was pregnant, and he felt his heart sink.

'Now what are we going to do?' she asked him in a strangled voice.

'What do you want to do?' he asked her, as he sat down on another packing box. 'Should I unpack? This is your decision, Valerie. I'm not going to force you to move to China if you're pregnant.' He was sure now she would want to stay home. And he wasn't sure he liked the idea of her being pregnant in China.

'I don't know.' She thought about it for a minute.

'You could come back and have it here. When would it be due?' She calculated the dates in her head.

'February.' It was a hell of a shock. She hadn't expected to get pregnant. But they had been a little cavalier about it a couple of times when he came home in May. They had been so happy to see each other that they had taken a chance, and figured they'd get away with it. They hadn't. And they had put it out of their heads. Till now.

'You'd have to come home by Christmas if you want to have it here. Is it worth going for six months?' She looked at him and smiled.

'I really wasn't expecting this,' she said thoughtfully, trying to figure it out. This put a serious kink in their plans, a major one.

But he didn't want her pregnant alone in Paris either. It could mean that he'd have to leave the job. There was only so much he could ask of her, and she had been so patient for the nine months since he left. And they'd been so excited about her coming to China. And then she looked at him and laughed.

'This is crazy, isn't it? I find out I'm pregnant while we're packing to leave.'

'It's a good thing you checked. I don't know what we'd have done if we found out once you were there.'

'And what if I had? Women have babies in China all the time. Not as many as we have, but they do.' Most people in China still only had one child, and very rarely two. Now she and Jean-Philippe would have four, which they had always said they wanted, just not now, when they'd be living in Beijing. 'Would it be so unthinkable to have it there? There have to be good doctors in China in the big cities.'

'I don't know anything about medical conditions there, but we can check.' She had had easy pregnancies and deliveries before, and she was remarkably calm about it.

'Chantal said her grandchild was going to be delivered in a water birth at home,' Valerie said, grinning at him, and Jean-Philippe looked horrified.

'Please tell me you're joking.'

'I am,' she said, serious again, and then he sat next to her on the box, and she put her arms around him. 'We're blessed. We're having another baby. We always wanted four.'

'Yes, but not now.' He looked disappointed. He was sure that now she wouldn't come. Their plans for living in Beijing together were about to go out the window again.

'Women have babies all over the world. So can I. I'm not afraid to have a baby there, if you're with me. And as long as we can find a European or American doctor I can talk to, I'd feel fine about it. And there must be at least one in Beijing.' She didn't look worried as she smiled at him and kissed him.

'Are you sure?' She was an incredibly game person, and he loved her more every day. Every time they had a problem, she found a way to solve it, just as she had figured out a way to work there for a year, and hang on to her connection at *Vogue*, without risking her future there, and she had even come up with a consulting job. 'This is a major deal, Valerie. I don't want to take you there pregnant, if you're uncomfortable about it.'

'I think it'll be fine. If I have problems with the pregnancy, I can come home. But why would I? I never have before. And I'd really like to go. I think it will be exciting.'

'It will be wonderful for me if you're there,' he said, looking at her adoringly. 'And I'd rather be with you when you're pregnant, to keep an eye on you.' He knew what she was like. She always did too much. She had left her office to have Damien after a shoot, and almost didn't make it to the hospital on time. And she'd almost had Isabelle at a show during Fashion Week.

'I want to go,' she said firmly, with a determined look in her eye. 'Let's keep packing,' she said, and stood up.

'No! You sit down. I'm not going to China

with you pregnant, unless you're reasonable,' he said sternly.

'Yes, sir,' she said, and he smiled at her and kissed her as the realization that they were having another child washed over them. For a minute, the logistics had almost stopped them, but nothing could stop them now. They were going to China, and their fourth child would be born there. It made it suddenly feel more like home, and they would have a sentimental bond to it forever with a child born in Beijing. She went back to the bathroom to pack the rest of her things to be shipped.

Jean-Philippe walked into the bathroom while she was putting over-the-counter medicines for the children into a box, and she turned when she heard him come in, and stood there facing him. She was the woman he loved and the mother of his children, and he knew he had almost lost her this year, and now they were having another child. It was a blessing beyond measure, for both of them.

'Do you have any idea how much I love you?' he asked her with a lump in his throat. He had been thinking about it while he packed.

'As much as I love you,' she said gently, and slipped into his arms again, as he held her, thinking about their baby inside her, and the happy times ahead of them. He knew he could do anything with her at his side, and she felt the same way about him.

'Thank you, Valerie,' he said and held her tight, as she closed her eyes and smiled.

22

The email came from Jean-Philippe that morning. He had already heard that the first meeting place was at the Palais Royal. It was an interesting location, because it was two blocks from the Louvre, three from the Place de la Concorde, and just as close to the Place Vendôme. So the White Dinner could be in any of several locations. But most alarming was that it had been raining buckets since the night before.

Chantal looked out the window that morning when she got up and told Xavier there was no way the White Dinner was going to happen this year.

'Yes, it will,' he said calmly, as he read the paper before he left for work.

'The weather is never going to clear, not with rain like this.'

'Don't be such a pessimist. Of course it will. It will stop raining before tonight.' He looked totally unconcerned as he put the paper into his briefcase, gave her a kiss, and left. And at regular intervals throughout the day, Chantal glanced out the window in despair and watched the rain come down. If anything, it got steadily worse.

She had already picked her outfit for that night, white slacks and a white sweater, with a white jacket, in case it got chilly. She had cute white shoes. And all their china, silver, and crystal were already in the rolling caddy. Their meal was in the fridge. She had the wine. And the heavens were still dumping everything they had. It looked like a deluge, and she was waiting for Noah's Ark to show up on the Seine. The weather report was for more rain that night. And she had no desire to sit in front of any monument in Paris, no matter how beautiful, romantic, or grandiose, and get drenched while she tried to eat her sopping dinner with Jean-Philippe and their friends. Xavier was crazy if he thought it was going to stop.

She texted him several times that day at the office, and he kept responding that everything would be fine. He had his box of lanterns waiting next to the caddy, and he had devised a system for carrying it like a backpack, so he could still manage their table and chairs.

At four o'clock the sky got darker, almost like the end of the world. There was a clap of thunder, a bolt of lightning, and a few minutes later hailstones were raining down on the roof and bouncing off the windows. It was ridiculous, and the White Dinner appeared to be doomed.

At five, it lightened up a little, and the rain slowed down. And when she glanced out the window at six, a patch of blue sky appeared, and a few minutes later a rainbow streaked across the sky. She stood and stared at it for a minute, and wondered if he was right. Something was happening, and in the next half hour, all the clouds disappeared, the rain stopped, and the sky was blue. Xavier was right. The White Dinner was going to happen, and the magic had begun.

She would never have thought it possible that a sky that had been dark all day, with pouring rain, could turn blue by the end of the day.

Xavier came home from the office at seven with an I-told-you-so grin on his face.

'Okay, okay, I get it. Tonight is special. Apparently God thinks so too.' Jean-Philippe called and told them the first location had been confirmed. They were to meet at the Palais Royal at eight-fifteen. And she and Xavier tried to guess where the dinner would be held. She thought it would be the Place de la Concorde, Xavier guessed the Louvre. When they had asked Jean-Philippe, he said he didn't know, which was most likely true.

They both got dressed then, all in white, and as they were about to leave the apartment at a quarter to eight, Xavier looked at her and smiled.

'A year ago tonight I was going out with friends, to a dinner I'd never been to before, and thought might be boring, so I bought the Chinese lanterns to liven things up. Little did I know I'd find you.' She smiled at him, and they walked out, drove to the area around the Palais Royal, and found a parking space. Chantal rolled her caddy into the gardens, where they saw thousands of people in white congregating, shouting to each other, finding friends, and calling others on their phones to locate them in the crowd.

It took them a few minutes to find Jean-Philippe, who had an arm around Valerie's shoulders, and their friends were standing with

338

them. Jean-Philippe had invited nine couples, as he did every year. It was the same group as the year before, without Gregorio. Benedetta came with Dharam, and they were beaming at each other. He greeted Chantal warmly, remembering that he had been her unofficial date the year before. Most everyone knew Xavier by then, but Chantal introduced him to the few he had never met. They were all talking animatedly, and at eight-forty-five, the announcement came, and Jean-Philippe smiled as he told them the location of the dinner. Xavier had been right, it was the Louvre. They would be seated between the ancient palace that was now a museum, and the two glass pyramids by I. M. Pei. And they would have a spectacular view of the sunset, as night fell. Everyone was excited when they heard the location, and there were rumors that the other location that night was the Trocadero under the Eiffel Tower, but no one knew for sure. They were told that there were eight thousand people in the garden of the Palais Royal, but it didn't look it, as people got moving, and Jean-Philippe's group stayed close to each other, as they crossed two streets and entered the archways of the Louvre and walked through them into the square. And suddenly they were in front of the palace, with the pyramids sparkling in the sunlight. It would be light for another hour, and the sky was as blue as it had been for the last two hours.

All the men unfolded their tables, as they found their designated spots. Jean-Philippe was laughing and in high spirits, as Valerie shook out her tablecloth, and Benedetta and Chantal and the other women in the group unfolded theirs. They had all brought linen napkins, white china, and crystal glasses. Benedetta had brought Buccelatti candelabra, and Chantal had brought some votives, along with the silver candlesticks from her dining table. The ten tables in their group, set down side by side in their numbered spots, looked beautiful, but so did all the others. By nine-fifteen, the tables were set, and by nine-thirty, all eight thousand revelers were seated and pouring wine. And as Chantal looked across the table at him, Xavier was beaming at her.

'I can't believe I'm here with you,' he said only for her ears, and he toasted her with champagne. Dharam had brought caviar for all of them, as he had before. Hors d'oeuvres were passed around. They all set their food out, and the hubbub of laughter and lively conversation could be heard throughout the square, and by the time they began dining in earnest, the sun had set, the candles had been lit, and the square was alight with the glow from four thousand beautifully set tables, and eight thousand good friends enjoying each other's company on a starry night.

'Last year I could only dream of being here with you,' Dharam said to Benedetta, and she smiled at him. The disaster of the year before had become a dim memory, when Gregorio left the table and disappeared. In fact, their marriage had ended that night when the twins were born. And now she was here with Dharam, the kindest man she'd ever known.

340

As he always did, Jean-Philippe walked along their combined tables, making sure that everyone was happy, and he kept coming back to Valerie and kissing her. It was a tender evening for all of them, and by the end of dinner, at eleven, the sparklers were handed out and lit up the whole square, and the band began playing. Benedetta and Dharam were among the first to head to the dance floor, as the others chatted and ate dessert.

And then half an hour later, Xavier took his mysterious box from under the table, opened it, and began handing out paper lanterns, and as he looked at Chantal, he thought of something. 'This is our anniversary, you know. It all started a year ago tonight.' And now they were in love and living together. Xavier kept one lantern aside for her. And one by one he lit the others for their group, the group at a table behind them, and another to the side. And at each of the tables, people were lighting them, and holding the lanterns as they filled with air and grew. And when they were full of warm air and brightly lit, people released them and watched them fly into the night sky. It was as beautiful as it had been before. Chantal watched as Xavier reminded people to wait until the lanterns were full of air, and then make a wish and let them go.

There were dozens of them sailing through the sky, when Xavier turned to her, and beckoned her to come to him, and she stood next to him as she had a year before. They held the frame of the lantern together and watched it fill and stand to its full height of about three feet.

'Make your wish,' he said gently, with his arms around her.

'I already got my wish,' she whispered to him, and he smiled.

'Make another one,' he said softly. 'And I'll make mine.' He didn't tell her that he had had the same wish as she did the year before.

People were dancing in the aisles then and watching the Chinese lanterns, and Chantal and Xavier lifted their lantern high over their heads, and let it go, as it sailed almost straight up and then veered toward the roof of the Louvre to sail over it, and then rise into the Paris sky until it was out of sight. It was just a pinpoint of light when Xavier turned to her and kissed her.

'Thank you for making all my dreams come true,' he said gently. They both agreed that the evening was full of magic and unabashed expressions of love.

'Thank you for the lanterns,' Jean-Philippe said to Xavier. The two men exchanged a smile. They had used them all by then, and they were sailing high overhead as people watched, entranced by the beauty of the sight.

'It's magical,' Dharam said to them as he and Benedetta came to stand with the rest of the group.

'It's always the most exquisite night of my life,' Benedetta said, and she looked straight at him as she said it.

It was always a night of love and friendship, and generosity, in the shadow of the most beautiful monuments of Paris. Jean-Philippe thought he had never seen a better White Dinner than that night, the atmosphere was perfect, and he had been coming for many years.

Conversations were lively, as people drank and smoked and talked among their friends. The music was playing in the background, and some people were dancing. And then at twelve-thirty Jean-Philippe gave the signal to his guests, and each one took out a white plastic bag and began filling it with their refuse. Not a single shred of evidence of their dinner there could remain. There was very little left of dinner, and Jean-Philippe's tables had finished their wine and champagne. All of Dharam's caviar was gone and had been a major hit. Everything about the evening was. Someone asked Jean-Philippe and Valerie when they were leaving for Beijing, and Valerie said in a few days. This was going to be a night to remember Paris by. The next day they were going to a hotel with the children, while the movers packed.

They all hated to leave their tables and the evening, but the witching hour came. Their guests hugged and kissed each other and Valerie and Jean-Philippe, and wished them well in Beijing. They wouldn't have time to see their friends again before they left. Valerie had a thousand things to do, and she had to get the vaccination certificates of her children stamped. She seemed full of energy that night at dinner, and Jean-Philippe never took his eyes off her. And Dharam had stayed close to Benedetta. He had waited to celebrate this moment for a year.

The magic of the White Dinner had happened before, was happening that night, and would

343

happen again. The square had been lit with the glow of eight thousand hearts, thousands of candles, with the lanterns blessing them from above before they disappeared. Chantal and Xavier could feel the magic, as could the others. And they floated out of the square, carrying with them the spirit of the White Dinner. It had been once again a night of magic in an extraordinary setting.

'Ready to go home?' Xavier asked her gently, and Chantal nodded with a smile, and then followed him to the car, after they said goodbye to their friends. She looked into the sky one last time to make sure her lantern was still there somewhere, carrying her wish up to the stars. But it was already there.

Books by Danielle Steel
Published by Ulverscroft:

SUMMER'S END
THE PROMISE
SEASON OF PASSION
LOVING
TO LOVE AGAIN
THE RING
REMEMBRANCE
A PERFECT STRANGER
NOW AND FOREVER
GOLDEN MOMENTS
CROSSINGS
ONCE IN A LIFETIME
CHANGES
THURSTON HOUSE
GOING HOME
FULL CIRCLE
DADDY
STAR
MESSAGE FROM NAM
HEARTBEAT
NO GREATER LOVE
JEWELS
MIXED BLESSINGS
WINGS
THE GHOST
THE RANCH
LIGHTNING
MALICE

We do hope that you have enjoyed reading this large print book.

Did you know that all of our titles are available for purchase?

We publish a wide range of high quality large print books including:
Romances, Mysteries, Classics
General Fiction
Non Fiction and Westerns

Special interest titles available in large print are:
The Little Oxford Dictionary
Music Book
Song Book
Hymn Book
Service Book

Also available from us courtesy of Oxford University Press:
Young Readers' Dictionary
(large print edition)
Young Readers' Thesaurus
(large print edition)

For further information or a free brochure, please contact us at:
Ulverscroft Large Print Books Ltd.,
The Green, Bradgate Road, Anstey,
Leicester, LE7 7FU, England.
Tel: (00 44) 0116 236 4325
Fax: (00 44) 0116 234 0205

Other titles published by Ulverscroft:

THE MISTRESS

Danielle Steel

Discovered on a freezing Moscow street by Vladimir, a Russian billionaire, Natasha Leonova has lived for seven years under his protection, though she is careful not to dwell on his ruthlessness or the deadly circles he moves in. Until she meets Theo Luca, who owns a restaurant filled with his late father's artwork. There, he first encounters Natasha, the most beautiful woman he has ever seen — and there, Vladimir lays eyes on Luca's artwork. Theo, himself a gifted artist, finds himself feverishly painting Natasha's image for weeks after their first meeting. Enraged that the paintings are not for sale, Vladimir is determined to secure one at any price. And Natasha, who knows that she cannot afford to make one false move, nevertheless begins to think of the freedom she can never have as Vladimir's mistress . . .

THE AWARD

Danielle Steel

France, 1940: When the German army invades, sixteen-year-old Gaëlle de Barbet loses her family, and her closest friend is sent to a detention camp. Joining the Resistance, Gaëlle takes terrifying risks to fearlessly deliver Jewish children to safety, and later to help save France's art treasures. But when the war draws to a close, she is falsely accused of collaboration, and flees to Paris in disgrace. There, she begins a new life that eventually takes her to New York, from a career as a Dior model to marriage and motherhood, unbearable loss, and mature, lasting love when she returns to France. No matter where she goes, however, her label as a collaborator remains — until her granddaughter, a respected political journalist, embarks on a journey to see Gaëlle recognized as the war hero she was.

RUSHING WATERS

Danielle Steel

As Hurricane Ophelia bears down on New York City, millions are caught up in the horrific flooding it unleashes. Interior designer Ellen Wharton flies in from London, heedless of the hurricane warnings, intent on seeing her mother. British investment banker Charles Williams is travelling on business but is also eager to see his young daughters, who live with his estranged ex-wife. As the hurricane rages, he desperately checks the shelters where thousands have taken refuge to find them. Juliette Dubois, a dedicated ER doctor, fights to save lives when the generators at the hospital fail. The day of chaos takes its toll as New Yorkers struggle to face a natural disaster of epic proportions. But as lives are shattered, heroes are revealed — and then the real challenge begins, when the survivors face their futures . . .

A PERFECT LIFE

Danielle Steel

An icon in the world of television news, Blaise McCarthy seems to have it all: beauty, intelligence and courage. But privately, there is a story she has protected for years ... Blaise's daughter Salima, blinded by juvenile diabetes, now lives in a year-round boarding school with full-time assistance. When the school closes suddenly, Salima returns home to Blaise's New York apartment with her new carer, Simon. He rapidly shakes up their world, determined to help Salima find the independence she never thought possible. Then Blaise's personal and professional worlds collide: a young rival at work attempts to take over, and the well-guarded secrets of Blaise's home life are exposed. Suddenly her life is no longer perfect, but real. Can mother and daughter learn together how to face a world they can't control?

PEGASUS

Danielle Steel

In the German countryside, on the cusp of World War II, everything is about to change for two lifelong friends. As widowers, Nicolas and Alex are raising their children alone, but lead contented, peaceful lives — until a long-buried secret about Nicolas's ancestry threatens his family's safety. To survive, they must flee to America. The only treasures Nicolas and his sons can take are eight purebred horses. These magnificent creatures are their ticket to a new life, securing Nicolas a job with the famous Ringling Brothers Circus. There, he and the white stallion Pegasus become the centrepiece of the show. But as the years of war take their toll, Nicolas struggles to adapt to his new life, while Alex and his daughter face escalating danger in Europe. Then tragedy strikes on both sides of the ocean . . .